Jon smiled slightly, gazing at her. *Look at me,* he willed her.

She glanced at him, then blinked, startled, and went back to staring at her screen. "I'm sorry," the doctor said in a low voice. "You're obviously someone famous, and I'm making you uncomfortable...." Blood seemed to drain from her face.

Usually, he would interject, reassure her and make *her* comfortable, but...he was genuinely interested in hearing what she had to say. And he got the feeling she didn't speak her mind very often to people—preferring to keep things to herself.

"I've...had a bad morning," she continued, still not looking at him. "I just got some...difficult news. If you'd like, I'll have another anesthesiologist called in to assist with your surgery. But I assure you, I'm very capable at what I do, and once I'm with the rest of the team, I will be fine—"

"I want you," he blurted.

She blinked at him. Her eyes lingered on his, then traveled the length of him very quickly, up and down. She swallowed. "Why?" she asked.

Dear Reader,

Where I grew up in New England, following baseball was an important tradition spanning the generations. As a child, I remember visiting Boston's Fenway Park on "Family Day," a baseball glove in hand in case any errant foul balls came our way. During summertime, the game was always on the radio or television in our homes. And all the kids in the neighborhood knew the name and uniform number of every player.

This book's hero is one such player. Everyone loves Jon Farell, a left-handed pitcher for the New England Clippers. A local guy, he wants nothing more than to be re-signed to his team in the big leagues, but a medical issue and a clubhouse scandal threaten his future.

When Jon performs community service at the cancer hospital where he was treated, he falls for the one woman in Boston who has no idea who he is. Dr. Elizabeth LaValley has good reasons for being cautious, as her introverted world is sent into upheaval when she's temporarily assigned responsibility for the care of her eight-year-old nephew, a cancer survivor.

But Jon, the extroverted, likable pro baseball player, is determined to bring Elizabeth out of her shell. And this man that her nephew adores is the one man that prickly, privacy-minded Elizabeth can't seem to scare away...and she's not sure that she really wants to.

This is a story about opposites attracting and, most of all, about the joy and power of falling in love. I hope you enjoy Elizabeth and Jon's story.

All the best,

Cathryn Parry

Out of His League

Cathryn Parry

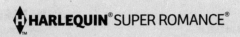

HARLEQUIN® SUPER ROMANCE®

Recycling programs
for this product may
not exist in your area.

ISBN-13: 978-0-373-60787-7

OUT OF HIS LEAGUE

Copyright © 2013 by Cathryn Parry

Printed in U.S.A.

www.Harlequin.com

ABOUT THE AUTHOR

Cathryn Parry is a lifelong baseball fan. She also loved playing first base on her childhood softball team, coached by her mom. Today she lives in Massachusetts with her husband, Lou, and her neighbor's cat, Otis. When she's not writing romance, she enjoys figure skating, plans as many vacations as possible and pursues her genealogy hobby. Please visit her website at www.cathrynparry.com.

Books by Cathryn Parry

HARLEQUIN SUPERROMANCE

1756—SOMETHING TO PROVE
1820—THE LONG WAY HOME

Other titles by this author available in ebook format.

For Lou. Thanks for the inspiration,
the meals and all the love!

Thanks also to Karen Reid for your help in making this
story the best it could be!

And to my three brothers—baseball players all—for
the many games of catch, pitch-back fun and pickup
games in our sandy backyard. I'll be forever grateful
that you taught me how to not throw like a girl.

CHAPTER ONE

WHEN DR. ELIZABETH LAVALLEY approached the elevator bank on the third floor of her Boston hospital, a crowd milled in front of the nurse's station. Her department was uncharacteristically buzzing.

"Somebody famous," she heard an aide say. Instead of joining the mix, Elizabeth skirted the chaos and quickly stepped inside the elevator, heading in the other direction.

Privacy and peace, that's what Elizabeth craved. Outside, the city was waking.

She cut across the hospital complex until she came to a red-painted stripe that ran along the sidewalk. Boston's famous Freedom Trail. Appropriate, because this was what Elizabeth's job meant to her: freedom. An escape from the turmoil she'd grown up in.

But that was behind her. She'd worked hard for the life she led now, and she would do anything to keep it.

Her surgical scrubs fluttered in the slight breeze. A half hour before the first surgery in her morning shift, it was a sunny, blue-sky, early October day. She strode, focused, down the red-painted line, more crowded with people than usual. A cruise ship was docked in the harbor—likely one of the fall "foliage" itineraries that went from New York up to Canada, though it was early for the peak of the autumn leaves' spectacular color. Still, it seemed passengers and crew members from around the world were crowded into town today.

Maybe someday she would take one of those cruises, albeit to Rome, Greece or Turkey, where she could focus on her love of archaeology and antiquity. Surely there would be a way to find a single berth and keep herself sequestered.

Maybe, if she were bold and asked him, Albert would go with her.... But on second thought, Albert didn't like vacations. And he certainly didn't share her curiosity for ancient civilizations. A seminar on the latest techniques for inserting prosthetic heart valves, perhaps.

But that was the kind of man she preferred. A safe man, one who didn't push her from her comfort zone, question her or make demands on her time. Really, she only wanted to be left alone. She was independent, and she was…not understandable to the world at large. Only a man who lived in her world—this world, not the world of her past—could possibly understand.

She stepped aside as she saw a man, a cruise ship passenger—judging by his tote bag that said *SS Holland*—eye her, and then his camera. Even though he smiled at her, obviously intending to ask her to take a photo of him, she tightened her grip on the bag in her hand and drilled her gaze into the pavement as she walked away, faster now.

She did feel a twinge of guilt, because she wasn't a rude person at heart. But people didn't always understand that. She was awkward at small talk. Someone else would be a much better photo-taker for the man than she would ever be.

She hastened around the corner, out of the tourist area and back to her hospital. Just a small escape, a short bit of exercise before her workday in the operating room, where she'd be sitting hunched over her equipment for hours straight. She had a full morning and afternoon of procedures—typically three to four scheduled surgeries, as well as whatever emergency situations came their way. She would be busy, focused and absorbed in her job—just the way she liked it.

Checking her watch, she headed into the underground tunnel that led to Wellness Hospital, then felt a flash of cold that made her skin prickle. Jogging ahead, she rubbed her arms and went inside to the main lobby.

She was still breathing heavily when the receptionist stopped her. "Dr. LaValley! Your department called down looking for you."

Elizabeth felt at her waist, but she'd forgotten her beeper. "What's wrong?"

"Your sister is upstairs."

"*My* sister? Are you sure?"

"That's what they said."

Elizabeth's heart sank. All the goodwill and euphoria slipped away. The panicky, unsafe, confusing world she'd escaped was colliding with the orderly, private, secure world she'd created for herself as an adult.

She hurried for the elevator, wondering if something was wrong with their mother again.

A fall, a blackout, an arrest. Which one would it be this time?

That was the only reason she could think of for Ashley to contact her. Either way, Elizabeth had no choice but to see her sister.

JON FARELL SAT beside his agent's daughter in the waiting room. The hospital had cleared out a private room for him, thankfully.

Not that he didn't love signing autographs. Under regular circumstances, he could interact with people all day. As a pitcher with the New England Captains, he made it a point to hang out by the bullpen before home games, making himself available for any kid with a pen and a slip of paper. And why shouldn't he? He was living the dream life—pro athlete for a big-market team, a local guy made good.

Everybody in the region knew the Captains, and most rooted for them, as well. Even this morning, strolling through the hospital before elective surgery, he'd noticed half the people waiting wore blue Captains caps with the distinctive "C" logo. Jon had been mobbed when he and Brooke had first shown up in the admitting area. Despite being on a food-

and-drink fast since midnight, with nothing in his stomach and worry on his mind, Jon had signed a few autographs before a nurse took pity on him and hustled him into the empty examination room.

Jon scratched his right hand. He'd gotten used to the throbbing. Thankfully, it was his nonpitching hand.

But still...

It might be malignant.

That one, offhand comment from the doctor had shaken him to his core and thrown him off stride. Still did.

What would Jon do if it was cancer?

Do. Not. Go. There.

Mom was twenty-eight when she died of cancer. Your age now.

Jon swallowed, tried to keep his face a mask.

Next to him, Brooke tapped away on her smartphone. He hadn't told her about the cancer part of the consultation. Hadn't told anybody, except for Max, Brooke's father and Jon's agent since he'd been a high school kid drafted in the fourth round.

Where the hell was Max, anyway? Why had he sent his daughter in his place?

Brooke glanced up and smiled at him. She'd been flirty and full of attention toward him, and that had set Jon on edge. The only thing he wanted to talk to her about was her father, and that was the one topic she'd been closemouthed about since picking Jon up at his apartment. "Dad's busy" had been all he could get out of her on the subject, though she'd chatted nonstop about baseball and Jon's chance at a contract, which unnerved him. *She* wasn't his agent; her father was.

"You can head out now," he told Brooke. "Grab some breakfast. I'll have the nurses call you when I'm out of surgery."

She stood and stretched. "I shouldn't. My father will kill me if I don't stay here and report back everything to him."

"I won't tell him," he said.

She patted his shoulder as she brushed by him, and he caught a whiff of perfume, sharp to his nose. Her pants were tight, showing off her behind, which jutted out with the high heels she wore. She strolled across the room, "working it." She was too much like the groupies who were always around guys like him, doing their best to tempt him away from his game, and it made him uncomfortable.

"I'll call the team doctors once you're in surgery," Brooke said.

Don't do that. "Max can handle it," he said mildly.

"Enough with the 'Max.'" She pouted. "I don't know why you don't trust me, Jon."

He clenched his right hand. *Malignant. It might be malignant.*

"I'm just caffeine-deprived," he said. "Have a coffee for me, will you?"

She frowned at him. "I think you should give me your valuables to hold. Wallet, keys, jewelry." She eyed the chain around his neck—the medallion was tucked under his shirt and she couldn't see it. His mother had given him that, the last Christmas she was alive. He didn't take it off for anybody.

But damn it, Brooke had a point. The doctors would want him to strip to nothing, and anything personal belonging to a celebrity, even a local celebrity, tended to grow legs and walk off. He took out his wallet, handed it to her, then pulled his keys from his pocket and unclasped the chain from his neck. She was Max's daughter. If she lost any of it, Max would disown her.

A smug smile on her lips, she deposited his life inside her big, gold satchel of a purse. "How about a phone?" she asked.

"Nope, didn't bring it," he answered, doing his best not to show his irritation.

Thankfully, she left the room then. Sashayed right on out. Her perfume lingered, so he closed his eyes and transported himself someplace safe. He'd had so much practice as a kid. Man, he was thinking about those days too often lately. His chest throbbed right along with his hand.

Another nurse came in and set him up with a hospital gown and plastic bag to hold his clothing and shoes. He smiled at her, was polite and personable, even though he wanted to lie down and grit his teeth. But if he did, it might get caught on camera, might change the public's opinion of him and jeopardize his job.

He was up for a contract. The season was over. He'd done okay—he was a back-of-the-rotation starting pitcher and had won his last two games—but the team had gone down in flames, anyway. The radio guys and the sportswriters were on the warpath; you'd think he and his teammates had all mugged little girls and stolen their lunch money.

Yeah, he understood fan loyalty. But there was real suffering in life, and, unlike most of these media people, it seemed he understood that while they didn't.

"It was a shame about the Captains," the nurse remarked to him. "My son stayed up late and watched all your games this month. He was hoping you'd make it to the playoffs."

Him and about a million other people.

"Would your boy like an autograph?" Jon asked. His finger was really goddamn killing him. Had to be psychosomatic. It knew a knife was going to be slicing right into it, down to the bone, and cutting off a tumor the size of a pistachio nut.

"He would love that." The nurse pulled a marker out of her pocket. "Are you sure you're offering? I don't want to bother you."

He hid a smile. "I know I've got a job most kids in Boston would do anything for."

Under normal circumstances, there was nothing he liked better than taking care of people—making them happy.

He glanced at his bum hand. The past couple weeks wearing a baseball glove rubbing against the knuckle hadn't helped it. Still, unless a person knew what they were looking for, the growth on the bone of his right ring finger wasn't apparent. He'd kept it from the team doctors, wanting to finish the season and make it into the playoffs.

Playoffs hadn't happened, but he had finished the season, pretending nothing was wrong with him. Then he'd gone for an appointment earlier in the week and...

Here he was. Scheduled to get the tumor immediately removed and tested.

A chill socked him in the gut. This could not be cancer. *Could not.*

What would Bobby and Francis do if it was?

His smile stiffening, he turned to the nurse. "What's your son's name?"

"Kyle." She pulled out his baseball card from her bag and handed it to him. "He's a Little League pitcher, but he missed his spring season because he broke his arm."

"I'm sorry to hear that." Jon signed his name on the card. "Do you have a piece of paper? I'll write him a personal note."

The nurse produced a memo pad, and on it he scribbled, "To a fellow pitcher. Hope you stay healed and well for next season."

He handed the card and the note back to the nurse. She was looking at him thoughtfully. "You're very good at being a public person. You have a way with people."

Jon shrugged. "I'm the oldest in my family. Two younger brothers." Bobby and Francis. And if it weren't for this issue, he would've told them he was going to be here today, and Francis probably would've come, Bobby, too, seeing as he was a college student in Boston, just back from Italy on a junior semester abroad. "So I know what kids are like."

The nurse put a blood pressure cuff on him. "We get celebrities and famous people in from time to time. But usually, they have entourages who instruct us not to interact with them."

Because it sucks thinking you might have cancer. Jon smiled at the nurse as he watched the needle move on the gauge. "No worries."

But there *were* worries. Tons of worries. Maybe after today, he'd be unemployed. Or worse, handed a death sentence. Then what would his family do? His father...cripes, he hated to think what Dad would do. He'd barely survived what had happened to their mom. Jon had held them all together emotionally, for years. It gave him a purpose, and with the money from his contract, he was taking care of them still.

The nurse handed him a paper cap for the operating room. "They might ask you to tie back your hair," she said, winking at him. "I know how the girls love it. Getting long, isn't it?"

Yeah, it was his thing—his trademark. Shoulder length now, he had promised not to cut it until the Captains made the playoffs, and then he'd lined up somebody to shave it off for charity. The team had been planning to make a big deal of it for their *cancer* charity.

That word again. Not that he'd ever told anybody on the team about his mom.

He forced himself to smile. "It's fine."

He was a good liar, when he needed to take care of others.

Finally, the nurse left him. He was used to people lingering over him, and that was okay. Being famous served a purpose. It was the thought of not having a purpose that threw him into a tailspin. *Just get through today.*

He changed out of his jeans and long-sleeved T-shirt into the hospital gown.

A male aide entered his room. "Hey, man! I love you guys!" he said. "You were the best pitcher on the team this September—they should put you at the top of the order!" Then the man wheeled Jon into what looked like a holding room for the O.R. His gut twisted into a million knots.

Do or die. Cut the friggin' thing out and test it. Am I done, or do I get to come back for another season?

But as someone pricked his arm—shit, his *pitching* arm—with a needle for an IV, he looked away, knowing that it wasn't the season that counted.

It was his family. And for them, he was flooded with the worst fear he had ever felt in his entire life. And that was saying something.

He squeezed his eyes shut. He felt more helpless and alone than he wanted to admit to himself.

More preoperative patients were wheeled into bays; the room became busy. As doctors, nurses and orderlies came inside, they all looked his way, to the farthest corner.

Word was out that he was here. Publicity-wise, Jon had it covered. A tweet was prepared to go out this evening, if necessary—Routine elective surgery on a stiff finger, non-pitching hand. Looks good. Thanks to Wellness Hospital. For now, though, he just needed to calm down, get the knots out of his stomach. He closed his eyes again.

"I'm Dr. Elizabeth LaValley. I'm your anesthesiologist this morning."

He opened his eyes a slit. Saw a pretty doctor with chin-length, glossy hair. A cute pug nose. Slight but sure hands that gripped an iPad to her chest.

He opened his eyes all the way, because he needed to pay attention. It was his body that they'd be cutting into. But when he looked up at the doctor, it was what he saw in her eyes that made him sit up.

From the dampness in her lashes, and her puffy face, he could tell she'd been crying. And whatever the reason, she was trying to hide it. She kept her gaze drilled on her tablet computer instead of looking at him.

"And you are..." Blinking fast, she touched the screen. "Jon Farell."

She pronounced it wrong, like "barrel," which was his first clue.

"It's *Fair-ell*," he said.

Her brow knit. He waited for her to recognize his name.

Nope, nothing.

"You're here for surgery on your finger..." She swiped another page. Tears were welling in her eyes, and she blinked fast.

"Are you okay?" he asked.

"Of course." She seemed to shake herself. Tapped at the screen. "Do you have any concerns I should know about?" she said to the tablet's screen.

Other than the fact that he might have *cancer?* And that his pretty anesthesiologist had just been *crying?*

"Are you sure you're okay?" he repeated.

"Yes." She took a breath. "I need to double-check some questions. Are you..." She squinted at whatever his computer files were telling her. "Right-handed?"

A *very* good question. "I'm left-handed," he said. "I pitch left-handed. This is my catching hand." He held it up to her, as if that made a difference.

"I see." She glanced at the chart. He noted that she wore no rings on her left hand. "And you...play sports?"

The one woman in Boston who appeared not to know who he was. He would have laughed if what he was facing wasn't so important.

"At a very high level," he said. "They pay me lots of money to do so." At least, he hoped they still did after today.

She nodded, still staring at the tablet. "You are worried that the surgeons might cut into your left hand by mistake. Duly noted."

"You've never heard of the New England Captains?" he asked her.

"I…don't follow sports."

Even more fascinating. "Do you know *anything* about baseball?"

"I… No." She blinked. Again, those eyes were filling up. Eyes that were warm and brown. Like the root beer he'd liked as a kid.

"My nephew likes sports," she whispered.

His antennae went up. He was absolutely certain she hadn't meant to divulge this fact, that she was nothing at all like the others—people who knew he was coming into surgery, knew he was good-natured by reputation, and had therefore used the opportunity to provide a gift or a story for their own children.

Not that he blamed them. It was just…refreshing… to meet somebody—especially a single woman his age with a solid career and goals in her own right— who didn't look at him as public property.

"Please sit down," he said to her. "I'd like to ask you some questions, if that's all right." There was a chair next to his gurney.

She continued to stand. "Certainly. In five minutes, your surgeon will be stopping by, and after that I'll put a relaxant in your IV drip. Do you have any allergies?"

He'd been through all of this at his last appointment, but he just smiled at her. "No allergies. Tell me what's upsetting you?"

She wouldn't meet his gaze. "I'm fine, Mr. Farell."

"Fair-ell," he said. "And it's Jon."

She licked her lips and stared hard at her tablet. "Have you ever been under general anesthesia? Do you have any concerns about it?"

Dr. Elizabeth LaValley, the name stitched across her white lab jacket said. Her scrubs beneath it were bright turquoise. She was medium height, and she was attractive in a fresh-faced, studious way. Obviously she was smart, or she wouldn't be a doctor.

"Mr. Farell?" She said the name correctly this time.

He smiled. *Look at me,* he willed her.

She glanced at him, then blinked, startled and went back to staring at her screen. "I'm sorry," she said in a low voice, "you're obviously someone famous, and I'm making you uncomfortable…." Blood seemed to drain from her face.

Usually, he would interject, reassure her and make *her* comfortable, but…he was genuinely interested in hearing what she had to say. And he got the feeling she didn't speak her mind too often to people, preferring to keep things to herself.

"I've…had a bad morning," she continued, still not looking at him. "I just got some…difficult news. If you'd like, I'll have another anesthesiologist called in to assist with your surgery. But I assure you, I'm very capable at what I do, and once I'm with the rest of the team, I will be fine—"

"I want you," he blurted.

She blinked at him. Her eyes lingered on his, then traveled the length of him very quickly, up and down. She swallowed. "Why?" she asked.

He liked the sound of her voice—soft and calming. And it was completely inappropriate for the situation, but his body was giving a sexual response....

He crossed his arms over his lap. Smiled nonchalantly at her and gave her an uncharacteristic, honest answer. "Because I'm scared as hell at what's going to happen to me, and I don't want anybody else but you to know. Okay?"

"Me?" She put her hand on her heart.

"Uh, I figure you've already seen me at my worst. I don't want to have to explain it to anybody else again."

She nodded slowly. "That's logical."

"It is."

Their gazes held for just a split second too long. There was…something there. An attraction, and on her part, too. And no, it wasn't as meaningless to him as overcoming a challenge—getting a woman who wasn't impressed with his celebrity to come to his side. It was…deeper than that.

And it was crazy to think so based on a two-minute meeting. Maybe he was just so scared witless about the cancer talk, it was making him think crazy things.

Carefully, Elizabeth LaValley put down her computer tablet. He got the impression that this action in itself was significant for her.

"Mr. Farell," she said slowly, "your surgeon is very good. He's our best, in fact, and I can vouch for him."

"Not all cancer can be cured," he murmured. "People die. I've seen...people die."

Again, that pale face. "I know." Her voice caught, and her hand went to her mouth.

"Tell me, Lizzy," he said softly. "Uh, is it okay if I call you that?"

"I... Yes. I'm fine, really. It's fine." She waved her hand, looking flustered. "It's just...we had a cancer scare in our family five years ago. My three-year-old nephew had leukemia. Today is the day he gets tested, to see if he's really cured."

"And you're worried?"

"My sister thinks he's sick again." She shook her head. "No—we're supposed to be talking about you. This is *your* surgery. *Your* anesthesia. In a minute, your surgeon—the head of the team—will be coming to see you."

She picked up the tablet again and very carefully sat to read his case notes. There was fresh concentration in her gaze. Her blinking had stopped. Her hands weren't shaking.

"Lizzy, I'm sorry about your nephew."

She shook her head again. "He'll be fine, Mr. Farell. Today, we'll be removing a tumor from your right ring finger—a growth on the bone—but from your tests, there are no solid indications it's cancer.

Of course, the tumor will be tested as soon as it's removed, but that is standard procedure."

He'd lost her. But she needed to prepare for her job performance in the minutes ahead—of anyone, he could understand and appreciate that. "How long will it take to get back the results?"

"Typically, a few days for the lab work," she said. "But, once the doctor opens up the finger and sees the tumor, he can usually rule out cancer by sight."

Jon drew in a breath. She was gazing at him, her forehead creased. He got a feeling she didn't look at too many of her patients like this. Really look at them, really let herself see them as people instead of as medical problems to be solved.

"Thank you, Lizzy," he said quietly.

She blushed. "It's Elizabeth."

"Call me Jon."

Her teeth bit down on her lower lip.

And because things were looking so much better now, he pushed his luck. "I have another request that I was wondering if you could help me with."

TALKING INAPPROPRIATELY TO a patient? This was so unlike her; it was surreal.

The only thing that explained Elizabeth's uncharacteristic unprofessionalism with Jon—with this *patient*—was that, silly as it sounded, her grandmother had called her Lizzy.

And her grandmother had died when Elizabeth was eight, the same age her nephew Brandon was now.

Fresh tears sprang to her eyelids. She bit down on her lip again. *Control. Stay in control.*

She was just so vulnerable now, ever since Ashley had told her about Brandon. She pressed her hand to her mouth, trying to stop the trembling.

The surgeon approached Mr. Farell. A professional athlete getting the most experienced doctor on staff… no surprise there. Elizabeth stepped aside, relieved to be able to step into the shadows.

Talking to the patients presurgery was the least favorite part of her job. She would as soon die as admit this to anyone, but she'd chosen anesthesia as a medical specialty because the bulk of her duties involved dealing with patients while they were unable to move or speak and therefore couldn't interact or cause conflict with her. All that was required, interfacing-wise, was typically a five-or ten-minute consultation before the procedure. Right up Elizabeth's alley.

But this man…Jon Farell…had just blown all her experience out of the water. Even now, as the surgeon talked on and on, regaling Jon, asking him questions, adding to his "cocktail banter stories" by interacting with a Captains pitcher, Jon kept glancing at *her*. Meaningfully, as if the two of them shared a secret.

She rarely stared at men. Her life was too private for that, Albert not considered. But this man…

She'd been fighting an urge to lean closer and smell him. Very strange, but she did understand the scientific principal behind it. Sex pheromones, it was called. The theory stated that Nature, in her infinite wisdom, ensured that people with complementary genetic traits were attracted to one another. Someone with a family tendency for diabetes, say, was attracted to someone else with specific immunity against it. A way for survival of the species, so to speak.

Scientifically, then, *she* wasn't physically attracted to Jon Farell, but her DNA was.

Intuitively, it made sense. Jon was the physical opposite to her. He was athletic and strong, with ice-blue eyes. His face bore the fine, delicate features of Nordic ancestry, but mixed with something else—a blending of another culture that gave him bronzed, sun-kissed skin and long brown hair, mysteriously streaked on the left side with white. His hair wasn't *dyed* white, but was naturally white, as in, the absence of color. Somewhere along the line, probably through blunt trauma, a small section on his scalp, about a quarter inch wide, had been injured such that he no longer had any pigment in the hair follicles.

Overall, it made Jon Farell look…beautiful. And with his warm, musically pitched voice, it gave him the mysterious aura of some past, mystical culture.

He set her workaday French and Scottish genes on fire. Which had probably contributed to her opening her mouth and admitting things to him that she would never in a million years tell anybody else.

It made him uniquely dangerous to her.

The aides prepared to wheel Jon's gurney into the operating room, and she stepped forward, doing her job. As the rest of the team moved into position, she put relaxants into Jon's IV line. Waited until those ice-blue eyes flickered closed.

She felt her shoulders relaxing. He was in the customary pose of her customary patients. He was no longer a threat.

"Lizzy," he murmured suddenly, and she jumped.

"Yes, Jon?" She leaned closer.

"Please tell me afterward what the doctor said about the malignancy. Can you do that?"

"I'll…"

But he was out. It was just as well.

They wheeled him into surgery, and she set him up to monitor him with her equipment. Waited while the nurse—that lucky woman—tied his beautiful hair up into a cap before placing pads on his chest and a cuff on his arm. Elizabeth eased him into unconsciousness by selecting a syringe and inserting the drugs into his IV.

He was truly out then.

Briefly, Elizabeth wondered how she could possibly communicate to Jon afterward, as he had asked, but she put that out of mind and went back to her customary, safe place. With deft hands—she'd done this hundreds of times, after all—she intubated him.

For the first time, she was touching his body, albeit with gloves on. She gently placed a tube into his airway to take control of his breathing during the operation.

Then she sat back at her cart behind the surgery

drape and observed her machines. That was what anesthesiologists did.

He was not the famous Jon Farell now. He was any patient.

But still, when the surgeon isolated and removed the tumor at long last, she couldn't help searching the doctor's eyes.

Good news or bad?

And either way, how would she tell Jon?

CHAPTER TWO

AFTER THE SURGERY, and with Jon wheeled safely to the recovery room, Elizabeth hurried to the hospital day care center where her nephew and her sister waited for her.

In a private room, she gave eight-year-old Brandon a cursory checkup, questioned him and checked his vital signs.

The outgoing, towheaded boy showed no symptoms of renewed cancer. Nothing that Elizabeth could outwardly see. On the contrary, he seemed as energetic as ever—he fidgeted and had a difficult time sitting still. Elizabeth told him to wait for his mom in the hospital day care center, and then she led her sister to a long, quiet corridor, encased in glass, that overlooked the Boston skyline.

In the midday light, Elizabeth stared at the thin, stylishly dressed, older sister who was so different from her, it was hard to believe they'd come from the same parents.

Ashley paced back and forth, jittery, her high-heeled boots clicking on the floor. She was rubbing her arms as she walked. "It's happening again."

Elizabeth's pulse sped up. "*What* is happening again?"

"I can't take it," Ashley said. "The tests…the trips to Boston…the stress of worrying…"

"Ashley, he seems fine. A normal, active eight-year-old. Give the tests a chance to ease your mind. What time is his appointment?"

"Twelve o'clock, and I can't be there." Ashley stopped pacing. "Lisbeth, I need you to help me with Brandon, just for today while we get through this."

"You know I can't do that," Elizabeth said as calmly as she could. There was a reason she kept her family at arm's length. Ashley's appearance this morning was the least of it.

But her sister's chin took on a stubborn tilt. "If Brandon is sick again, you work at the hospital. You're the best person to help him."

"I'm glad you've come to that conclusion." Five years ago when Brandon had been diagnosed with leukemia, Ashley had refused to allow Elizabeth to have anything to do with Brandon's treatment. She'd been the devoted if slightly martyred mother who had hovered over him at every appointment.

Elizabeth's reaction to the boy's sickness, on the other hand, had been to study all she could about the illness. She'd consulted with Brandon's doctors, and, as a medical student affiliated with the hospital back then, surreptitiously checked to make sure that he was getting the best and latest of care. All of it done behind the scenes, of course, with the guarantee of no attention drawn to herself.

"Ashley, I am not good with children. You know this."

"You work with sick people," her sister insisted.

"Brandon is not sick! He is healthy and he needs to get back to school!"

"You have a car," Ashley said, hugging herself and staring out the window. "The school's not too far from here…"

She didn't appear to be listening to Elizabeth. Then again, she was Ashley. Even as a girl, she'd been fueled by emotion. A queen of drama. Born pretty, Elizabeth's older sister had been the head of a clique of girls who'd ruled the neighborhood. Maybe that had been her coping mechanism to their chaotic home life. Elizabeth had coped by hiding in the public library, doing her homework or looking at *National Geographic* magazines. She had skipped two grades and had been accepted at college in Boston at sixteen, which had been her escape, and from which she'd never gone back.

Elizabeth tapped her foot. This meeting was unnecessary. She could spend precious time—time she did not have, since she was on duty and had a case to prepare for—explaining to her sister why she could not drive Brandon a half hour to school, in the opposite direction, and then back again, cutting out of her job at the hospital to pick him up. It didn't make logistical sense.

But Ashley's mind was not logical or ordered. Elizabeth needed to cut to the heart of the matter for her.

"What's really going on here?" Elizabeth asked quietly. "Why can't you sit with Brandon through his tests and then take him to school as usual?"

Ashley stopped pacing. But Elizabeth stepped closer and noticed her sister's body was twitching. Her skin seemed clammy, and she smelled like...

No. Oh, no.

Their mother drank, but to Elizabeth's knowledge, her sister never had.

Elizabeth certainly never did. She didn't chance touching the stuff. That behavior was common, she had read, in children of alcoholics.

"Ashley?"

"I...have an appointment with a counselor today," her sister confessed.

"That's...good." It was excellent, in fact. That showed Ashley was taking charge in an appropriate manner. If Elizabeth had the time, she'd delve into the how and where...check out this counselor and offer her sister medical advice.

Elizabeth glanced at her watch. In another minute the surgical nurses would be paging her. "Ashley, I really need to get to my next patient."

Ashley's thin shoulders straightened. She'd lost weight, Elizabeth noticed. "I'm leaving Brandon with you at the hospital today."

"That isn't possible." The emotional response was

elevating her pulse, but Elizabeth willed it away. "I have a full schedule of surgeries."

"I know. I already talked to a nurse about the emergency child care program for employees that you have here."

"You did?" Elizabeth said drily.

"Lisbeth, here is his insurance card and hospital ID." Ashley shoved the patient cards at her. Then she tightened her jacket around her as if to close the pain inside. "Please kiss Brandon for me." Her voice wavered. "And tell that lady 'thank you' for watching him while you and I talk."

"Ashley—"

"I have to go!"

Elizabeth watched, gaping, as her sister hurried away down the corridor.

"What time will you pick him up?" she called after her, but Ashley just waved her hand and disappeared around the corner.

Now what?

Elizabeth racked the logical side of her brain. Actually, her *entire* brain was logical. She dealt in facts, not "what if" flights of fancy.

Fact one: Brandon needed to be escorted to his appointment. Thank goodness for the aides in the child care department. Of course she would normally accompany Brandon herself, but a patient receiving scheduled wrist surgery needed her care as his anesthesiologist.

She quickly dropped off Brandon's insurance cards

at the Emergency Hospital Day Care, and then rushed back to her post.

On the way, she passed the post-op room where Jon Farell would be recovering.

She wanted to slow. She wanted to stop in and see how he was doing. Catch a glimpse of those ice-blue eyes.

He might be lucid by now, and she had embarrassed herself enough already. Nearly losing her reserve and showing tears in front of a patient—it was so uncalled-for, so unlike her normal personality that the entire event had been…ludicrous.

She was Dr. Elizabeth LaValley, and she did not drop her veil of privacy for anybody.

Not even for men with understanding eyes and pheromones that smelled like heaven to her.

IN JON'S DREAM, he was sitting in a room, brightly lit by white light, on one side of a conference table. On the other side was a kindly, older man who looked familiar but who Jon couldn't recall ever meeting. Max, his agent, was there, too, but he wasn't speaking, he was just listening.

Jon seemed to be having an earnest conversation; he was telling the man what he was doing in baseball. He was trying to explain why it was imperative that he be allowed to continue.

"I'm not ready to stop," Jon told the man. "I still have so much to do."

He said a lot more to the man, too, but as soon as

Jon spoke the words, he seemed to forget what he'd just said. He was trying to concentrate, but it wasn't possible.

"I understand you," the man said, something Jon clearly remembered. "It's time to get serious."

Yes! Jon understood exactly what he meant. He'd been coasting for too long. If he worked harder, he would be allowed to continue playing pro ball. He would not have to stop this life that he loved so much.

It's time to get serious.

The thought filled him with hope. Even Max seemed to agree.

When Jon woke, his heart was pounding, the dream fresh on his mind. He knew exactly where he was. Inside a brightly lit recovery room. He felt groggy, his throat sore, his nonpitching hand numb. He looked down and saw it was bound in a thick bandage.

He tried to sit up, but nausea swept over him. He put his head back down. All of a sudden, he heard a child's voice whisper next to him, "You're Jon Farell!"

The nurse hustled over and bundled the child off.

Jon turned his head right, then left. "Where's Lizzy?" he asked thickly.

"Lizzy? Is she the woman in the waiting area who keeps asking about you?" the nurse asked. "I told her that as soon as you eat some crackers and drink some ginger ale, we can call the doctor and get his okay to sign you out."

"No. I want Lizzy. My...other doctor."

"Dr. LaValley? She's presently administering to a patient in surgery."

"I need to see her. Elizabeth…LaValley," he enunciated as best he could, but his words were slurring.

"That's my aunt!" a voice piped up. It was the kid. The boy who'd recognized Jon.

"Brandon," the nurse said to the boy, "you know you're supposed to be in the day care center." She picked up her telephone and made a call.

"Leave him," Jon muttered weakly. He still felt so…sluggish yet full of purpose. He supposed dreams did that to people.

No, not a dream, a vision. And it was so clear. He had to get out of here. Had to get started.

The kid trotted over to his gurney. Jon blinked at him. Whatever medication they'd pumped him full of, he would be shaky for a while. He squinted, concentrating as hard as he could.

The kid was about eight, Jon estimated, with sandy hair and those sneakers kids wore that lit up when they walked. He shrugged out of his backpack and grabbed for a pen.

"Can I get your autograph?" the kid asked. He was missing one of his front eyeteeth.

Or maybe Jon was hallucinating. "How do you know who I am?"

"Everybody knows Jon Farell. You have twelve wins, eleven losses, a four-point-one-five season ERA, and one hundred forty-two strikeouts."

Huh. Jon didn't even know all that. He usually ignored his stats.

Those numbers weren't great, though. He should be doing better. If he were honest with himself, he'd slacked off this summer. The playoffs had seemed a certainty, so maybe the team had socialized and hung out partying together more than they should have.

He had a vague feeling that had been part of his dream. He wasn't sure, but he thought they had touched on the topic....

He struggled to sit up.

"Hurry!" the kid whispered. "The nurse is coming back."

"Maybe you should get your aunt," Jon said.

"She's in surgery." The kid looked at him earnestly. "She's a famous doctor."

"When I see her again," Jon slurred. "I'll give her an autograph for you to take home."

"You should drive to her house and give it to her there. I'm eating dinner at her house tonight. I'll tell her you're coming to see me." The kid turned around so his back was to Jon. Dangling from the boy's backpack was a cardboard address label, freshly filled out in blue ink. "That's where she lives."

With Jon's good hand—his pitching hand, which, thank God, felt fine—he drew the label closer, just out of curiosity. Dr. LaValley's address was in Medford. Huh. That's where he'd grown up. The vision meant something, but he'd known that before he even saw where Lizzy lived.

He squinted at her street address. He was vaguely certain it was near the school he'd attended as a kid, but Jon's GPS would know for sure. He dropped back on the bed.

"Brandon! Leave the patients alone!"

Brandon let the nurse take his hand and lead him away. Jon thought the boy might have winked at him.

He still felt so groggy and confused. A second nurse brought him a plastic cup filled with ginger ale, and a packet of saltine crackers that crinkled in its cellophane wrapper.

"Can you ask Dr. LaValley to come here, please?" he asked, pushing away the crackers. "I have a question for her."

"Let me know the question, and I'll get it answered for you." The nurse was speaking loudly. She didn't need to. He understood her perfectly.

"I want to talk to her," he said as clearly as he could. The words weren't coming out so easily. His throat felt sore. Why was that?

"I'll tell her that you asked for her," the nurse said.

"I need to talk to her…about the surgery. About what happened to me…" Damn it, he was getting tired. And his finger was starting to throb.

The nurse walked away. Jon peeled back the sheet that covered him. Swung his bare feet to the cool floor. He could feel himself tottering.

In a split second, two nurses were at his side, swinging him back onto the bed.

"He wants to talk to Dr. LaValley," one of the nurses said to the other nurse.

"Mr. Farell?" The second nurse was in his face now, talking loudly. "Jon?"

"I want to speak to Dr. LaValley," he repeated.

"That isn't possible. She's in surgery. But she left a message for you. She said to say that the procedure went favorably. She said to emphasize the word *favorably*."

That was code: Lizzy didn't think he had cancer. That was good. That was...

Exactly what he'd asked for in the vision. His wish was coming true.

But he still had his end of the bargain to hold up.

Jon leaned back on the pillow. There was so much he could do to improve himself during the off-season. And now that he was out of surgery, he would get right on it.

CHAPTER THREE

JON DIDN'T LET Brooke accompany him in the elevator up to his penthouse, and he remembered to ask for everything back that he'd given her to hold for him: wallet, keys, medallion. He wanted no excuses for her to contact him later under pretext of forgotten belongings. The sooner he was back to focusing on his baseball career and in the care of Max alone, the better off he would be.

Once in his apartment, he crashed on his pillow and slept off the aftereffects of the surgery. He woke at midafternoon, his mouth dry and his finger throbbing with pain, but he refused to take the painkillers the doctor had insisted he leave the hospital with. Instead, he swallowed two acetaminophen tablets with a huge glass of water, before falling back into bed and lapsing into a sleep that felt like a coma. He didn't wake again until his phone rang.

"Yeah?" he mumbled into the mouthpiece.

"Jon Farell? This is Dr. Morgan from Wellness Hospital."

"Yes." Jon sat up, his heart pounding. He held the phone between his ear and his shoulder while he groped for a pen and pad of paper in the drawer by his bed. He didn't want to miss anything the surgeon said. "Go ahead," he said, pulling off the cap to the marker with his teeth.

"We expedited the lab work for you. The tumor is benign. Cancer-free."

The pen cap fell from Jon's mouth and bounced off the pad of paper. Thank God. Thank God, thank God, thank God.

"Thank you," Jon said to the doctor, once he was breathing normally again. "I appreciate your taking the time to call me."

He also appreciated that they'd rushed his test through the system. Another advantage of playing for a big-market sports team.

"I'll see you next week at your checkup," Dr. Morgan said on the other end of the line. "We'll remove your stitches then. Until that time, follow the directions the nurses sent you home with. If you have any questions, you can call me at this number."

"Will do." Jon disconnected the call and felt the smile spread over his face. For the first time in weeks, the worry he'd been carrying with him lifted.

He'd told no one about the growth on his finger. He couldn't, because the season had been still underway, and the Captains were in the hunt for a playoff berth. And then when it officially ended, he'd made an appointment and, less than a week later, was in surgery. He hadn't told his dad, because he didn't want to worry him about the cancer scare. Ditto with his brothers.

Jon took care of *them,* not the other way around.

The only reason Brooke had been with him at the hospital was because at the pre-op checkup, the doctors had insisted he designate a person who would escort him home after the procedure. Of course, he'd called Max. It was Jon's agent's job to keep the team informed as to his medical status, but whether Max had done so or not, Jon wasn't certain. The season was over, and Jon was no longer in day-to-day contact with the general manager and team staff. Things were loose....

They were worse than loose. Jon's contract was up, and he needed the Captains to offer him a new one. That had been step two, after step one—get his tumor taken care of. Max had warned him to be cautious about discussing injuries or medical issues when he had a contract to re-sign.

Now, especially, Jon wanted to shout his good news about the cancer-free diagnosis to the world, but it just wasn't possible. He wished, at least, he could tell Dr. LaValley.

She's waiting for news about her nephew.

Mentally, he smacked himself. He had met the nephew in the recovery room, and it hadn't even occurred to Jon that the kid was in the same boat he was. What kind of guy was he?

It's time to get serious.

He strode into the bathroom and took the world's fastest shower, his nonpitching hand—his *cancer-free* hand—sticking out the side of the curtain so it wouldn't get wet. There was probably stuff he needed to take care of in regard to changing the bandage, but he didn't have time to read the instructions the hospital had given him along with a bunch of bandages and tubes of ointment. He would worry about that when he returned home. For now, he gingerly threw on fresh jeans, a T-shirt and a pair of loafers—seeing as he couldn't tie shoelaces with one of his fingers bandaged—and grabbed his SUV keys, wallet and phone.

It was dark outside. He'd slept the whole damn day. Some of that was the anesthesia and painkillers wearing off, some of it was just sheer exhaustion from a week of private worry.

He called down to valet parking and had Josh bring his Ford Expedition around front to the curb for him. Jon attempted to put on his medallion, but gave up trying to work the clasp and instead shoved it into his front pocket.

On the way downstairs, he called Max again. As before, the call went straight to voice mail. He shut off his phone without leaving a message.

He'd deal with his agent later.

For now, he was driving to Medford to see how a little kid with a cancer scare, like him, was doing.

And, oh yeah, sign him the autographs he'd promised.

ELIZABETH PUT HER hands over her ears. Her chest felt constricted and her pulse was elevated. Her living room, usually her sanctuary, blared with jarring music from an overloud children's cartoon. Her nephew bounced on the couch and hummed to himself. "Brandon, please turn down the television so I can hear myself think."

The boy gazed back at her with a wide-eyed look that made Elizabeth feel guilty. His mom was staying at an alcohol treatment center in town—unbeknownst to him, thank goodness—and she'd asked Elizabeth to take care of the boy for the next twelve hours. Elizabeth wanted to help them, she truly did.

"It's only for one night," Ashley had said. "Brandon loves sleepovers."

With that, Elizabeth had driven Brandon from the hospital to his house, two towns over, to pick up an overnight bag, and then she'd dropped off Ashley's small dog with one of her coworkers at the beauty salon Ashley worked at. Brandon had chattered and fidgeted nonstop, playing with the radio dials, and when she'd asked him to stop with the radio, he'd fiddled with her cell phone. She had felt so overwhelmed she'd ended up giving in. She just didn't know what to do with a young boy in her busy life. Not even for one night.

In no universe would Elizabeth ever be called a nurturer. She was the absolute wrong person to have an active eight-year-old boy spend the night with in her small condominium.

"Brandon, *please,*" she asked.

Blinking, he took the remote and turned down the volume exactly one notch.

"Thank you." She sighed.

"Auntie, what's for dinner?" He jumped back on the couch and put his feet up on her formerly pristine cushions.

"I...don't know." She stared as Brandon kicked off one sneaker with a thump to the floor. Then his other sneaker dropped onto the magazines on her table.

Her favorite magazines.

She closed her eyes. She was so not cut out for babysitting young boys. This was going to be a long night. And she didn't have a bed for her nephew, or even a guest bedroom—just her office. She didn't have a toothbrush for him, either, and he had announced that he'd forgotten his, halfway up the stairway to her condominium unit.

Add that to the shopping list.

She turned back to her dilemma in the kitchen.

Every can of soup and package of cereal was emptied from her cupboard and spread out on her countertop. She had found nothing in her pantry or refrigerator that her nephew could eat.

This was her fault. She'd been so flustered over the fact that her sister had expected Brandon to stay with her—on one night's notice—that'd she'd forgotten to stop at the supermarket. It was clear she needed to journey outside and brave traffic again. But there was no way she could leave an eight-year-old unattended. What to do?

She needed a babysitter, that's what she needed.

Sighing, she crossed to the bulletin board where she'd tacked a slip of paper with the scribbled phone number for Mrs. Ham, the widow who lived in a condominium apartment downstairs. Elizabeth hated to ask people for favors—but the elderly lady was the only neighbor Elizabeth knew by name. Mrs. Ham walked with a cane, made it a point to talk to everybody and was home most of the time. Elizabeth remembered her talking about raising two boys, now grown and married and living in other states. Maybe she wouldn't mind watching Brandon for fifteen minutes in her apartment while Elizabeth ran out to the store.

Before she could agonize over the decision, she made the call. Quickly, like ripping a bandage off a cut.

Mrs. Ham picked up on the first ring.

"Hello, this is Dr. Elizabeth LaValley from upstairs," she said all in one breath. "I'm wondering if I could ask you a favor for tonight."

"Tonight?" Mrs. Ham rasped. "It's not a good time." A television set blared in the background. "I'm watching the Eastern Series playoffs."

"The...?" Elizabeth had no idea what the elderly lady was talking about.

"Auntie!" Brandon called from the living room.

"Excuse me for a moment, Mrs. Ham." Elizabeth covered the phone. "Brandon, please, I am on the phone."

Her nephew picked up the pillow from her couch and tossed it into the air. "Who are you talking to?"

"A babysitter. Put your shoes on, please, you're going downstairs for a few minutes to watch the, uh, Eastern Series playoffs while I go out to the store."

"But I can't go downstairs." Brandon sat up with an urgent look on his face. "I have to stay *here*. In your house."

"You can't stay here without me." Elizabeth continued to cover the phone. "You're eight years old."

"But I *need* to. Just in case."

"Just in case of what?"

And then the buzzer from the lobby rang. Elizabeth blinked, the meaning not registering at first. People did not visit her. She worked long hours, and the short amount of time that she spent at home she kept to herself.

Brandon perked up. "Can I answer the door?"

"No, I'll do it." She uncovered the phone and lifted it to her ear, intending to beg Mrs. Ham to watch the boy for just a few minutes, but it slipped from Elizabeth's fingers and clattered to the counter. When she picked the phone up, she saw that she'd turned it off by mistake.

"Auntie!" Brandon nagged.

This was why she lived alone. To keep to herself.

Oh, God, she felt like weeping. How was she supposed to manage sharing her time when she was just so greedy for privacy?

It couldn't get any worse.

Her nephew tugged on her shirt. "I think it might be Jon Farell at the door."

Jon? Her patient from the morning, with the beautiful blue eyes?

"I asked him to come," Brandon said softly.

But it couldn't be. It just could not be.

JON WAITED IN the lobby, wondering if Lizzy was home. But at last he heard her voice answer from the intercom:

"Yes?" She sounded frazzled. In the background, the *Scooby-Doo* theme song played on a television set, a blast from his past.

That made him smile. "Hi, Dr. LaValley. It's Jon Farell. Ah…I hope it's okay, but Brandon asked me to stop by. I'm dropping off the autograph I promised him."

"Jon! Jon! I knew you would come!"

A buzzer sounded, and Jon was on his way upstairs. She waited for him in the hallway before an open door, the light from an apartment shining behind her. Also behind her was Brandon, bouncing from side to side in his stocking feet, and wearing the huge grin of a typical, energetic eight-year-old glad to see his sports hero.

Jon felt relieved. The kid really didn't look sick with cancer. Maybe he was okay?

Lizzy closed the door behind her so she was in the hall alone with Jon. "You should not have come," she said to him in a low voice. Her face was pale. For the first time it occurred to him that this wasn't a good idea to stop by unannounced.

"Sorry." He held out a game ball he'd grabbed from his car for her nephew. He gave Lizzy his best "Mr. Helpful, I'm a Good Guy" smile, but she didn't seem to be buying it. He shrugged. "I promised Brandon. The ball is from my last start of the season, against Toronto. We won."

But New York had won their game, too, so the Captains hadn't made a wild-card slot into the play-offs. Still, Jon had done his part, and Brandon, numbers kid that he was, should appreciate Jon's stats from that outing.

"*When* did my nephew give you my private address?" she asked, not taking the baseball he offered. Her arms were crossed, and she was rubbing them, as if worried.

"Ah…Brandon and I talked in the recovery room. He asked me to stop by tonight to deliver an autograph for him."

Her eyes grew huge. "*Brandon* was in the recovery room?"

"It's okay, Lizzy. Lots of local kids are baseball fans. He probably just heard I was in the hospital, and he came to check it out. I'd have done it, too, at his age."

"I did *not* give you permission to come to my house, and do not call me Lizzy."

He gazed down at her. Why this woman intrigued him so much, he had no idea. She was buttoned up so tight—or in her case, zipped up, with a gray fitted turtleneck sweatshirt that went right up to her chin. He couldn't help staring at that zipper pull, swinging back and forth from the force of her flustered breathing, and then he looked at her mouth.

Bow-shaped lips, without a speck of gloss or lipstick on them. They weren't all plumped up, either. They were good, old-fashioned naked lips, and he would love to—

"Jon Farell!"

His gaze jerked to her face.

"Are you even listening to me?" she asked.

"Yes." And she had said his name correctly, so that was a good sign. He smiled at her again.

Before she could react, pounding started on the other side of the door. Lizzy put her head in her hands.

"Let Jon Farell in, Auntie!" Brandon yelled.

"It's okay," he said to Lizzy. "I'll give him the autograph I promised, then I'll leave."

"I don't want you inside with us," she hissed. "You can give the ball to him in the hallway, out here."

"Sure." He shrugged. "If that's what you want."

"It *is* what I want."

"Auntie!" came Brandon's muffled yell.

She seemed to cringe. "And furthermore," she whispered to Jon, "you'll tell no one you've been here, do you understand? I am a private person, and I find your public lifestyle abhorrent."

Abhorrent, that was a big word just to say she didn't like it.

"You don't have to worry about me," he said gently. "I won't tell anyone I was here. And it's not like I'm Brad Pitt. I don't have paparazzi tailing after me everywhere."

She still didn't seem mollified. "I value my independence."

And then she opened the door a crack and said to Brandon, "Please watch your TV program and be patient. Just give us a moment."

There was her problem—she was too formal and too much of an adult with the kid.

She turned back to Jon, her gaze narrowed. "I do not want my name associated with a public person, do you understand?" Again, that whispering, as if he were a criminal at her door.

"I will honor your rules." He crossed his arms now, to match her stance. "Remember though, *you* were the one who left *me* a coded message. In the recovery room. And your instincts were right. The lab called me already—it's not cancer."

Her breath expelled. "That's...good." She was nibbling those naked lips again, just like this morning. "That's very good." Her expression had softened.

"What about you?" he asked in a low voice. "Have you heard about Brandon?"

"No." She sighed. "But I'll be shocked if the test results aren't favorable."

"Why do you say that?"

She let out a breath, and her eyes darted from his face to his chest. She was starting to open up now ever so slowly, and it was fascinating to watch.

"It turned out my sister was being overly dramatic in thinking the cancer was recurring," she said.

"Wow. That's gotta be hard for Brandon."

"He doesn't suspect anything. He thinks it's just a sleepover." Again, that frown.

He squinted at her. "And you're not comfortable with that?"

"I'm used to living alone."

"Auntie!" Brandon was through being patient; he resumed his hammering on the door.

A door opened farther down the hallway. A head popped out.

Jon blocked Elizabeth from view by standing with his back to the curious neighbor. "You should let Brandon out to see me before the neighbors come over to investigate," he pointed out.

She looked horrified. "Get inside," she hissed. "Quickly."

He'd never met a woman like her. Jon was willing to bet she didn't know many of her neighbors. Holding out his hand, indicating she lead, he followed her inside. He liked the view of her in her street clothes rather than her hospital scrubs. This was the real Lizzy that she hid from the public. He appreciated seeing it.

Inside her apartment—smaller and homier than his, with lower ceilings instead of wide-open windows, and curtains drawn tight—he could see straight away that she'd been in the process of foraging up a meal in the kitchen. The wall cabinets were open, and cans of soup—he saw one labeled chicken noodle—were spread over the counter. An empty pot sat on the stovetop.

Brandon came up behind him, clasped Jon's elbow and clung to him. Jon stiffened. *Not cool, Brandon,* he almost said.

"You can give him his autograph," Lizzy remarked, "but then you have to leave. I need to run out to the store to grab us something for dinner."

Her mobile phone rang and, flustered, Lizzy excused herself to go answer it.

Jon stared from Lizzy—in the kitchen whispering into the phone—to Brandon.

Maybe the boy just didn't like chicken noodle soup. His own younger brothers were finicky eaters; one of them had consumed nothing but peanut butter sandwiches until he hit school age. Jon smiled at Brandon and took the boy's hand. He thought again about telling the kid that it was a bad idea to grab a pitcher's throwing arm—sort of like tugging on Superman's cape—but given the kid's and his aunt's riled-up emotions, he figured he would let it go. The kid had been through enough. "I brought over the autograph you asked me for. Plus a game ball from my last start of the season."

Brandon brightened. "That was your Toronto game!"

"It was."

"I watched the whole thing on TV! My mom let me stay up late."

"Are you behaving for your aunt tonight?"

Brandon scratched his head. "I'm hungry."

Jon sat on the couch and motioned for the boy to sit beside him. He noticed a half-written grocery list on the coffee table. Lizzy obviously wasn't used to having people drop by her house unexpectedly, like he was. She probably didn't cook much for herself, either—too many long hours at her job. He could certainly relate.

Lizzy was still murmuring into her phone, in a low voice. She was flustered and out of her element with her nephew and him in the house. While she spoke on the phone, she glanced nervously at them, then opened her refrigerator and stared inside.

Jon smiled quietly at Brandon. His experience bringing up rambunctious younger brothers had taught him that if he acted calm, they were more likely to follow his lead and act calm, too.

"So you're staying here for the night?" he asked Brandon.

The child nodded. "Do you want to see my room?"

"In a minute. For now, I'm wondering why you're

not in your pajamas. It's pretty late. Do you have school tomorrow?"

Brandon brightened. "I didn't go today, but Auntie is driving me tomorrow. I'm going to tell everybody I met you."

"You can do that. But you know, it would really make me happy if you made things easy on your aunt. She works hard. Did you know she took care of a problem with my catching hand today?" Jon held up his bandage.

The kid looked awestruck. Jon's wound did look impressive, all wrapped up like Frankenstein's finger. It throbbed, too, but he was going to overlook that for now.

"It's important you sit still and not bump it," he told Brandon. "That way it will heal properly. Do you think you can do that?"

Brandon's eyes widened. "Are you on the D.L.?"

Disabled list. Jon smiled to himself. Yeah, this kid was a baseball fan. "I wish. That would mean the season wasn't over for us yet."

"I wish the season wasn't over yet, too. Because then you could get tickets for us. We could sit in the players' box and watch you pitch, couldn't we? We could be on TV."

"Ah…" The kid was a live wire, that was for sure. Jon stood and motioned for Brandon to follow. Jon would do this small act to help her, and then he would leave. Now that he knew Brandon was probably okay, he was feeling much better. "Let's get you into your pajamas so you can eat dinner and go right to bed afterward for your aunt. Does your mom like you to take a bath at night, or do you do that in the morning?"

"I take a shower in the morning," Brandon said. "But I don't have my toothbrush with me. I forgot it."

"We'll add one to your aunt's shopping list. What kind of toothpaste do you like?"

"The blue kind."

"What's that? Bubble-gum flavor?"

"Excuse me, Mr. Farell, but the five minutes is over and you're going to have to leave now."

He and Brandon stopped talking and stared over at Lizzy.

You're in my bathroom, she mouthed to Jon, obviously annoyed.

Yeah, he was. But if anybody needed help with the boy, she did. Maybe it was time she removed that bug she carried up her butt.

Slowly, Jon straightened to his full height. "Brandon's going to get into his pajamas for you, and I'm gonna take your shopping list and grab us all something for dinner. Then I'll get out of your hair. Is that okay with you?"

She pulled him angrily aside, out of earshot from Brandon. He got that he was overstepping his bounds, and that she was probably going to throw him out the door, into the hallway.

Still, he rather enjoyed the feeling of her palm, curled into a fistful of fabric from his T-shirt and pulling him around the corner into her...bedroom.

It was Spartan. Too Spartan. A plain cotton comforter, beige walls, miniblinds. Not a throw pillow in sight. No television. No comforts or interesting things to look at. Certainly no silk ties, lubricant or sex toys…

"I," she said, jabbing a finger to his chest, "can take care of my own nephew. Alone."

"Yeah, I'm sure you can. All I'm doing is helping you."

"Auntie?" Brandon said, standing plaintively in the doorway.

"In a minute, Brandon. The adults are busy having a conversation." She shut the door.

He raised a brow at her. "I'm not up for it tonight, Lizzy. I'm still under the weather from all that anesthesia you pumped into my system this morning."

She gasped. Her face went bright red.

He winked at her. "Kidding. I never sleep with women on the first date, much less women with kids. It sets a bad example."

"He is my *nephew!*"

Interesting reaction. She wasn't denying him access to her bed, just correcting his misstatement about son versus nephew. He would remember that.

"Yep, got it," he said. "Never in front of the kids."

She shook her head, obviously flustered. He loved seeing her with her hair messed up like that. He was willing to bet that in her starched-up world, people didn't tease her. They didn't come into her house and help her. And they certainly never made it over the threshold into her bedroom.

She ran her hands through her glossy hair. She really was a natural beauty. Lots of players had wives or girlfriends from the television reporting or modeling worlds—typically brassy women who, when all decked out and made-up, were eye-catching and flashy.

That wasn't Lizzy. He was taken by an urge to draw her close to him. But…that would be a huge mistake.

Don't push it, something told him. *Get too close to her, and she'll throw you out for good.*

He didn't want her to throw him out. So he hung back, waiting. Kept his hands glued to his side. Didn't say a word. Let her know that he wasn't a threat to her.

Finally, a sigh shuddered out of her. "Look, Jon, I have a downstairs neighbor who brings in my deliveries sometimes so they don't get lost," she said, like a confession. "She is elderly and doesn't walk well, so she's usually at home. I called and asked her to watch Brandon for me while I ran out to the store, but she just called back and said she doesn't want him down there, bothering her, because she's watching the baseball game. She doesn't want to come up here and watch him, either, even if he's waiting quietly in my bedroom, because I don't have an HD television."

"Seriously?"

"I know." She rolled her eyes. "Who needs high-definition television to watch baseball?"

"Maybe she has a crush on the pitcher."

A noise burst out of Lizzy, something between a giggle and a snort. She clamped her hand over her mouth, but it was too late.

Aha. So his studious, buttoned-up anesthesiologist had a fun streak in her after all. It was just buried, layers and layers deep.

"Give me your shopping list," he said gently. "I'll take care of it. It's not a big deal."

"It is to me. I don't want you buying things for us. And also…" Lizzy gestured to his bandaged hand. "Did you not read your postoperative instructions? You aren't supposed to be driving, not with the medication you're on. I won't be responsible for that."

"I'm not on medication," he said quietly. "Just acetaminophen."

Her mouth dropped open. "Then you're in pain."

Maybe, a little bit.

He shrugged. "It doesn't matter. I don't want to chance messing with my health by taking heavy drugs like that. My body is how I make my living."

She rolled her eyes again.

He grinned at her. "Lizzy?" he said, at the same time that Brandon whined plaintively through the door, "Auntie?"

Jon opened the door. Brandon was dressed in Superman pajamas. "Excellent job," Jon said to him. "I'd like to reward you for that."

Brandon beamed at him. Before Lizzy could say another word, Jon pulled his wallet from his back pocket and tossed it on the bed. He pulled out his phone, too. "My team's owner sits on your hospital board. Go ahead and call her assistant, she'll vouch for me. Then go out and shop for as long as you need to—I'll wait here with Brandon."

"Yesss!" Brandon pumped his fist and did some kind of rap dance around the bedroom.

Lizzy glowered at Jon. Yeah, he'd pay for making the kid part of their negotiations.

"How do I know you're not a pedophile?" she asked in a low voice. "Perfectly respectable-looking football coaches have been found to be abusive to children. If there is one thing we've learned, it's that we can't trust somebody else vouching for our kids' caretakers just because they have a prestigious job."

Uh, she had a point. A twisted point, but then again, these could be twisted times.

He turned on his phone and called up the video interface. "In that case, we'll use my phone like a nannycam. You can go about your shopping and still see everything Brandon and I are doing."

"You're crazy. I am not going to let you stay in my home, Mr. Farell. I'm a private person."

"And I'm a public guy. I have a lot to lose, too, if you were ever to come out with allegations against me."

That made her pause. "Why?" she asked finally. "Why do you care so much about helping us?"

Damned if he knew. His finger was throbbing again, he was tired, and well… "I'm hungry."

He walked over to Brandon, who said, "I'm hungry, too."

"Then this is what we'll do, kid. While your aunt is out shopping, we'll have quiet time together, under her supervision. So get one of your books and show me how well you read."

"I don't have any books," Brandon said.

"You have books at home," Lizzy corrected him.

"No," Brandon said. "I don't."

He and Lizzy both seemed to still at the same time.

Then she seemed to snap. Scowling, she stomped toward her closet. "Fine." She reached for a plastic box on the top shelf. "I have books." Lifting off the lid, she rummaged inside before handing Brandon a hardcover kid's book.

A very old, very worn-out copy of *Curious George Goes to the Hospital*.

A lump formed in his throat.

He'd read that story many times to his brothers, many nights when they were left alone that one, hard year.

He looked at Lizzy, locked gazes with her.

It was strange, but he could swear she was thinking the same thing.

"This is what we'll do," she said, shaking her head, suddenly straight and crisp again, no sign of apprehension in her root-beer-colored eyes. "Both of you will go down to Mrs. Ham's apartment. While she watches baseball and ogles the real, live baseball-playing pitcher sitting in her living room, the two of you can read your book. And the minute I return, Jon can go home."

CHAPTER FOUR

ELIZABETH PUSHED A grocery cart down the frozen-foods aisle, only halfheartedly paying attention to the waffles and pancakes in the gluten-free breakfast section. Most of her concentration was on the video-phone in her hand.

On the small screen, she saw Jon Farell sitting on the couch beside her nephew in Mrs. Ham's apartment, the child calm, dressed in his pajamas and leaning against Jon's shoulder. Brandon read the book aloud in a halting, unsure voice while Jon patiently encouraged him.

Tears sprang to her eyes, unbidden. Jon didn't know it, but he touched a lode of emotions buried deep inside her.

She quickly wiped her eyes, glancing up to make sure that nobody saw her. It was obvious that this man was dangerous to her sanity. There was a reason she had been so harsh with Jon.

But now everything had flipped around, and she did not want to like him. This public, professional baseball player was so easy with people, while she was so uncomfortable. She certainly did not want to feel these emotions she was feeling—the tenderness toward a man who seemed to have given her fatherless nephew a role model who treated him with respect. How had this man—this man she'd been so inexplicably attracted to—ended up being more good-hearted than she ever would have guessed?

Any man she chose to speak with outside of the work environment—and for her, that was a rare occasion—had to be dispassionate and private.

Jon Farell was the opposite of that kind of person. He was far too outgoing. He didn't seem to have any boundaries—he was the take-charge type. Being drawn to him at all had to be a tragic mistake of her DNA.

As soon as she got home, Elizabeth would shake off her tender emotions and make sure to bar the door to Jon. Brandon wouldn't be happy, but he was going home to his mother tomorrow, after breakfast. Then Elizabeth would have her ordered world back to herself, and all would be well.

By the time she finished up her transaction and drove home, Elizabeth was ready to say goodbye to Jon, once and for all.

Steering her Prius into her numbered spot, she parked and then grabbed the grocery bag from the seat beside her. The carton of eggs wasn't packed properly—she'd been distracted at the checkout counter by staring at her cell phone, watching Brandon reading the book to Jon—and hadn't paid close enough attention to the bagger. Disgusted with herself, she reached over to her purse and shut off her phone inside without looking at it. It was obvious by now that Jon wasn't a predator, just a guy who was extraordinarily good with kids.

She would lead Brandon upstairs to her condominium and then send Jon on his way. She'd picked up a hot takeout pizza for Jon, as a thank-you, from the supermarket's prepared foods section, as well as a frozen gluten-free pizza to heat up and feed to Brandon—something that Brandon's stomach could tolerate. Brandon was allergic to anything with wheat in it. The kid just didn't have a lot of luck in the health department. But, he seemed happy enough—his prior illness and her ineptness about how to deal with him notwithstanding—and she was thankful for that.

Elizabeth shoved her key into the lock and elbowed open the main door to the building. She knocked on the door to Mrs. Ham's unit. She heard the thump of a cane on hardwood floor before Mrs. Ham opened her door.

"He went back to your unit a few minutes ago." Mrs. Ham had a beatific smile on her wrinkled face. She looked ten years younger. "Brandon was drifting off to sleep, so he carried the boy upstairs." She sighed. "I really do like Jon Farell."

"You let him into my apartment?"

"Yes, lucky you."

Elizabeth groaned inwardly. "Thank you, Mrs. Ham."

Then she took the stairs two at a time. When

she came to her unit, she tested the knob. The door opened easily, no key needed.

A shot of panic went through her. Jon had neglected to set the dead bolt? Then again, he was a big man. Six foot two, one hundred ninety pounds—she'd seen his electronic medical record. If she thought rationally, it should be comforting knowing that somebody capable was inside with her nephew, keeping him safe and holding down the fort. He had to be fairly responsible to be part of a professional team, didn't he?

The New England Captains were followed by many children. It wasn't like they were disreputable.

Calm down.

She dropped her keys on the hall table and set the grocery bag down on the kitchen counter. The television was on, the volume low. Jon sat on the couch. Head back, legs stretched out and relaxed.

He was asleep.

Her breath exhaled as she studied him. His eyes were closed and his lashes rested against tanned skin. A lock of hair fell across his cheek. His chest rose and fell softly.

Her chest felt warm and fluttery, which was not rational. She should feel threatened—he was in her space, after all. But everything about her feelings for Jon made little sense to her.

She tore her gaze away, shook off the feeling and tiptoed across her small apartment. She'd told Brandon he could sleep in her bedroom tonight because she didn't have a guest bed for him—she used her second bedroom as an office. Later, she would set up an air mattress for herself there. For now though, the door to her bedroom was open and light from the overhead lamp shone across Brandon's head. He was sleeping on his stomach, cocooned under the covers.

Snug as a bug in a rug, she thought, the phrase a remnant of a short, rare time of stability in her and Ashley's childhood.

A lump in her throat, she shook under the force of her memory. Maybe that was the source of her mixed-up emotions toward the baseball player on her couch. Swallowing, she slipped off her shoes and crept back into the living room in stocking feet, crossing the cool hardwood floor to the couch where Jon was still asleep.

She felt an inexplicable longing in her heart.

Who *was* this man? She didn't understand anything about him. *Why* would he bother with them? It couldn't be just the shared worry of a cancer diagnosis.

His bandaged hand was flung carelessly across the couch. She'd never heard of a patient so unconcerned with himself. Jon had undergone surgery today; he should be at home recovering from the trauma to his body. Where was his sense of self-preservation?

Crowd noise erupted from the television behind her. The baseball game was in full swing. She never paid any attention to the sport, but now...what if she watched, like Mrs. Ham had said? Just until Jon woke up and she could send him on his way.

She pushed aside her magazines and sat quietly in her armchair. Studied the action that so consumed Jon's life.

The image of a broad, commanding player filled her television screen; he toed white rubber on a dirt pitcher's mound. Elizabeth knew that much about the game from long-ago required-attendance gym classes, like any public school kid. She watched the player—the pitcher—stare down the batter. Shake his head slowly to one side, then to the other.

"He's shaking off the catcher's signals," the television announcer said. "It's a full count. Three balls and two strikes."

Elizabeth nibbled her lip. From what little she remembered, if the batter swung and missed a pitch, or did not swing on a pitch that was thrown within the specifications of a "strike zone"—the space over the home plate from batter's knees to his chest—then a strike was called. Three strikes, and the batter was out. A "ball" was called if the pitcher's throw went outside of the strike zone and the batter did not swing at it. Four balls, and a batter advanced to first base.

A walk is as good as a hit.

Elizabeth froze. That voice inside her head was an upsetting blast from her past, from the earliest days of her childhood, when she was younger than Brandon. She never thought of her mother's boyfriend.

Elizabeth's biological father.

Never, ever did she allow herself to think of him as *Father,* because he most assuredly was not. Anger consuming her, she gripped the arms of her chair. *He* had followed baseball like a religion. Why hadn't she thought of this before?

On television, the camera angle swung to the pitcher, a look of concentration on his face. Elizabeth pressed her hand to her throat and forced herself to focus on the pitcher on her TV screen. He had a look of intelligence about him.

"We have a classic dilemma," the television announcer said. "It's the bottom of the ninth inning. Two outs. The tying and winning runs are on base, and it's a full count."

"The question is," a second television announcer said, "does Martinez do the predictable and deliver his trademark fastball in the strike zone, or does he risk throwing the changeup that Bates has already smashed over the right field fence?"

"He shouldn't risk it," Elizabeth muttered.

"Martinez is shaking off his catcher's call," the first announcer said. "His hand is inside his glove. What we're seeing here today is a showdown of baseball's top ace versus the leading home run slugger. If the ace wins, his team wins the series and moves on to the Eastern League finals. Otherwise, they're out until spring."

"Martinez is a pitcher's pitcher," the second announcer said. "Better than anyone in the game today, he throws the batters off their rhythm. As a batter facing an ace, you never know what he's going to do. Is he going to speed up your rhythm or slow it down?

"The thing about Martinez is that he's developed his technique, his windup, such that the batter can't see his grip position on the baseball. He has no clue whether to expect a curveball, a fastball, a changeup…until the ball is right in front of him and it's too late. Very few pitchers have the skill to do this, and it's what makes Martinez great. Barring any unforeseen scandal, he's a future Hall of Famer."

"A legend," the first announcer agreed.

"What will it be?"

She found herself holding her breath. The noise from the crowd was a buzzing hum. In the stadium, it would be deafening. She wondered which side the fans were on, the pitcher's or the batter's?

Elizabeth sat forward in her seat. She was concentrating so hard her focus had narrowed to a place where all that existed was the pitcher on the screen. His slow, careful windup. His arm stretched back, his leg in the air.

He fired the pitch like a rocket, with a skill that seemed superhuman. In a blur, the slugger swung hard and missed. The ball smacked inside the catcher's mitt.

"Game over!" the announcer cried.

Elizabeth jumped up from her chair and squealed. She'd had no idea baseball was this exciting.

"I knew there was a reason I liked you, Lizzy," Jon's quiet voice said from behind her.

She gasped. She'd been so absorbed in the game, she'd completely forgotten about Jon.

Now he was awake. He had a faint smile and a twinkle in his eye. He wasn't even watching the television screen, the commotion of celebration and the jostling of reporters crowding onto the field.

He grinned at her. "You were rooting for the pitcher."

"I was not!"

He grinned harder. "Sure you were."

She glanced to her grocery bag on the kitchen counter. She needed to get Jon out of here and on his way. "I brought you a pizza from the ovens at Whole Foods. You can take it home with you and eat it there."

He cocked his head at her. "Why can't you admit that you were enjoying watching the baseball game?"

"I wasn't *enjoying* anything. It was strictly intellectual curiosity."

"So you admit that you find baseball intelligent," he said quietly. "Good. Because it is."

"Whatever you say," she snapped.

That seemed to deflate him. Touched a sore spot with him, maybe.

She felt angry at herself. Confused…and she was a woman who was rarely confused. But her actions made no sense. She should not be interested in Jon, or his sport—she had her own, critical business to attend to.

Stalking to the kitchen, she headed for the counter.

"Here's your pizza." She pulled the warm, delicious-smelling box out of the bag.

Jon followed her. "Thanks." But his face looked pale, and he seemed to be...wincing.

He put his hand on the tabletop to steady himself. "I'm...sorry I didn't help you carry the bag upstairs," he murmured.

She stared at his bandaged finger and saw the red stain. "Are your sutures bleeding?" she demanded.

His ice-blue eyes considered her. "I'm okay, Liz."

"You are *not* okay. You've been through surgery and you need to take care of yourself."

He winced again, and she remembered that he'd said he hadn't taken painkillers. She opened a cabinet and grabbed some over-the-counter acetaminophen and wound-dressing supplies.

She hadn't bandaged a patient since her rotation in emergency medicine, but she owed him that, at least. "Let me change your bandage as a thank-you. Then you should go home and rest. Surgery is difficult on the body." She handed him a glass of water and shook out two tablets. "Take these. You'll still be able to drive."

He took them from her outstretched palm. His hands were...overly large for his frame. Long fingers, the nails groomed short.

"Do you ever watch baseball, Liz?" His voice was so low and warm it made her shiver.

But she shook the thoughts of him out of her head. Those pheromones were wreaking havoc again.

"Never," she said firmly, turning to the sink to soap up her hands, then she smeared them with Purell almost to her elbows, by force of habit. "I already told you that."

He said nothing. Sat still, at her kitchen table. She bent over his splinted finger, and squinted into the light.

She could feel the steady rhythm of his breathing, she was so close to him, their heads almost touching. She was horrified to find that she was matching her inhales and exhales to his.

Stop it, she told herself. Switching into professional mode, she removed the bandages the surgical nurse had placed around Jon's finger. The stitches beneath were small and even: expert. Typically, the residents stitched up the incision after the surgeon cut, but in Jon's case, he had wanted to do everything himself, carefully and by the book; he'd even forbidden the team from playing music in the operating room.

"Do you have any idea how much money this guy's hands are worth?" Dr. Morgan had remarked to Elizabeth. At the time, she'd had no clue. Now, after watching that clip on television, she had a better idea.

She kept her gaze on Jon's finger, and on the sterile gauze and tube of antibiotic ointment she was opening. Jon said nothing, and that was worse than his teasing earlier in the night had been.

He wasn't throwing roadblocks in her way now. So why was she delaying sending him home?

She drew in her breath. "Thank you for watching

Brandon for me," she said crisply, "but I see no reason for our continued acquaintance beyond tonight." Her heart rate was elevated again, but she forced herself to continue. "I understand that Brandon and you may have formed an attachment, and I think that's wonderful, but tomorrow Brandon goes home, and tomorrow you can take up the matter with my sister if you wish."

"I'm not interested in your sister," he said quietly.

"Don't say that until you've met her," she said beneath her breath.

His ice-blue eyes seemed to bore into her. Seeing too much beneath the surface, more so than she was comfortable sharing with anybody.

She made as much noise as possible, tearing at the packaging for the sterile gauze. Anything to distract herself from his presence.

"Does she suck up all the attention, Liz?" Jon asked quietly.

"What? No!" She jerked her gaze to him. "Stop questioning me. You have the wrong opinion of us."

"What's wrong about it?"

"You would like my sister. Everybody does."

"I'm not everybody."

He did not understand. "You in *particular* would like her, I mean." Elizabeth slapped the bandage onto his hand. Or, she wanted to slap it on, but years of training betrayed her. *Be gentle with the patients.* "I'm saying that because right now she is helpless and in need of assistance, and you seem to be drawn to helpless women, one of which I am not."

He frowned, pulling back his hand. "You think you're helpless with Brandon, don't you?"

"Did I say that?" she demanded. "Don't put words in my mouth!"

"You're prickly." He smiled. "I touched a nerve, didn't I?"

She really did not like him sitting so close to her, seeing too much inside her life. And yet, she had finished bandaging him and he wasn't pulling away, despite what he saw of her. She leaned the tiniest bit closer, into his space again. It had to be the pheromones.

She shook it off. Remembered why she was pushing him away. "You stayed here, Jon, and you took right over from me because you like being in situations where people are helpless. It allows you to be the hero. I can see it, and I don't want that in my life. It goes against everything I've set up for myself."

He stared at her. "You are so wrong about me," he blurted.

Yes, she thought, *that's good. Get mad at me and then leave.*

But at the same time she felt sadness. She didn't know why. Maybe she'd hoped he saw beyond the prickliness of her delivery into the truth of what she'd observed.

She fought her own inner resistance. Pushed back from the table—from him—and grabbed the pizza box she'd bought him, which was quickly getting cold. She shoved it forward, against his chest. "Thank you for your assistance. Tomorrow I go back to my normal life and Brandon goes home to his. Please be careful driving home, and follow all the instructions on your postsurgical papers this time."

"I didn't come here intending to help you with Brandon," Jon said, standing to his full height and towering over her.

"Maybe not," she replied, looking up into his face, "but that's the instinct that took over, isn't it? Maybe subconsciously, that's how you're used to handling difficult situations."

Real anger flashed in his eyes.

A textbook reaction—and she knew, because she'd completed a psychology rotation. Jon seemed to be experiencing classic denial symptoms.

"Excuse me?" he said. "You don't know me at all."

Perhaps, but she knew a textbook case. Psychology fascinated her. And why not answer his question? It's not as if she would ever see him again after tonight.

"You're a pitcher, Jon, right? You play in the major leagues. That took years of training to attain—I'm assuming it was as long and as grueling as it was for me to become a doctor. I'm also assuming that in order for you to make the major leagues, and stay there, you have to love your sport the same way that I love my job. So if that had been me tonight in your shoes, I would have been watching that game very closely, and not at all caring about somebody else's reaction to it. And yet, you weren't even interested in watching that guy—Martinez, the ace pitcher—seeing how he did it. You were just staring at me."

"I'm friggin' tired," Jon said as he shoved the pizza box back at her, which was the first instance of hostility she'd seen from him. Maybe it was for the best. That meant he didn't like her, either. That meant she had nothing to fear from him.

"I had surgery and I was pumped full of chemicals today," he continued. "Your chemicals."

She nodded vigorously, walking him toward the door. "And yet you came here to see us—to see Brandon. To help Brandon. As I said, you have a white-knight complex."

Those ice-blue eyes bored into hers. "Lady, you have no idea who I am."

Bull's-eye, she thought. And it gave her no comfort to be right. That wasn't why she was pushing him. Being prickly.

"Why are you always so prickly?" Ashley often asked her.

Because I want to be back on my own track away from everybody else, she silently answered.

Jon Farell was…not good for that. He threatened her autonomy.

She opened the door and stood beside it. She felt sad all of a sudden—lousy. Being prickly and irritable was not what she'd wanted. She was not a cruel person. But Jon was in her lair, and she wanted to be—needed to be—alone. She was yearning for it, in fact.

"You're right," she said firmly to him. "I don't know you. I don't want to know you. You were simply a patient to me. Please go and help somebody else."

He walked out and didn't look back.

Inside, she closed the door and leaned against it, her back to the cold, hard surface. Her hands were shaking as they curled around the edges of the now-cold pizza box. Her heart rate was elevated, and she appeared to be having palpitations.

It was crazy, but a part of her still wanted him here with her.

And she had blown that from ever happening again.

CHAPTER FIVE

SHE WAS DEAD wrong about him.

His pulse throbbing in his neck, Jon yanked open his SUV door and fumbled with his key in the darkness in an attempt to start his engine. He had the key lined up, but damn it, he couldn't turn it in the ignition easily with his right finger in a splint.

White-knight complex? Give me a break. At the moment, he couldn't even help himself out of a paper bag.

Jon laid his head against the seat back and let the motor quietly run. Condensation covered the windows. It was a cool night after a warm day. Lizzy could probably explain the scientific reasoning behind the fog that blocked him from seeing where the hell he was. In so many ways—education-wise, her doctor status, her aloofness to sports teams—she was out of his league. Made him feel inadequate. Tossed him around like nobody else did.

He blew out a breath. He wasn't an idiot. He was a self-aware person, smart enough to know that he'd been thrown for a loop over his cancer scare. That, and then the euphoria over learning he was cancer-free had sent him spinning, all in the course of a few hours.

He'd wanted somebody to share his excitement and relief with, somebody genuine, a person who didn't have any skin in the game with his career, and somebody who understood what he'd been going through. He'd thought that person had been her.

Wrong. Lizzy wanted nothing to do with him, and she'd told him so from the moment he'd rung her doorbell. Maybe, for a brief time, he'd managed to change her mind. When Martinez had thrown his ninety-eight-mile-per-hour four-fingered fastball, low and in the corner, and had psyched out Bates into swinging too late, she had been hooked, and Jon had felt hope.

But then…somehow her prejudices against him had kicked in, and the moment had gone to hell. He hadn't managed the situation right at all. He'd blown it; he'd been the one to walk out in anger.

No highs, no lows. The best fielding coach Jon had ever known had taught him that, early on during his rookie year in the minor leagues. Don't get too far emotionally up, and don't get too far emotionally down, the mantra meant, or you'll ruin the game plan. If you wanted to win—at baseball and at life—then it was necessary to take everything as it came, with an even temper.

He knew what he had to do. He felt calmer now. The windows were getting clearer.

His stomach growled. He should have taken the

pizza when he had the chance. Pride be damned, he was starving. Still, it wasn't wise to go back up to Lizzy's apartment to have her psychoanalyze him again, even if—in her defense—she was probably terrified over having him and Brandon inside her normally ordered, doctor world, and was making up theories in order to push him away.

He was *not* drawn to helpless women. He never had been, and everyone knew it.

He dug his phone from his pocket and scrolled the contact list to call up the number for Brooke. He would stay cool. His plan of action was clear: *get your baseball life back on track.*

"Patch me through to Max," Jon said to Brooke when she answered the phone. "I want a three-way call with all of us on board."

"What's going on?" Max asked, his voice faint. "You've left me a few messages this evening."

"Yes, I have." Jon's SUV windows were clear now, so he pulled the Expedition out of the lot. "I need my contract signed for next season, and I need to get going on that as soon as possible."

"That's…good. Brooke is sitting with me." Max did sound weak. Why was that? "She was just about to send you a text message. Are you listening to radio sports talk?"

"Ah…no. I don't pay attention to that stuff."

"Jon…turn on the radio…and listen…"

"Now," Brooke said insistently. Jon could hear

the radio playing in the background. "Turn it to SPK FM."

"Call us back in a few minutes." Max disconnected the call.

This was not good. But Max had never steered him wrong. Jon eased up on the accelerator and slowed for a traffic light.

While the light was red, Jon took a swig of water from the bottle in his cup holder and then fumbled with the radio dial to find SPK. He would subject himself to the negativity for just one minute, and then he'd turn it off.

"…he's a local guy. What are you ragging on the local guy for, the only pitcher who won his last two games?"

Jon almost spit out his water. That was Francis! His brother had called into the radio show. On top of everything else, this had to happen?

Jon turned the volume louder.

"…come on," the radio host was saying. "Local or not, you can't argue with his numbers. They're terrible."

Great, Jon thought. The host's gravelly voice made him sound like a tough guy, but Jon had met him in person. He was short, overweight and wore thick glasses. In high school gym class, he likely would have been picked last, every time. Maybe Lizzy would know if there was psychology that drew guys like him to working on these sports-team criticism shows.

"Farell just did not have a good season," the second sports host said. "I'm sorry, but you can't spin the numbers. Overall, he was a disappointment to Boston fans this year."

That particular host had played in the big leagues. Jon actually respected his opinion, and that comment hurt.

"But he won his last two games! You guys aren't even considering that. It shows you don't know anything. You don't know what's happening in that clubhouse," Francis said again, spouting off, and Jon knew he had to do something, because this would not end well.

When the light turned green, he hooked a left turn and drove the mile out of his way through thickly settled neighborhoods to his father's house—Jon's boyhood home—where Francis still lived in a bottom-floor apartment. Jon had even helped build and convert it for him. And when Jon got there, he would physically hang up the phone on his well-meaning but hotheaded younger brother, before he could do any real damage to Jon's name.

Fortunately, the show cut Francis off. Fuel added to their fire, the two hosts segued to a discussion about how they would like to dump the entire Captains starting-pitching rotation, front to back, and start over with new recruiting, because they thought that the existing attitudes were poisonous to the rest of the clubhouse.

Jon switched off the radio. Talk like this could

spark a revolution. The cries and calls from fans and press—especially in a big-market team like Boston—did affect management's personnel strategy, as much as everyone liked to think it didn't.

This was worse for him than his evening's troubles with Lizzy. He fumbled with his phone and dialed Francis's number. "Don't you ever do that again," he said when Francis picked up.

"I hate those jerks," Francis sputtered.

"Then why do you listen to them?"

"How can you *not* listen to them?" Francis shouted.

"Because it helps nobody," Jon answered calmly. "Don't you get it? They're looking to cast blame. These guys live and die by their ratings, and they'll be happy for any kind of outrage they can stir up to explain our lousy September—how we blew such a huge lead in the standings and lost so many games that we missed making the playoffs. If I were a fan, I'd be interested, too."

"Why *did* you lose so many games?"

If Frankie was questioning him, then he was really in trouble.

"In reality, Frankie, sometimes stuff like this just happens. For no reason. Okay? And then we deal with it and we move on."

"How *are* you dealing with it, Jon?"

"By planning for the future. My agent and I have a plan." Okay…not yet, but they would. "What I'm getting at is that I have to be irresistible to the team for next year so they'll sign me again. And if people are bringing up my name in public in a bad way, then that can only hurt me. Do you understand, Frankie?"

It was the bluntest speech he'd ever given Francis. There was silence on the other end of the phone. Hopefully, his brother was digesting the message.

"Yeah, man," Francis said, but in a smaller voice.

"Look, I don't want to hurt your feelings, man," he said. "I appreciate you caring about me."

"I'm…sorry," Francis said. He paused—it sounded like he was conducting a muffled conversation on the side. Jon couldn't be sure, but he'd guess it was with a woman.

A *woman?* With Francis? Since when?

Jon glanced at a passing street sign. Just a few more blocks to go. "Don't leave, okay?" Jon said, stepping harder on the accelerator. "I'm almost at the house. We'll have a beer together in Dad's kitchen when I get there."

"I'm, ah, not at home," Francis said.

How could he not be at home? His life was at home. Him and their dad, home together every night after work. Why did Jon get the feeling that his life was quicksand all of a sudden?

"Where are you, Frankie? Do you want me to drive over and pick you up?"

"No, Jonny, I'm good. I just…don't know what I'll do if you lose your place with the Captains, okay? It's…it's…" He lowered his voice. "It's the best thing in my life."

Jon gripped his hand on the steering wheel. There

was something just so sad about that statement. Did his brother really believe that?

Yeah, he did. And if Jon were honest, it had been that way since childhood. That, at least, hadn't changed.

"It will be okay, Frankie," he said quietly. "You'll see. Everything will turn out."

"I have to go," Francis mumbled. "I'll see you on the weekend, okay?"

Before Jon could answer, the call disconnected.

He tossed the phone on the seat. But now, he was there, at their dad's house. Jon slowed the SUV to a stop.

The porch was lit by a single bulb, and in the diminished light, the place didn't look much different from when he was ten and Francis was eight. Back then, Jon had the weight of the world on him, because nobody in his family could pull themselves up from their sadness and their grief without his encouragement. He'd cajoled and helped his brothers and his dad every step of the way. And it had eaten at him. Some days, Jon didn't know how they were going to all make it through to the end—himself included.

A car came up behind him, high beams bouncing off Jon's rearview mirror. The single lane street was narrow, lined on both sides by parked cars, so Jon had to either pull his SUV over or drive on.

Shaking off the maudlin feelings, he executed a quick maneuver and backed the Expedition into the empty on-street spot beside the driveway. There was a pecking order with neighborhood parking spaces, and the local owners and tenants knew enough to leave this particular space open—for him or for his brother Bobby—or else face the pain of Francis's wrath raining down on them. Not that Jon insisted on the spot remaining open—but Francis did. And they were a family, so Jon embraced it.

The car with the high beams roared past him. Jon wondered why he hadn't driven off, too. Why sit and stare at his boyhood home, thinking depressing thoughts? The place was in darkness, and it was obvious that nobody was home, either in his brother's downstairs rooms or his dad's upstairs apartment. At ten o'clock on a work night.

Jon frowned. Where was his dad, anyway? But Jon had no idea, because he hadn't checked in with him since before the season had ended. Jon had been too preoccupied with his cancer scare, trying to hide that from his family so they wouldn't be upset if they found out.

His phone beeped, alerting him that he had a new text message—which reminded him that he really should drive home and call back his agent. Surprisingly, when he checked the phone's readout, he found that the message wasn't from Max but from a young Captains pitcher just up from the minors, his first year in the big leagues. Jon had been mentoring him this season. Calming him down before all his big starts.

Jon, help me out here. I don't like the sound of what I'm hearing about us on SPK. What should I do??

Jon stared at the screen. Fixated on that word *help*. Focused on the question marks just begging for his assistance.

Twenty-four hours ago, Jon would have happily tapped out his advice and sent it to the newbie. Now, he was doubting himself.

Lizzy was in his head, obviously. Her psychoanalyzing was causing him to see things differently. He wasn't sure he liked that.

Maybe he did like helping people now and then. So what? It didn't mean that they were helpless, or that there was something wrong with him. He just…hated when people felt bad. Like Francis, in childhood. Jon needed to see people smile. He needed them to have an easier time in life than they were having when they were upset.

But Lizzy did have a point. Maybe he did tend to help people a little too much, at the expense of himself.

When he really thought about it, hadn't all this helping and protecting and watching out for people gotten him into a bad spot with the team? He'd spent too much time worrying about—frankly—the crappy attitudes of some of the Captains' leading aces. It had trickled down to the younger guys on the pitching staff, and the team's cohesion had been affected.

The sports talk radio guys were right—there was a reason their team had imploded.

For the second time that night, Jon leaned back with his head against the seat. He should have focused more during the season on his own pitching, his own numbers. Things had slipped by, and now he didn't have what he wanted: the team breathing down his neck, eager to sign a contract with him for next year.

He held his throbbing finger in his lap and just closed his eyes. *Lizzy, what did you do to me?* But nobody had ever pointed this out to him before.

A knock sounded on the window. Jon snapped to attention. His old neighbor, Mr. Yanopoulis, was peering at him. Jon turned off the idling engine and stepped outside into the cool night air to greet him.

"I knew it was you!" Mr. Yanopoulis grinned and held out a gnarled hand. When Jon didn't shake it because of the splinted finger he hid behind his back, Mr. Yanopoulis lifted his hand to pat Jon's shoulder, undaunted. "It's good to see you, Jonny. You don't visit us often enough. You're our neighborhood celebrity. When you're pitching, we throw a big party."

"It's good to see you, too." Jon smiled at his elderly neighbor and knelt down to pet his little dog, yapping and straining on his leash. "My dad isn't home?" he casually asked, straightening.

"Nope. I'm feeding his cat for him." Mr. Yanopoulis pulled on the leash. "Your dad called me today.

Said he was extending his trip and going with a group down to the Grand Canyon."

"The Grand Canyon?"

"Sure. Jean and I went there last year, flew out and rented a motor home in Denver. I showed him the pictures when we came back—I guess he liked what he saw."

Jon nodded. "How long has my father been gone?"

"He left for Vegas the day after…after the season ended." Mr. Yanopoulis looked embarrassed for him. "It was a last-minute decision."

His dad was gone, too? Why not, Jon thought. His dad had probably left after it had been clear the Captains wouldn't be in the playoffs. Dad would have been bitterly disappointed. Jon wasn't feeling so great himself.

"Can I ask you a question?" he said to his neighbor. This was stupid of him, but… "Did I ever help you when I was a kid?"

"Help me? You helped everybody." Mr. Yanopoulis pulled on the leash again. "Why? What's this all about?"

"I'm just wondering…what do you remember most about me from those days?"

Mr. Yanopoulis smiled. "You know what I remember?" He pointed at the narrow strip of grass—barely the width of a dugout bench—that separated Jon's family's driveway from the Yanopoulis house. "You, at about ten years old, out there for hours, hurling a baseball against that screen thing."

"The pitch-back net," Jon said.

"Yeah, the pitch-back. You threw baseballs at it every night. Jean stayed up late, worrying. She wanted to complain to your father, but I told her, no, leave the boy alone, he is going to be a star someday." He pointed at Jon. "And I was right."

Jon felt shaken. He remembered perfectly—the glow from the reflective tape of the strike zone he'd measured out, the squeak of the springs when the ball bounced back on the net at him, the satisfying feel in his muscles of hurling the ball with all his might, getting out his frustrations.

At first, he'd shredded those pitch-back toys. There hadn't been just one; there had been half a dozen he'd gone through, at least until he'd figured out how to reinforce the sides with PVC piping and duct tape. To make them, he'd saved up bottle-and-can collecting money, plus payments for neighborhood shoveling and grass cutting, and bought the equipment at a sports store downtown, hauling it home on his bike with Frankie's help. Jon had needed that ritual. His mom was gone—dead from bone cancer—and his dad was in a serious state of depression. His father had been—still was, in a sense—a lost soul. Francis, even more rage-filled back then than he was now, was constantly in schoolyard fights, and Jon had felt compelled to defend him. Bobby, the baby, had needed Jon's help with everything—getting dressed, getting fed, being told to brush his teeth and to turn off the TV. He had been very much like Brandon in that respect.

Those hours with the pitch-back—that had been Jon's outlet for blowing off steam. His way of calming himself down. Getting centered so he could sleep.

It had only been an accident that he'd turned himself into a pretty good pitching talent. A talent that, luckily, some world-class coaches along the way had noticed. They had seen enough potential in Jon to take him on board and train him seriously. After that, life had gotten measurably better, for everyone in his family. He'd brought them hope.

He didn't want to lose that.

He blew out a breath. Everything felt clearer. Maybe there was even a reason he'd met Lizzy. He'd needed that message—her message—to focus on himself.

No highs, no lows.

"Thanks," Jon said to his neighbor. "You take care." He turned and stared at the narrow strip of grass one last time.

After Mr. Yanopoulis had left with his dog on the leash, Jon climbed back into this SUV and typed out a text message to his agent.

I need to give the team reason to sign me again. I'm adding a fourth pitch this winter, a changeup. I also need to do some visible fund-raising with Vivian's charity at the hospital. Call me back and tell me what you think.

Then, and only then, did he reply to the text from the young guy he'd been mentoring. This would be the last time Jon would expend energy on a fellow pitcher for the foreseeable future. Jon had his own work to do.

Talk to your agent. Listen to whatever advice they give you, and follow it.

Then Jon took his own advice. He set his phone in the SUV's cup holder and, while he waited for Max to call back, he headed home to Boston. He was trying a new way of living. *Not helping,* he would call it. *Focusing on himself and getting his own work done.*

"I am not a helpful guy," he said aloud to himself.

"Jon?" Max said when he finally called Jon back, as he was driving across the Zakim bridge. "That sounds like a good plan you came up with."

"I'm glad you think so."

"We made some calls," Max continued. "Management is marching to the drumbeat that they're blaming the team's collapse on the pitching falling apart."

Little surprise there. Jon pinched the bridge of his nose with the fingers of his good hand as he fixed his gaze on the headlights and road before him. "Yeah, I heard the gist of it from the call-in program."

"*Your* pitching staff," Max said. "So you'll be painted with the broad brush. It won't be smooth going."

"I know." Jon turned the wheel with his left hand.

"That's why I'll be working on my changeup pitch again."

"It can't hurt." That was Brooke speaking. "But we think you should focus most on appealing to Vivian. She's hosting a charity fund-raising event early next month. I can get you an invitation near her table."

"Max," Jon asked, "are you passing me on as your daughter's client?"

"How's your finger doing?" Brooke asked, unperturbed by Jon's question.

"Fine." The over-the-counter painkillers Elizabeth had given him had finally kicked in. "The surgeon called me and said everything is fine." He paused. "Max, are you fine? What's going on? Why is Brooke with you?"

There was only a slight hesitation. "I'm headed into surgery myself," Max said evenly. "It's routine—nothing for you to worry about, but Brooke will be in charge for the next few weeks while I recuperate. Pay attention to her—I've taught her everything I know. Don't discount my daughter. Do you hear me, Jon?"

He was really being tested today. "Yeah, sure. As long as you're the one negotiating my contract."

"Of course," Max answered. "But in return, I want you to implement Brooke's ideas with Vivian."

Jon grunted into the phone, paying closer attention to traffic in the intersection as he stopped the SUV at a red light. "I already do fund-raising for Vivian's Sunshine Club project." Such as, writing lots of checks behind the scenes. "I just don't trumpet it."

"Well, now you'll be trumpeting everything to the high heavens," Max said. "Vivian may be the team's majority owner, and as such, normally stays away from operational issues, but she's taken it upon herself to give input on contract decisions. If she likes you personally, you stand a better chance of things going your way."

"And you shouldn't have any worries in that department, Jon," Brooke interjected, "but just in case, I'll work on other ideas for your fund-raising participation."

Jon hated having cameras in his face. But for the sake of getting serious… "Yeah, sure, everything is on the table."

"Excellent," Brooke said. "I'll talk to the program directors at the Captains front office and at Wellness Hospital."

Lizzy's hospital. But knowing Lizzy, she didn't get involved with the public programs.

"Fine," Jon said. "Sounds good."

"All right," Brooke said. "I'll float some ideas when I have them."

"Great." In the meantime, Jon would line up his changeup coach.

Jon hung up the phone.

He drove home and just slept, as long as he needed to, which, thankfully coincided with the crack of dawn. When he got up, he cooked himself a big breakfast: eggs, toast, bacon, orange juice, coffee. He made an early phone call, checked the internet and, in the process, tracked down the one man in Boston—the pitching wizard—he could trust to help him add a changeup pitch to his repertoire.

That was all Jon had in his power to focus on at the moment. Yeah, his day of "not helping" other people, just himself, was starting off fine. Coach Duffy—his high school mentor—still lived nearby. Now, all these years later, he worked at a local college with a top baseball program. Not Jon's alma mater, but that worked out for the best. His "changeup" project needed to be top-secret in order to get him anywhere.

Feeling better than he had in weeks, Jon showered and dressed and called down for his SUV. Then he drove out to the suburbs and approached his old coach on the back nine of his weekly golf game.

Since it was a tiny municipal course, the back nine was the same as the front nine, meaning there were only nine holes, played twice. Perfect for Coach Duffy, the biggest "duffer" Jon had ever known. Lousy at golf, he was a great pitching coach. But woe to anyone who told Coach Duffy he was terrible at golf.

Coach Duffy was teeing up in front of the clubhouse when Jon found him. Focusing intently, his old coach was trying his hardest—as usual. A cap was tucked over his balding head, and his feet and hips were lined up at the perfect angle.

Jon crossed his arms, his splinted finger tucked up under his biceps, and waited for Coach Duffy's swing. Studied, technically perfect...but awkward.

At the moment the club head connected with an off-kilter *thwap* against the golf ball, Jon timed his entrance. The other three members of Coach's foursome recognized Jon immediately and crowded around him. That's what Jon had been counting on.

The drive hooked left into the trees. "Almighty Chr—" Coach Duffy saw Jon and did a double take.

"Hey, Coach," Jon said, grinning.

Coach Duffy tossed his club into the bag and stalked to his golf cart.

"Do you mind if I ride along with him?" Jon asked the rest of the foursome. When the other men nodded, Jon jogged across the grass and climbed into the cart beside his old mentor.

"Blast from the past," Coach said drily.

Jon settled into the seat, his splinted finger still tucked under his arm. "I know. I should have sent you some Captains tickets at some point."

"What, you mean they didn't get lost in the mail?" The low-putting engine kicked in, and Coach swung the cart down a bumpy gravel pathway.

"I promise I'll send you some for the spring training games." Assuming Jon got a contract for next year. "A plane ticket, too."

"What do you want, Farell?" Coach growled over the whine of the engine.

"What? Can't I visit with the guy who made it all possible for me?"

Coach snorted. "I made squat possible. You were

the most talented young man I ever taught, and when you weren't distracted, you worked your ass off."

The implication was that Jon had been distracted far too often. He gazed out over the sparse fairway, a few of the leaves on the maple trees in the distance just turning red with the autumn season. "I paid the price for it."

"No, Jon, you didn't. Not yet. You're squandering your talent." Coach Duffy glared at him. "Do you know what people would *give* for what you had?" He thumped the steering wheel. "Natural talent plus the combination of hard work—that's the only formula for success. I tell it to my students, and they never believe me." He threw up his hands. "Imagine that."

Thinking back to his teenage years, Jon couldn't remember Coach Duffy being so bitter and frustrated. Or maybe, back then, he hadn't been.

"You know, maybe you're selling yourself short," Jon said. "You could be a big-league coach if you wanted. I know—I've worked with some of the best out there."

"What do you *want,* Farell?" his old coach asked again.

It was time to take a chance. Jon needed this, because he couldn't go to the Captains showing the weakness of his wounded finger. Not now, when he had so many other strikes against him.

"I need to work on my changeup pitch, and I want you to be the one to help me do it."

There was a moment of silence as Coach Duffy

swung the golf cart into a small parking area and cut the engine. He stared into the distance. The other golf cart in his foursome was chugging up behind them.

"Please," Jon said quietly. "You're the only one in the business who gets what I'm trying to do. You know where I came from. What…I was dealing with as a kid."

"Are you past that?" Coach Duffy asked.

Bringing his brothers safely through childhood and getting them started in life after his mom's death? If that's what his old coach was talking about… "Yeah. Yeah, I'm over that."

Coach nodded slowly. "You were working on the changeup in high school as I recall."

"I was." But he'd abandoned it. It had been too much to handle at the time. His fastball, his curveball and his sinker were his reliable pitches—the arsenal that worked for him. "The changeup…I just never had a handle on it." It was an off-speed pitch, meaning that when thrown, it looked like a fastball, but it arrived at the plate at a slower velocity.

The lower speed and the deceptive delivery confused a batter's timing. When thrown well, it was lethal. When executed improperly, a batter could hit the hell out of it.

Coach glanced at Jon's finger. "What's that splint on your hand?"

"Nothing." Jon hid it under his biceps again. "Elective surgery."

"You can't work out with that," Coach said bluntly. "How are you going to hold a glove?"

"I can condition myself. Work on grips. Some light throwing."

Coach Duffy stared at Jon. "You're serious about this?"

Jon's heart beat harder. Those words…that's what his dream had been about when he'd been under anesthesia. Maybe Coach Duffy was the man in the dream that he couldn't remember? Maybe this was all about getting closer to who he really was. Finding his purpose and getting centered.

"I've never been more serious," Jon said.

"Then you'll need to work your ass off. Unlike what you've been doing in your big-league career."

"You've been watching me, huh?" Jon smiled, but Coach Duffy didn't like the joke.

"I'm committed," Jon said quickly. "I'm in a fight for my life."

The other cart pulled up beside them, and Coach stepped out to join them. At the last second, he turned to Jon. "You know that the Captains might drop you, trade you or move you to the bullpen, don't you?"

Don't say that. Don't even think it. "I'm a starting pitcher with a changeup pitch in my future."

Coach Duffy's smile crinkled. "That's the spirit." He strolled to the back of the cart. "You could be an ace, Jon, if you let yourself have it."

"Does that mean you'll do it? You'll help me?"

"Only if I see commitment from you. This, right now…this is just talk."

"I'll start today," Jon assured him.

Coach Duffy selected a seven iron from his golf bag. "Meet me in my office on campus at eleven in the morning. If you're late, it's over." He pointed at him with the end of the grip. "Consider it your first test."

Jon went home and got his gear together. Coach Duffy didn't know it yet, but Jon wasn't going to let anything stand in his way.

With his good hand, he tossed in a small cooler full of ice packs. He even threw in his glove, though he didn't know why he was bothering, because with the splint, he wouldn't be wearing it. It just felt like the right thing to do.

The day would probably be a session of loose stretching. Of easy, long tosses. Just getting back into a regular workout routine after the break caused by the surgery. Then, in a few days the stitches would be taken out. For now, he just wanted to get going on discussing the mechanics of the changeup pitch. He felt an urgency to begin anew.

With the address of Coach's campus plugged into his GPS, he swung his SUV into traffic. It was a bright autumn day in Boston, windy and warm, and there were lots of tourists on the meandering streets built over Colonial-era cow paths. One of the big universities—MIT, BU, Northeastern—must be having Parents Weekend. It made Jon smile, thinking of his own college years in Arizona. That had been the time in his life he'd been most focused on himself, selfish even. He would do best to keep that in mind.

But he was sitting at a red light when his phone buzzed. Glancing down, he saw "Lizzy" on the screen.

That had to be a mistake. His pretty anesthesiologist would not be calling him. Not after the parting shot she'd given him.

It had to be a butt-dial.

As the traffic started up, he maneuvered his SUV around an obviously lost tourist from Pennsylvania, beat the left turn on the light and then answered the phone.

He didn't expect her to answer him back, but he spoke into the phone anyway. "What is it, Lizzy? I'm busy 'not helping' people today."

"Jon?" Brandon's thin, high voice cut in on the line.

Jon snapped to attention, steering the Ford away from a Duck Tour bus and into the lane behind a delivery truck carrying beer.

"Hey, buddy," he said into the phone. "What's going on?"

"I think I'm lost."

"Um. Okay." The beer truck stopped short—right before a green light—so Jon cut around the truck and made a forced merge into the left lane. A horn blared at him, but he ignored it. *Get used to Boston driving, out-of-towners.* "*Where* are you lost?"

"If I knew where I was, then I wouldn't be lost, would I?" Brandon said.

Smart-ass, Jon thought. Just like his brother Bobby.

But the good news was, Brandon didn't sound scared. Jon's instincts told him this was just a ploy. *Get-the-attention-of-the-big-league-ballplayer. Maybe he'll come around the neighborhood and impress your friends.*

Lizzy would not be happy when she found out.

"Are you with your aunt?" Jon asked.

"No."

So, the kid had taken it upon himself to look up the number that Jon had typed into his aunt's phone last night? "Are you with your mom?" Jon asked.

"No. I told you, I'm lost."

With a cell phone in his hand. Jon sighed. The entrance to the expressway was just ahead, beyond the lumbering Duck Tour bus, which had caught up with and then apparently bypassed him.

As soon as the light turned green, he was out of here. He checked his watch. Thirty minutes until his appointment on the South Shore with his new pitching coach. He really didn't have time for this.

"Brandon," Jon said patiently, "you need to use that phone you're holding in your hand and, instead of calling me, you need to call your dad."

"I don't have a dad," came the plaintive reply.

Damn. Jon was an idiot. What did he say to that— I'm sorry? Of course he was sorry…for being an idiot and bringing up the topic. But would that really help the kid if he told him so?

What could he say to help the kid?

"The people in my family don't have dads," Brandon said matter-of-factly.

Jon felt floored. Whether Brandon knew it or not, Jon felt the pain of his reality to his solar plexus.

The traffic light changed, cars and trucks crept forward, but Jon didn't move fast enough for them. Horns blared.

This time, Jon used his left-turn signal instead of just changing lanes like he normally did. *Giving intelligence to the enemy,* as his dad would say. A fresh barrage of horns rang out.

"Yeah, yeah," he said aloud, and then stepped on the accelerator.

He was met in a standoff, the intersection blocked by a guy in a clunker with a Rhode Island license plate.

Mr. Rhode Island wasn't giving an inch. Interesting, considering that Jon's SUV was three times the size of the clunker.

Then again, it *was* a clunker. The woman in the passenger seat applied toenail polish, her bare foot propped against the glove compartment. Jon was lucky—she could be hanging out the window and screaming at him.

Just another morning drive through Boston. He sighed. He needed to get out of the city and on his way.

"Brandon, seriously, where are you?" Jon hated to do this, but… "Put your aunt on the phone. Now. Okay?"

"I mean it. I'm really lost." Brandon's voice was

frightened now. Was Jon imagining it, or was he hearing the sound of blaring music, as if from the open window of a car passing by the little boy? "Jon...I'm scared." His breath sucked in, and he whimpered, "Boston is scary."

The only scary parts of Boston were the bad parts of Boston, and no kid should be alone in the bad parts.

Brandon started to cry. Jon knew little-boy tears, and this wasn't acting.

"Tell me where you are, Brandon?" Jon said, his heart racing. "Give me a building or a street name, and I'll come get you right away."

"Okay," Brandon said, "I see a street sign...."

Jon had sworn to stay out of Lizzy's business, but it looked like he had no choice.

CHAPTER SIX

"WHY ARE WE HERE?" Elizabeth said to her sister. "We need to get going."

They waited in a patient/family conference room not much larger than a library study cubicle—Ashley sitting tensely on an aged, beat-up leather couch, Elizabeth standing impatiently, squeezing her hands into fists.

"Please, Lisbeth," Ashley begged. "Sit with me for a minute." She patted a cushion beside her. "I have something I really need to tell you."

This could not be good news. Elizabeth had arrived at the alcohol abuse treatment center expecting to pick up her sister and take her home, but instead a nurse had led her upstairs—alone, without Brandon—under very hush-hush, mysterious circumstances.

And *now* Ashley wanted to have a family counseling session?

"I can't," Elizabeth said, backing against a wall. "Ashley, yesterday I called in to work and changed my schedule from morning surgeries to an afternoon and all-night double shift where I'll be sleeping in the on-call room, all so I could drive you home and then take Brandon to school. Why aren't you packed?"

Her sister didn't answer. Elizabeth got a bad feeling. Ashley looked like crap. She was shivering and picking at a loose thread on her sweater. "I can't go back," Ashley whispered. "Not yet."

"I don't understand." Ashley loved her son. Brandon was the sun and the moon to her.

"Do you remember how we would sit with Mom at night?" Ashley's voice was a whisper. "Mom would be waiting for Tony to call. And she'd be drinking vodka and orange juice—mostly vodka—out of that juice glass?"

Elizabeth sat heavily on the couch beside her sister. She didn't remember a juice glass. She did remember waiting, however, for the Tony who never came. Their biological father. But Elizabeth was younger than Ashley and she had only that one hazy memory of Tony's visits—the memory she'd thought of last night, during the baseball game.

Elizabeth shook her head. "I didn't sit up with Mom like you did." Elizabeth was usually behind a closed door in her bedroom, reading. Ashley had been the one who'd sat up nights with Mom.

"So…you think you're like that?" Elizabeth asked. "Is that what this is about?"

"I *am* like that. I even drink at *work*." Ashley got up and paced, rubbing her arms as if she couldn't get warm enough. "Mom is a functioning alcoholic, and I am, too."

"I…didn't know. About you, I mean."

Ashley stopped pacing and wiped her nose. She seemed to lift herself up. That's what Elizabeth had always admired about her older sister—she wasn't afraid to take charge, and she had determination. "I need to talk with Brandon. The counselor is going to sit with us and help me explain to him why I need to be away from him for a while. The counselor said he'll do it in a way that's age appropriate."

Poor Brandon. Elizabeth tried to put herself in the shoes of an eight-year-old. She'd been that age once. But she couldn't remember. Maybe she'd blocked it all out.

Elizabeth shook her head. What she most remembered was books. The cool, welcoming public library. The peace and escape of her schoolwork. The calmness of the rich, inner world of her intellect, the life of the mind and her ordered imagination.

Ashley had possessed none of that. Her sister was a social creature. She'd depended on the people of their neighborhood for comfort. "Ash, I am so sorry. For you and for Brandon."

"Do you think he's okay?" Ashley asked in a small voice. "He seems okay. He's so…bright. The teachers say he's top of his class, more like you in that way. But he is extroverted."

"A blend of both our personalities," Elizabeth muttered.

"I hope I'm not screwing him up." Ashley's eyes

were luminous and blinking. "I worry so much about him."

"You're *not* screwing him up. He loves you."

Ashley blew her nose on a tissue she'd scrunched in her fist. She looked more miserable than Elizabeth had ever seen.

"I'm sorry, Ash."

"I'm just glad you avoided the family illness, Lisbeth." Ashley gave her a small smile.

Elizabeth's heart went out to her. She commended her sister for trying to help herself, she really did. But here? In this facility? Elizabeth glanced at the dingy furnishings. Tried not to breathe too heavily of the stale air. "Why don't you let me research a nicer place for you to stay?"

"I did the research," Ashley insisted. "This place is good. My friend Sharma went here."

Sharma was a flake. She was also the friend who was taking care of Ashley's dog for her—Elizabeth wasn't sure *she'd* trust a dog to the woman. She simply sighed. "Who is going to watch Brandon for you? I know you don't want to ask Mom to fly up from Florida. How about your neighbor—Caitlin, isn't that her name—the one with all the boys? She seems responsible. And her kids go to Brandon's school, too, so it wouldn't be out of her way to drive him every day, right?"

Ashley squared her shoulders. "I'm leaving Brandon with you."

Oh, no. No, no, no.

"That's impossible." Elizabeth had barely survived the morning. His little-boy energy was simply too exuberant for her.

"I don't say this often enough," Ashley said, "but you're the best role model for him I know."

"Ash—"

"I've been terrible with him," Ashley whispered. "I can't stop myself from drinking." Her thin hand twisted and slid down her forearm. "I disgust myself, and I can't stop it. I don't know what else to do…"

"Has Brandon been physically hurt?"

"No." Ashley shook her head wildly. Then, in a lower voice, she said, "Not yet."

Not yet? Did that mean it *could* happen? Elizabeth swallowed. This was all so upsetting and sad and confusing. She felt blindsided by it.

Ashley paced from one end of the room to the other. She seemed lost in the past. "Do you remember that time when Mom passed out and she hit her head? There was blood everywhere and when we found her we thought…"

Yes. Elizabeth shivered. In her mind, she still saw the scene. Ashley, the older sister, thin and pale in a big shirt, straight-legged jeans and hair pulled into a high ponytail, racing through the snow in slippers and with no coat to a neighbor's house in order to call 9-1-1 because their phone had been turned off.

It was in the days before cell phones, the days before laptop computers and handheld screens everywhere. And still Elizabeth had found ways to hide from her home life. Curled up under her covers in a tiny room with a flashlight, the walls painted midnight-blue because that's how the rental unit had come from the previous tenants—and Mom hadn't been all that interested in interior decorating.

She had been interested in her water bottle emptied of water and filled with juice and wine, or juice and vodka. A secret she thought she successfully kept from everyone. And she had also been interested in her check that came every week like clockwork, even if Tony no longer did.

Or maybe, by that time Tony had moved to San Diego and the checks had stopped, and Mom had been trying to clean up her act, first with a job at the hospital sweeping floors. But even those jobs didn't last. Mom hadn't fooled anyone with her water bottles.

Ashley stopped pacing in her reverie. She was staring at Elizabeth, saying nothing.

"It's…really great you'll be talking to someone about it," Elizabeth said.

"For some of the sessions they have family days. It would be good for you to come, too."

Elizabeth opened her mouth to retort in the negative, then thought better of it and clamped her mouth shut. This was about Ashley, not her. Whatever Ashley needed, she would support her.

But not this. Not an entire thirty days of taking care of Ashley's eight-year-old son.

"I'm not the best person for him, Ash. I burned his toast this morning."

"He's eight. He's really great at making his own toast. Besides, I'll bet you bought him his gluten-free, didn't you? You're a doctor, you know how important that is."

"My apartment is small and not at all kid-proof!" Elizabeth's voice was sounding shrill, even to her.

"Like I live in a mansion." Ashley snorted.

"I don't have a bedroom for him," Elizabeth insisted. "He slept in my bed last night. I slept on a cot in my office."

"Honey, put *him* in the cot! He's a kid. Tell him it's an adventure, like a sleepover. He'll eat it up."

"But it's *not* a sleepover. Brandon has school. *Somebody* has to drive him to school on Monday!"

Ashley smiled and patted Elizabeth on the shoulder. She was much too calm about this. "I know with your busy schedule you might have to hire help. But you know I'm good for it. I will pay you back every cent when I get out."

"Ash, it's not the money—it's me! I'm terrible with people! I…" *I'm afraid of people,* was what she wanted to say, but instead she repeated, "I'm just not good with them."

"Well, Brandon is good with everyone," Ashley stubbornly insisted. "He's a people person. He's a joy, and I don't know what I'd do without him…." She covered her mouth with her hand. Tears were falling down her cheeks again. "Don't you think I'd be with him if I could? All *you* have to do is be yourself with him. He understands you. He knows that you're quiet and studious, and that you worked hard to become a real doctor. We talk about you, him and I. At night when he says his prayers, he prays for you, too."

"Ashley!" There was no way she could do this. *No way.* And yet, Ashley was making her cry. As siblings, they were the only two people who'd grown up in their house, who knew what went on, who shared the unique scars and the unique joys, too, because she supposed there had been those times....

"You don't remember this, Elizabeth, because I cleaned up the bad stuff before you saw, but sometimes, Mom would throw up on her bed. I would rinse the sheets out in the tub, and then wash them. Once in a while, I'd get a towel down in time."

"I didn't know that." Elizabeth sniffed.

"You were so little. You had these big brown eyes. So cute. Like a little doll. I wanted to protect you. I did a good job, didn't I?"

Ashley *had* protected her in her way. Elizabeth had never realized that until now.

Ashley smiled. "Well, maybe not so much in the teen years. I got a little rebellious. But by that time, you had your bike, and you knew the way to the library."

Her eyes watered. "You asked me earlier, why now? I'll tell you why now. It's stupid. I can't tell anybody else, but I can tell you, because only you get it." She turned her eyes up to Elizabeth, miserable. "Two nights ago, I threw up in my bed."

Elizabeth exhaled. "Because you were worried about Brandon having cancer again?"

"No, that was just my excuse. In reality, I'm an alcoholic who thinks she's functioning, thinks she's keeping it from people. Like Mom."

Elizabeth let that sink in. It was strange, but she felt proud for Ashley. Still… "What did the counselor say? Does he really think you belong here with these people?" Elizabeth thought about the drug addicts Ashley might have to interact with. "I mean, junkies and criminals and such?"

Ashley wiped her tears away. "Don't be prejudiced. Besides, once I'm processed and checked in, you won't *have* to come back here again for thirty days. My only hard part will be saying goodbye to Brandon."

Which led Elizabeth back to the main problem. "You should leave him with your friend Caitlin. The woman with all the boys Brandon's age."

"No," Ashley said stubbornly. "I want Brandon to stay with you."

But Elizabeth didn't want Brandon to stay with her. *Don't make me say that aloud,* she thought. "I can't handle him."

"You can. You have to."

"Why not your friend?"

"Because this is a private, family affair, and if

Caitlin has him, then Caitlin will *know*." Her chin set as if she was closed to discussion.

"So what's the story you're telling everyone?" Elizabeth asked. "What's the lie?"

"No lie. Just that I'm gone away on business, for occupation training, and that Brandon is staying with his aunt until my training is over. In a sense, that's the truth."

"Ashley—"

"I cleared it with my boss at the salon. He supports me. He's juggled my clients for me before. He's the only one who knows where I am this month, besides you and Sharma, and that was because I had to tell him."

So why couldn't *her boss* take Brandon? But Elizabeth bit her tongue, even though the panic was swelling, the nerves were jumping and that shaking, lost, hollow feeling in the pit of her stomach was overwhelming her.

She leaned over and placed her head between her knees. *Breathe,* she commanded herself. She was a doctor; she knew human physiology, had taken semesters of course work on human anatomy. In the most technical sense, her emotions were shutting down her system, and that was just…not good. She needed a rational way to deal with Ashley and her commendable but misguided plan for her and Brandon.

Elizabeth was in no way equipped for a little boy. Not in her home, her job, her life…

Her throat squeezed. Her life! Her beautiful, happy, comforting bubble of a life! The only thing that kept her independent.

And thus, safe.

WHERE THE HELL was Lizzy? Jon felt steam coming from his ears. Was she completely clueless, letting a kid walk around alone in this part of town?

He pulled over to the spot where the GPS indicated he stop. He was in an urban neighborhood, with six-family, boxy-style homes that had seen better days. A redbrick tower-style housing development was on the corner of the busy, four-lane intersection. Jon glanced up and down the sidewalk, saw a man loitering in the doorway, looking him up and down. Or, maybe looking Jon's SUV up and down.

Damn it, where was the kid? And what had happened to Lizzy?

He saw Brandon then, sitting in the passenger side of a parked car in front of him. Jon lightly knocked on the window of the small green Prius. "Brandon, open up."

The kid opened the door and propelled himself into Jon. Jon wrapped his arms around the boy's thin shoulders and his small head. A warm, tender feeling came over him. This is what he knew. This is what he missed.

This is what centered him.

He knelt to Brandon's height. The child wore a blue Captains cap low over his eyes, his shoulders hunched as he slouched against Jon, his aunt's cell phone still clutched in his fingers.

Behind him, the door was open, and a woman's purse—Lizzy's purse?—was opened and dumped across the seat.

His heart hammering, he asked, "Where is your aunt?"

"In the doctor's office." Brandon sniffled. "She told me to hold her p-pocketbook and wait for her, but I don't remember where the office is now."

"Are you okay?"

The boy nodded, staring at his sneakers.

Jon tipped up the boy's chin and looked into his sheepish face. "Did you wander off from where your aunt told you to wait?"

Brandon scuffed his toe. "Yes, but I got bored in there and I didn't like it." His lip trembled. "I'm sorry, Jon," he said in a small voice.

Jon glanced at the buildings surrounding them. Which one would be a doctor's office? There was a church on the corner. A Salvation Army store. A small bodega.

And an alcohol and drug treatment center.

Jon took Brandon's hand into his and pointed to the building with his still-splinted finger. "Is that where you were waiting?"

"I don't know."

Jon gathered up Lizzy's purse and handed it to Brandon. She had her car keys attached with a clip to the outside of her purse, so he used that to lock what he assumed was her car. He locked his SUV, too. He didn't like leaving it in this sketchy neighborhood, but he didn't see a valid option. He gripped Brandon tightly by the hand and steered the boy toward the building and then up the concrete stairs, which were swept clean, and into a check-in area that did look like a large-scale doctors' office. The woman behind the desk was busy on the telephone, so Jon stood to the side and waited. In a sitting area, a television mounted on the wall showed a weather report. There were the standard stiff, uncomfortable, doctors' office chairs and a large central table loaded with magazines.

Jon sat and motioned Brandon to sit beside him. Jon didn't speak; he just kept holding the boy's hand. Brandon was shaken. On his small lap, he gripped his aunt's large purse.

At some point, the woman behind the reception desk finished her phone call. She stretched, glanced into the waiting room, and when she saw Jon, did a double take.

For once, Jon didn't smile back.

The woman stood and peered over the counter at him. "Are you the boy's father?"

"No. Could you please ask Dr. LaValley to come see us right away."

The woman reached for the phone. Jon glanced at Brandon, who had gone pale. "She's gonna be mad at me," he whispered to Jon.

"Maybe. But next time you'll think twice before

wandering away from her in a strange environment, won't you?"

Brandon gave him a panicked look, but Jon just returned his measured poker face. The no-jokes gaze that had worked so well with his younger brothers when he needed them to stop fooling around and get serious.

Brandon sat straighter in his chair.

Jon was not prepared for what he felt when Lizzy strode into the room. But he kept his poker face and stood, slightly inclining his head. He'd decided to let her know up front that he wasn't amused, and he wouldn't be cowed by her brusqueness.

Her eyes widened, and she inhaled. Whatever she'd been about to accuse him of, she kept to herself.

"I'm sorry, Auntie." Brandon's plea was small and plaintive.

Her lips trembling, Elizabeth glanced down at her nephew. "It's okay, honey. Your mom is ready to see you," she said gently.

Brandon nodded, and both he and Lizzy stood silently while a nurse led Brandon from the waiting area.

It was just Jon, Lizzy and the weatherman on television talking about a tropical depression gearing to roar up from the Caribbean and into the Gulf coast of Florida.

Jon waited, saying nothing. *I am not helping you. I have my own problems* were the words he'd been planning to say to her.

But he hadn't expected to be affected by her the way he was at that moment. There was something about her—a vulnerability and a promise of what she could be, if only she would let down her guard. It pulled at his heartstrings even though he didn't want it to.

He did not need this maddening, self-righteous woman needling him about what was or wasn't wrong with him. He deserved an apology from her. He was now late for his conditioning and pitching session, destroying the credibility of his commitment to Coach Duffy and, by definition, to the game of baseball and his future in it. He had risked everything, and for what?

But when he looked into her eyes, he saw the remnants of tears. *Something* had happened, something bad. She wasn't even thinking about him.

Because they were at an alcohol and drug treatment center. Jon gave himself a mental head slap. It had to be for Brandon's mother.

"I'm assuming Brandon called you?" Lizzy asked.

"Yes."

Reaching into her purse, she took out her cell phone. She scrolled through it until she came to her outgoing calls history. He looked over her shoulder.

"Is there a way to delete a phone number from your outgoing calls list?" she asked.

"Yes, there is," he said. "By all means, do it."

Biting her lip, she made a tentative swiping movement with her thumb.

Something—anger, a moment of pride—reared its head, and he took the phone from her. He deleted all traces of his phone number, then handed back her phone.

A stricken look crossed her eyes, just for a split second, and he felt ashamed.

"You really should go," she said.

"That's it? No 'thank you'? No acknowledgment that I've come out of my way, derailing my own plans?"

"I'm sorry." She dropped her gaze and then lifted it to him. The sadness in her eyes was still there, and she was blinking rapidly. "Please accept my apology. You can go now."

He hesitated, confused. He'd gotten what he'd wanted from her, and now he should leave. But somehow, his feet seemed rooted. "What's going on with Brandon's mom?" he asked. "Is she okay? What's going to happen to Brandon?"

"That's none of your business," Elizabeth said.

The breath died in his throat. "I was scared to death when I got his call. I thought that Brandon was being kidnapped, possibly injured, and you're telling me it's not my business?"

"I didn't ask you to come to my house last night. I didn't ask you to befriend my nephew."

"Lady, you are really a piece of work."

"Jon, please. Take your concern and give it to somebody else. Somebody who wants to accept it from you."

ELIZABETH WAS BARELY hanging on, she was so close to tears. She couldn't remember a time in her adult years when she felt so upset, her foundation so threatened. She just wanted to shut her proverbial door and hide away from the world.

What she wouldn't give to be able to get in her car and just go to work. Oversee an operation. Open a book and read about another time, another place, other people's problems.

She turned, but Jon put a hand on her shoulder.

She froze. Could not move. His hand was warm, and it comforted her, just a little bit. But at the same time, he unnerved her. "Why are you doing this?" she whispered. "Why can't you just go away?"

"It's…Brandon. He reminds me of my brother Bobby in the years after our mom…was gone. Brandon is a little older than him, but…"

She turned and faced him then. His eyes were glassy, maybe a bit dead. His face had a saddened expression. He wasn't lying to her.

"So what do you want?" she asked him. "To save the world?"

His hand dropped from her shoulder. He looked like she'd struck him.

He *did* want to save the world. Or maybe just to be a white knight in his corner of the world.

But Jon hadn't yet learned what she already knew: that some people could not be saved. He had never pronounced a patient's death. She had. He surely hadn't spent time in private therapy over a mom that was so troubled and dysfunctional that she made her kids feel unsafe growing up. Elizabeth had done that, too. And what Elizabeth had learned from that experience was to accept that life was the way it was. Accept it, and stop trying to fix it for other people.

Jon needed to develop protection and harden his heart the same way she had. Her voice shook. "My sister—Brandon's mother—is an alcoholic. Brandon is facing that reality. I have faced that already, and if anyone will be helping Brandon with his new reality, it will be me."

Jon looked at her for a long time. "I don't see it happening," he said.

She blinked, surprised. "Excuse me?"

"The kid doesn't need to be given anesthesia in order to cope. He needs somebody to talk with. To hang out with."

The nerve of this...baseball player. "I don't see an M.D. degree hanging on your wall," she said.

"Of course you don't. You don't see my wall, because you don't pay attention to anybody who isn't in your direct line of sight."

She opened her mouth, and then closed it again. Pulled her arms around herself, hugging herself.

Nobody talked to her this way. Nobody was so blunt to a doctor.

"I'm sorry for Brandon," he said quietly, and she

saw in her heart how much he did feel it. "I'm really sorry."

And then he turned for the door and headed outside.

Her heart in her throat, she followed him. "Wait…"

But he didn't hear her. Or if he did, he didn't stop. She watched him walk over to his truck—a big, huge, gas-guzzling SUV—and swing into the driver's side like a confident, capable cowboy. Leaving her little, practical Prius alone on the corner by itself.

He didn't look back at her. Not once.

On the street, the light turned green, and he took off through the intersection. She watched until his truck turned the corner around a building and she could see him no more. He was gone.

She rubbed her arm where his hand had touched her.

Why did she feel so lousy?

So…alone?

She turned and hurried back to the counseling room where she'd left Ashley. She still had so many questions about how to care for Brandon. She had no idea how she was going to cope for these next weeks.

When she got to the room, the door was open. Both Ashley and Brandon had their backs to her. Ashley was sitting in the chair, and Brandon was half sitting, half leaning beside his mother, his head on her shoulder. She was speaking in low tones to her son, ruffling his hair. She appeared to be calming him. Not a counselor was in sight.

Elizabeth backed against the wall. How did Ashley do it? In her sister's place, Elizabeth would have run away from the conversation, or otherwise blocked herself off.

Maybe Jon was right: there was something she was missing…some skills she needed to learn. He'd been telling her she needed to pay closer attention to other people. Step beyond the curtain she'd drawn to keep people out of her life.

Elizabeth stepped just outside the door but could still hear what Ashley was saying.

"I love you," she heard her sister say to her son as she stroked his hair. "You're my best boy. We both need to be strong for a few weeks while I'm in the hospital. It's not a life-threatening hospital, like when you were in the hospital for chemo. It's…for my behavior. I drink more…wine…than is good for me, and I want to stop that. Because it's making me make poor decisions. But in thirty days, I'll be all better."

Elizabeth hoped so. She really, truly hoped so.

"Your Aunt Liz is going to be taking care of you," Ashley was saying. "Or actually, knowing you, you'll be taking care of her, too, because your Aunt Liz is a very famous doctor, but sometimes she…needs to learn to smile a bit more. And you're so good at smiling."

Elizabeth brought her knuckles to her teeth. *Oh, Ashley,* she thought. *I am sorry. I am so, so sorry.*

But Ashley kept soothing Brandon, oblivious to Elizabeth listening in the hallway. She really should make herself known, but she couldn't bring herself to do it.

"I will absolutely be back for you in thirty days," Ashley said to Brandon. "Just after Halloween. I will make sure of that. I'll look forward to seeing the costume that you and your Aunt Liz come up with together." She hugged him tighter. "And then, Thanksgiving will be a big reason for us to celebrate this year. But until then, I'm going to ask you to keep what I'm telling you just between you and me and Aunt Liz. Do you think you can do that?"

"I told Jon Farell," Elizabeth heard Brandon say in a small voice.

"Who is Jon Farell?" Ashley asked him.

"He's a New England Captains pitcher. I met him at the hospital and then he came to Auntie's house last night."

What would Ashley think about that? Her sister seemed to pause. Elizabeth dug her nails into her fingers. "Is he a friend of Auntie's?" Ashley asked Brandon cautiously.

"Not really," the boy said. "He likes her but she's kind of mean to him."

Elizabeth gasped.

"Auntie can be prickly," Ashley said.

Yes. Oh yes, and she had been much too harsh to Jon. Elizabeth regretted it already.

Ashley kissed the top of Brandon's head. "It's okay you told him, just this one time, but don't tell anybody else, okay?"

Brandon nodded. "Okay."

"Dr. LaValley, would you like to join us?" a male voice said from behind her.

Elizabeth jumped, swiping at her eyes. It was the counselor who'd said he would help Elizabeth say goodbye to Brandon in an age-appropriate manner.

Elizabeth shook her head. "No, thank you." She knew what she had to do. "I'll…keep in touch with you, though, sir. I'd like to be kept up-to-date on my sister's progress."

"Are you sure you wouldn't like to join us all while we talk?" The counselor took a sip from his coffee mug and looked at Elizabeth with kind eyes.

"No, thank you. I'm very sure."

Because now was the time for action. And Elizabeth knew exactly what she was going to do.

CHAPTER SEVEN

A WEEK LATER, Jon hadn't heard a word from Elizabeth, even though he was dying to know how she was doing with her nephew. He thought once or twice about finding some of his family's old kids' books for Brandon and driving them over to Lizzy's condo. But Lizzy had made it clear what she thought of his interference. Her rejection of him had been final, so the wisest thing he could do was to push it out of his mind.

He had his own problems to worry about.

The rumblings on sports radio increased with each passing day. Jon hadn't been mentioned by name, but a few of the guys on the pitching staff had texted him about the stuff the media people were dredging up. Most of it was garbage—they were misreading the situation, spinning it in the search for people to blame. But still, it was out there, and nobody on the Captains staff seemed to know what to do about it.

Jon was monitoring Twitter, just to see if team management was coming out with statements. They sent out one or two platitudes, but to Jon's mind, the responses were feeble. All it was doing was fanning the flames on the airwaves.

He felt he was in a holding pattern, waiting for a hammer to drop on him, crushing him into oblivion.

And there was still no talk of a contract for next year.

Meanwhile, Martinez's team was in the next round of playoffs. Jon watched the games at night as a distraction, while he spent his days working out, making snail-paced progress toward conquering the changeup pitch.

Coach Duffy had lost faith in Jon when he'd been late for their first meeting. He'd stopped talking to him, and the ramification was that Jon was now on his own. Jon wasn't giving up, though. He figured that until he proved himself to be committed by showing up every day on time and running endless "poles" (wind sprints from foul pole to foul pole on the baseball field), as well as working the machines in the weight room and doing whatever conditioning and throwing exercises he could manage without use of his right hand, he wouldn't get his old coach's respect back. Proving himself was slow going and painful so far. But all Jon could do was take it day by day and hope that he'd break through sooner rather than later.

Brooke called that night. Jon sat alone in his apartment, staring mindlessly at the game on TV while icing his elbow.

"Do you want to cut your hair for charity this weekend?" Brooke asked him. "I can set up a media event to get cameras on you for a special news segment."

All that would do was fan the flames further.

Didn't she have the instincts to see this? Jon put down the ice bucket and walked over to his living room penthouse window, the phone tucked against his ear, and gazed at the mind-boggling night view of Boston Harbor, all lit up. "No," he said to her. "Don't do it."

"But you've been telling people all season that you're going to cut your hair."

"Yes, followed by the sentence 'when the team makes the playoffs.' And since we didn't make the playoffs, Brooke, don't you think that will only draw attention to the scandal we're hoping will go away?"

Brooke sighed. "I concede your point. But you have to agree to something—something that would get you good press, and put you back in Vivian's good books. I can't help you otherwise."

"Fine," Jon muttered into the phone, not feeling up to this conversation. "Come up with something *not* the haircut."

"Do you promise not to torpedo my next idea?" she asked, a pout in her voice. "Because I'm working on getting you into something special that's part of the month-end fund-raising event. It's a charity bachelor auction."

Jon's blood ran cold. "A what?"

"Bidding should run high on you. You're good-looking, you're eligible, you're upbeat and easygoing. Women love being around you."

"Forget it." He went back and found his ice bucket. He didn't feel particularly upbeat and easygoing tonight. Maybe he was turning into Lizzy. "I want to do something meaningful that's about being more than a Captains player. How about a television pledge drive, something that will also educate people on the disease? That will help the kids."

"That's not going to happen, Jon. But the bachelor auction *is* going to happen. Vivian wants it. And you could raise lots of money, more than any other player if I do some behind-the-scenes work to get women into a bidding war."

The only person Jon wanted bidding on him was Lizzy, and that was an unlikely scenario. Just picturing her coming out from behind her curtain and pursuing anyone publicly like that made him choke out a laugh.

"Relax, Jon," Brooke said. "I'll make sure you don't get stuck with anyone distasteful. I'll have a plant in the crowd to make the final winning bid on you."

"Not interested, because I'd still have to go out on a date with the plant, right?"

Brooke made a tight, high-pitched giggle. "*I'm* the plant, Jon."

He blinked and held out his phone for a minute. This was surreal. He could never be entirely sure of Brooke's motives with him. Exactly why he wanted Max back as his full-time agent. "How is Max?" he asked her.

"He's recuperating. He just needs time to heal."

"Is he in the hospital?"

Brooke sighed. "I've said too much already. Let's

talk about you. Here's another idea—how about if we create an event—filmed for the evening news, of course—where you go into the children's cancer clinic—the Sunshine Club, I think Vivian calls it—and sign some T-shirts for the kids?"

The kids who were sick with cancer? The kids who were in a life-and-death battle with the disease? Jon shuddered. The last thing those kids or their families needed or wanted was to see him—or anybody else—signing T-shirts for the TV cameras. If he were in their shoes, he would hate it.

"Jon, what do you think?"

That my options keep getting worse.

He wasn't sure how to explain it to her, because unless a person had gone through a cancer death, how could they understand?

Lizzy would understand.

He could talk to her about this.

"Jon?"

"Let's table the discussion for now," he said, rubbing his head, which was starting to ache. "Tomorrow I have to head over to the hospital and get my stitches out."

With any luck he would bump into Lizzy. Just for a casual conversation, just to find out how Brandon was doing. He didn't even know if the kid had been cleared of his tests to see if he was cancer-free.

"All right," Brooke said, "but you're going to have to choose one of those options, because they're all we have. And my father agrees." She paused. "By the way, how is *your* part of the plan coming? Are you working on your changeup pitch?"

Jon gripped at the ice bucket in his lap. Inhaled the scent of menthol from the muscle ointment he'd rubbed on his quads. He was exhausted. Physically and mentally. But it was all good, because it was helping him not think during the day—of Lizzy and Brandon and how they were doing together, and of his predicament with the media.

"I'll be throwing more pitches after the splint comes off," he said.

"Good. Call me tomorrow when you're back from the hospital and ready to talk some more."

The next afternoon, Jon strode into the hospital complex. He rode up the elevators, feeling queasy as he retraced the route he'd made a week ago, prior to the rumblings in the media.

A foreboding settled in his gut. Maybe Jon wouldn't see the enthusiasm for his presence that he'd seen the last time he'd been in the hospital. Maybe the continuous, building hum of the background noise from the media assault on the pitching staff was doing its damage.

But once in the doctor's office, the staff greeted him warmly. Dr. Morgan himself removed Jon's stitches. A few of the aides and nurses and resident doctors who'd worked on him during the original surgery gathered and gave him a mini-celebration. Jon was deemed healed and given the green light to wear a glove and throw "bullpens," although he was supposed to stop if the affected finger bothered him.

He didn't bother to tell them he'd been pretty much working out all along. He also was biting his tongue to keep from asking where Dr. LaValley was?

And he'd been doing so well. *Just be serious,* he told himself. *Stay on track with the agenda.*

But on the way back to his SUV, two things happened. First, he had a long wait for the elevator to the garage. Second, this gave him time to look around.

Hanging on the wall in the brightly lit corridor was a huge poster for the Sunshine Club, the children's cancer clinic at Wellness Hospital sponsored by the New England Captains baseball team. Jon stared at the poster showing the smiling face of a beautiful young child clutching a teddy bear. He brought his hand up to touch the Captains team logo on the bottom corner of the glossy paper.

The bell for the elevator rang, and the doors opened. Jon's hand still on the poster, he glanced into the elevator and saw a boy, about two or three years old, slumped in his mother's arms. The boy showed the ravages of the chemotherapy that Jon remembered all too well. The bald head. The gray pallor to the skin. The look of general misery.

Jon closed his eyes. The poster on the wall was the whitewash. The kid on the elevator was the truth. He gripped his car keys, suddenly feeling as if *he* was in chemotherapy.

The elevator came and went, and Jon didn't go with it.

Instead, he walked over to the hospital directory posted by the elevator doors. The Sunshine Club was located just a few floors up from where he stood.

He was debating his options—either putting himself in the charity bachelor auction like a piece of meat, all body and sex appeal and very little soul, or taking a visit, just a short visit to the Sunshine Club to see if there was anything he could do there—something real and authentic. Something that could benefit the cause of helping kids and their families, without making it a platitude.

Max would tell him what to do. He would tell Jon to get on the damn elevator and go up.

The elevator dinged, the doors opened and…Brandon walked out.

Despite himself, Jon felt himself break into a grin. "Hey, buddy!" he said to the kid.

"Jon!" Brandon's moon-shaped face with the gap in his teeth where he was missing an incisor lit up at seeing Jon. His gaze went immediately to Jon's right hand. "Your splint is off!"

A tearing went through Jon's heart. After all the kid had gone through—his cancer remission tests, his mom going into rehab, his moving in with his aunt—Brandon's first thoughts were on somebody else.

Jon picked up Brandon's Captains cap, askew on his head, and settled it on properly. "The season is over for us, slugger. Don't you think it's time to move on to football?"

"Nope," Brandon insisted. "I'm a four-season base-ball guy, just like you."

Jon smiled wistfully. *How's your aunt?* he wanted to ask. "How's school?" he asked instead.

"Is it true what they're saying about the Captains on sports talk radio?" Brandon blurted. The kid looked distraught.

"Don't listen to that stuff, okay? It takes away your focus."

"Did you drink beer in the clubhouse with those guys during games?" Brandon asked.

Whoa. Is that what the media was saying now? Brooke hadn't told him that. *Damn.* Jon looked into that little boy's face, that little boy who had a mom with alcohol problems, and he could feel his heart squeezing. "No," he said firmly.

Brandon's relief was visible. "That's what I thought."

Jon knelt so he was eye level with the boy. "Let me give you a baseball tip, something that took me a long time to learn. Baseball is the great American game. If you're a ballplayer, people want a piece of you. But you can't listen to distractions. You have to focus on your own thing."

"I know," Brandon said. "Noah Devers told everybody in school that my mom is in alcohol rehab. But I told him to shut up and mind his own business, and then everybody was mad at him. Auntie went in and talked to the teachers. Then we all had a meeting." Brandon scratched his ear. "Oh, and you know what—I'm going to be in baseball tryouts this November. It's real pitching, not T-ball or coach-pitching. Can you show me some batting tips?"

Jon just knelt there, gaping. *Lizzy. Oh, Lizzy.* What he would have given to have been a fly on the wall in that school meeting.

"Ah...I don't work on batting anymore, slugger, sorry."

"How about pitching?" Brandon asked.

"Sorry, but your aunt doesn't really want me around, buddy." The thought depressed him.

Brandon cocked his head. "Didn't you get her voice mail?"

"What voice mail?" Jon drew his phone from his pocket. He flicked it on and stared at the rows of apps on the screen. One of these must be for voice mail—he didn't normally use it. In his line of work, people either texted him or if they called him and hung up, it showed as a "missed call," and then he would call them back.

Brandon sighed and took the phone from him. "Auntie stinks at using her phone, too. I had to go into her call log and get your phone number for her. She thought you deleted it, but you only deleted the call I made, not the one from the day before. Here." He looked up at Jon. "What's your password? I'll open the voice mail for you."

Jon took the phone back. *Scram, kid,* he wanted to say. He was damned if he would listen to Lizzy's message in front of her nephew. He had some pride left. "What are you doing in the hospital, anyway? Shouldn't you be at school?"

"No." Brandon shrugged. "It's a teacher training day at school, and my babysitter couldn't be at Auntie's house for me, so I came to work with Auntie this morning. She's busy now. But I know my way all over this hospital." He swept his arms in a circle. "I've been coming here since I was like, three." He rolled his eyes. Then he brightened. "Where are you going? I can help you find your way."

"Brandon." Jon gave him a warning look. "Didn't we just have a talk last week about the dangers of you wandering off without telling anybody?"

"But I'm not wandering! The lady in the day care lets me visit my old nurses from the cancer clinic! That's where I was! Come upstairs with me and see!"

Jon clearly felt the force of his pulse in his neck. "*You* go into the cancer clinic? The Sunshine Club?" *After what you've been through?*

"Yep!" Brandon nodded vigorously. "The Sunshine Club." He took Jon's hand, the one that had just been desplinted, and he pulled, dragging Jon forward.

Jon stepped into the elevator, not at all sure about this. But if Lizzy was facing up to her fears, attending school meetings and leaving him a voice message, then maybe he could face his, too.

Inside the elevator was another poster for the Sunshine Club. Jon's forehead felt tight. Not only didn't he want to go there, he wasn't sure he wanted witnesses when he did, either. "Just get me to the right floor, okay?" He pointed to the poster. "Then you can go back down to day care."

"They *like* me in the Sunshine Club," Brandon said, jabbing a button on the wall. "What are you going to do, just walk in without knowing anybody?"

Ah, good point.

The elevator doors closed. Thankfully, it was empty inside except for him and Brandon. The small space smelled like Chinese food from a take-out lunch someone must have brought in. It was that time of day. "Your aunt isn't going to get mad about you being with me, is she?" Jon asked.

Brandon picked at a mosquito bite on his arm. "Nah. She's pretty busy. Yesterday, she had to help sew back on a guy's toe that got cut off."

Jon couldn't help wincing. He wiggled his own toes. He could have done without that visual.

Funny, but Lizzy was the one woman he knew who was so immersed in her work—important work, too—that she was able to keep her focus fully on her own business. Like he should be doing at the moment. *She* followed the advice that *he* had trouble following.

"Has she, uh, been reading the newspapers?" he asked Brandon casually. "Specifically, the sports pages?"

Brandon shook his head. "She only reads hospital kind of newspapers." He picked again at his mosquito bite. It was starting to bleed. "She likes *National Archaeology* magazine, too."

The kid wasn't putting him on. Jon did remember seeing that reading material on her coffee table the one time he was in her apartment. "That's interesting."

"Yeah. She likes ancient worlds where people used to live, but then a volcano exploded and it ran down into everybody's houses, and, like, they all died. It happened a hundred years ago or something." Brandon decided to stop studying the blood on his arm and glanced up at Jon instead. "She read it to me at bedtime last night. I liked the pictures. This one guy, he was like, dying when the lava came and ran him over. He was a baker, I think. It was so cool."

Jon stared. "She showed you that at bedtime?" *Lizzy,* he thought, *You need help. Desperately.*

"Yup," Brandon said. "We read some books that Sharma sent over, too. But Aunt Lisbeth thought they were too optim…"

"Optimistic." The laugh caught in his throat. If she thought that way, she wouldn't disapprove of her nephew being exposed again to the cancer ward, that was for certain.

The elevator rang, and they came to their stop. Jon stepped out. The gleaming white floors squeaked beneath his sneakers. He felt underdressed in jeans and a T-shirt. Maybe it would have been better if he'd worn a team jersey. Then again, he wasn't an official representative of the team, not today.

This was just a…scouting expedition.

Jon paused in the long white hallway. Nobody had

recognized him. Brandon stood patiently beside him, his hand in his. Trusting him.

"This is where I used to come," Brandon said nonchalantly, as only kids could.

"Weren't you scared?" he found himself asking.

"I was too little to be scared."

Jon didn't want to be here, at all. But he held Brandon's hand and remained calm. The world didn't need to know he was too much of a softie to be able to handle seeing little kids with no hair and painful expressions, coming out of chemo with their upset parents.

"Come on," Brandon said, tugging at him. "I'll show you around. This is the community room." He dragged Jon through a doorway and into an open area with a television and grouped seating areas. Nobody was present except for him and Brandon.

"There's a TV and lots of toys here," Brandon said. "I used to like the puzzles."

"You can remember that far back?" Jon asked.

Brandon shrugged. "Well, I came in here last week. The day I met you."

"Why?"

"Because I like to remember."

"You like to remember when you were sick?"

"My mom was with me all the time then. My aunt and my grandmother were, too. Everybody wanted to help me. And I prayed to get better, and I did."

Jon eased his shaky knees into a chair and imagined Brandon as a younger kid, Bobby's age at the time Jon's mother had died. It was too much for him to comprehend.

The kid picked up a TV remote. Last winter, a group of local hockey players had been filmed visiting this very community room, signing caps and T-shirts for the kids and posing for photos as they gave interviews to the local newscaster. Jon had watched it at home on the television news, feeling slightly sick, thinking that could never be him in the hockey players' role. When his mom was sick, Jon would have hated cameras in his face. Hated public figures showing up to give him "joy."

How could there be joy when people were sick and dying in front of you?

And now he was going to be one of those people? Or, he was considering being one of those people. He hadn't taken the jump into being one of them yet.

He shook his head. *This* was the truth behind the ambivalence that he hadn't been able to articulate to Brooke. It wasn't that he was against charity. He did charity appearances, but quietly. Not in front of the cameras, and never in front of sick families. *Ever*. It just hit too close to home.

But he remained in the adult chair in the sunny children's room and watched Brandon hold out the TV remote and flip through channels, stopping only when he found a television station playing cartoons. Just as if the kid was at home, spread out on his own comfortable couch. Maybe Jon could handle coming here if he thought like that. There had to be something to the fact that he was with Brandon, himself a cancer survivor, while Jon had recently undergone a cancer scare himself.

He concentrated on relaxing his muscles into the chair. He let go of the proverbial pole keeping him close to the dock, and he waded through chest-high water, to the deep end of the pool.

But he heard movement at the door, and immediately he recoiled. A little girl, her skin bloodless, her head covered in a pink Captains baseball cap, had a thumb tucked in her mouth and her head leaning against her father's shoulder.

Jon stood, walked past them without looking and went back into the hallway. He sucked air into his lungs, but the corridor smelled like…chemicals. Syringes. Disinfectants. All the smells he associated with that time in his life when his family was in pain. All of those feelings he so studiously steered clear of. So reflexively avoided, his entire life.

How could Lizzy even work in a place that contained these things?

Brandon appeared at his side. "I know it's hard, Jon, but you have to keep a smile on your face."

Jon looked down at the kid. "A very good point. Which is why I'm leaving, buddy."

"Wait, Jon. I bet you can find *something* to smile about here," Brandon said.

"Is that what you do?" Jon asked. "Find something to smile about?"

"My mom says it helps people. Everybody likes to see a smile."

"Sometimes, kid, there's nothing to smile about."

"Oh, you can always find something. Did you see the cartoons on the TV?"

Jon shook his head. "That little girl looked...too sick for cartoons." She wasn't going to make it. He just knew she wasn't going to make it. It was like watching an execution in process and he was powerless to stop it.

It made him angry. Sick inside and wanting desperately to take action, but what?

Maybe he should just do the damn bachelor auction. Stand up on a block and let them bid on him. It was *abhorrent* to him, like Lizzy had said and, yet, easier than trying to smile in the midst of so many terminally ill kids.

The man who'd been carrying the sick girl came into the hallway and approached Jon, looking hesitant. "Excuse me, but I'm a big Captains fan. I recognized your hair. Are you...?"

"Yes, he is," Brandon piped up.

The man smiled at Jon and held out his hand. He seemed exhausted, tired and worn-out. "I just want to say thank you."

Jon kept his hand at his side. "Why? I didn't do anything."

"Yeah, you do, every time you pitch. My family has been here...lots of days and nights this past summer." He raked back his hair with the hand Jon hadn't shaken. "Rebecca…she's my daughter…she likes to sit with me and watch your games on television. It takes our mind off the chemotherapy, and…it's our escape. Our joy. No matter what happens, whether we win or lose, I'll always remember those good times spent with her. You helped bring that."

Jon's throat tightened with emotion. Never, not once in all his years playing baseball—a kids' game, once you got right down to it—had anyone ever said something like that to him.

"May I say hello to Rebecca?" he asked in a low voice.

The man brightened. "Please. Come in and meet her." He turned and held out his hand again. "I'm Frank, by the way."

The same name as Jon's brother. It had to be a sign. Jon returned Frank's handshake and followed him back to the community room.

Rebecca was inside, sitting limply in the corner of the couch. Her pallor was gray and her eyes seemed lifeless. But her dad sat beside her and lifted her onto his lap. "Becky, this is somebody we've watched on TV together. Jon is a Captains player."

Becky removed her thumb from her mouth and silently regarded Jon. A slight smile crossed her face. She didn't seem to have much energy, but she slowly placed her small hand in Jon's outstretched hand.

When she weakly clasped his fingers, Jon could feel the wetness from where her thumb had been in her mouth. But she didn't take her hand away. She left it there in his.

Jon sank to his knees. He stayed with Becky and her dad until Becky fell asleep. They'd shared no words. Brandon's cartoon played on in the background.

"Thank you," Becky's dad, Frank, said quietly to him. "This means a lot to us."

Jon nodded, feeling the lump in his throat. But at the same time, he felt…at peace, which was odd. He felt more true to himself, as well. He didn't want to leave Becky and Frank just yet. Their presence fed something authentic in him. But another little boy came into the community room, with both parents and what looked to be a grandmother walking beside him.

It was the grandmother who recognized Jon first. Apparently the stretch of "Captains Nation" extended to all generations, and both sexes in New England. The grandmother excitedly talked to Jon about watching Captains games with her own father, which led to her telling the sick boy about the great-grandfather he'd never met, and an exciting baseball game they'd been to together, just after World War II.

Jon loved the history. He'd grown up hearing these stories from his own dad and grandfather, and it made him feel good to think about his connection to the team this way. He loved the smiles that he and his team affiliation got from the family, who had definitely not been smiling when they'd entered the room.

They asked Jon why he was here, and Jon introduced them to Brandon, who was immediately in his element telling the other little boy exactly how he had been in his shoes once, too.

An hour later, when Jon left the community room, he was still dazed. Maybe a bit shaken, but refreshed. His experience talking with those families had shown him an entirely different perspective on his life, one he'd never anticipated.

He felt like his world was expanding. That he was bigger and more influential than he'd realized, but in a humble way that gave him quiet satisfaction and lifted his spirit.

Those kids and their families had helped *him* to see himself in a different light.

Astonished, he stood before the elevator bank.

"The next time," Brandon said to him, "you should bring some T-shirts or something like that with you."

Jon turned to him. "The next time?"

"The kids will like meeting you, Jon. You're good at talking to them."

Yes. Yes, he was.

And he was going to do something about it, too. He nodded to Brandon. "Can you take me to the lady who's in charge of the Sunshine Club?"

"Okay." Brandon showed him down a corridor to a small side wing. He pointed. "There are offices down there."

Jon checked the nameplates on the doors until he found a public relations manager.

Susan Vanderbilt wore a badge indicating that she worked for the hospital, but rather than wearing scrubs or a nurse's uniform—so prevalent on the ward—she was dressed in a professional skirt and blouse.

She recognized Jon right off the bat, which was helpful. Still, Jon introduced himself, shaking her hand, and ignored the flirtatious smile she initially gave him.

"I would like to help out with the Sunshine Club," he told Susan. "I hope it's okay, but I just spent time in the community room with young Brandon here. Brandon is a Sunshine Club graduate."

Susan's hand lingered in Jon's. She was definitely interested. "What did you have in mind?"

"Well, however I can be of best use to the program. I'm interested in fund-raising, but to tell the truth, bachelor auctions aren't my style."

"I do have another opportunity," she blurted out. Her face lit up like fireworks. "Vivian Sharpe, one of our board members, has asked me to organize the production of a commercial television video. I hadn't thought of using Captains players—we were planning on taking the cameras on the floor and filming the staff interacting with patients—but I'm liking the idea of trying you out instead." She put her finger to her lips and stared at him as if picturing him on television. "I'm liking it very much."

"Vivian is my team's owner," Jon said. "I, uh…

think I could do a video for her." Was this a gift horse or what?

Susan eyed him up and down. "Are you comfortable on camera? Because the purpose is to bring public awareness to the Sunshine Club. We'll be embarking on a fund drive this month, and if all goes well, you could be the face of the campaign."

A *campaign?* That involved much more than a single shoot on a single day. A *campaign* was more permanent. More…out there.

His palms felt sweaty. Now what?

Brandon nudged him.

"Ah, tell me what the campaign involves," Jon said.

"To begin with, we're talking two weeks to shoot video footage. Starting next week, you'll come in every other weekday for a full afternoon. We'll take time with some of the kids. Now and then we'll bring in different media—a camera crew, of course, and maybe some reporters or bloggers. It's a long-term commitment, if you have the availability."

"It's the off-season." Jon thought ahead to his pitching sessions…maybe he could duck out for a few afternoons a week. Max had said it was important to show a high profile with Vivian, after all. He would need to explain to Coach Duffy, but for this, he would understand. "I'll see what I can do."

Brandon tugged on his shirt. "I can help, too!"

"Is he your boy?" Susan asked.

"No, his aunt is a doctor at the hospital. Like I said,

he's a graduate from the Sunshine Club. He helped me today with the kids."

"I'm a survivor," Brandon said to her. "Jon needs me to help him!"

Susan gazed at him. Sadly, what Brandon had said was true. Jon shrugged. "The kid's good. He's smart and perceptive. I would welcome his help."

Susan bent to Brandon. "If your parents agree, would you like to work with us?"

"My aunt will let me." Brandon's eyes were wide. "I want to do it!"

Susan straightened, smiling brightly at Jon. "If you give me your email, I'll forward everything you need to know." She handed him a business card.

He would send her contact info to Brooke tonight. "That, ah, sounds great."

Susan peered at him. "Forgive me for asking, but if I'm remembering correctly, weren't you planning on cutting your hair for charity?"

"I…was," Jon said, "but we since we didn't make the playoffs, I don't think it would go over well if I tried to do that as a fund-raising event."

"Hmm. Yes, I know we've had Boston sports players shave their hair on camera, but I was actually thinking about something different for you—it doesn't require publicity, but would still help the kids. You see, we work with a charity that takes donated hair and makes wigs for the young cancer patients. If your hair is long enough, you could do that."

She took out a pen and another card, and jotted

down the information for him. "If you decide you want to check it out, tell them I referred you."

"Thanks," he said quietly.

Susan smiled. "It's great to have you on board, Jon."

JON WAITED UNTIL Brandon returned to day care. Then he went into a bathroom and splashed cold water on his face. It still felt odd to have his finger unsplinted. There was a red gash beneath the simple bandage the doctor had affixed. Jon stuck the bandage back on his finger and flexed his hand. It was stiff but okay.

He was lucky and he knew it. He had been given a fresh chance at achieving his goals.

Get serious. Do the community service. Learn the new pitch.

Some of the kids he'd seen today wouldn't get the chance to grow up and work on their dreams. He was blessed. And it was time to do something with that.

On the way out of the hospital, he stopped in front of the coffee shop. In a private place by the corner, he opened up the voice mail that Lizzy had left him.

The date and time were a few hours after he'd left the rehab center. *Lizzy,* he thought. *I'm sorry I didn't know you called me.*

"Hi, Jon," Lizzy had said. "I'm truly sorry over… the way I was harsh with you. I don't mean…to be prickly." A measure of silence passed. "Um, thank you for coming to Brandon's rescue. It's been a really hard day, and we're grateful." She had sighed audibly. There was a longer beat, and then a whispered, "Take care of yourself."

The recording ended.

His heart pumping, Jon listened to it two more times. He especially liked the ending. He felt good when she said, "Take care of yourself."

Instead of deleting the message, he saved it.

He shoved the phone in his pocket and stood there for a moment. Lizzy had obviously softened toward him. He felt an overwhelming urge to see her and talk to her about what had happened to him today. She alone, among everyone else he knew, would understand.

First, he would grab a coffee on the way out.

But as soon as he walked inside the café, he saw Lizzy. She was dressed in her surgical scrubs, and her back was to him. Her hands were curled around a cup of what was likely coffee.

It was fate. For a split second Jon was happy, until he noticed the man seated opposite her. He had a tray before him, eating lunch, and he also wore hospital scrubs.

Jon paused. He'd assumed Lizzy was more of a loner at work, but no. She was sitting with a handsome, serious-looking guy. His hair was cropped short and he wore glasses. His arms were bare under the scrubs, and it was obvious he worked out. The guy was no slouch. He was in shape, but brainy and serious. Like Lizzy.

Jon stood frozen for a minute. Felt self-conscious

about his long hair, scruffy razor stubble, and the T-shirt and jeans he wore. Not to mention his lack of an advanced college degree.

Was this a boyfriend of hers, or just a colleague she was having lunch with? Jon edged closer.

Lizzy and the doctor weren't talking. They seemed to be sharing a comfortable silence, which was even worse. At least if they had been talking, Jon could have told himself the guy was just a blowhard. Comfortable silence meant…intimacy. And there was no conflict between them, unlike the supercharged tension that always sizzled between Jon and Lizzy.

Jon had no right to care, about anything she did.

He stalked over and chose a bottle of iced tea from a display case in the corner, then walked to the cashier and paid for it. A slow, sad U2 song came over the store speakers—"I Still Haven't Found What I'm Looking For." The soundtrack to his life.

When he was out the door, he glanced back through the windows. Doctor Serious was throwing Lizzy's empty coffee cup away for her. Definitely intimate.

Jon was an idiot. He needed to get her out of his head. He had let her take up residence there for too long, and it was no good for him.

Because he was fine. He would be even better, once he got his contract with the Captains re-signed.

Get serious. Do the community service. Practice the changeup. Stay out of the way of sportswriters and media people.

And women who got too far into his head.

ELIZABETH KNEW THE moment Jon had entered the coffee shop. Her skin seemed to prickle, and she couldn't stop squirming. Her hormones always seemed to alert her when this guy was around.

Without turning, she could see his reflection in the mirror facing her table. Jon was behind her, staring at her and Albert. They were both halfway through a double shift, and they'd just finished the same case—a heart bypass surgery that had been particularly grueling, though more so for Albert than for her. He'd been the lead surgeon. Usually, surgeons and anesthesiologists were cut from completely different cloth—if anesthesiologists tended to be quiet and settled, surgeons were often more animated and dynamic. Surgeons cut. They developed and pioneered new methods to cut, while anesthesiologists kept their focus on the patients' medical well-being and stability.

Albert was different, though. He was quiet and ordered, like her. Focused and in his own world. He never spoke loudly. He valued peace. *The right way of things,* as he described it. Often, when they were together, they each remained quiet, contented in their own thoughts, unthreatened yet…comfortable in their separateness. Albert did not upset her. He did not challenge her.

Unlike Jon.

She watched him watch her, in the mirror. His face was…well, he looked shaken. Right away she noticed that his bandage was removed, which was surely his reason for being at the hospital. His hair hung loose and his jaw was flecked with dark, dangerous stubble—sexy stubble she wanted to rake her fingers over—and his lips were…mashed together and angry. Seeing her bothered him.

Her gaze flicked to Albert, fastidiously dunking his tea bag into the hot water. Up, down. Up, down.

She gazed back to Jon's reflection in the mirror. Held her breath. His eyes seemed to burn like ice-blue fire.

Come over to me. Please come over to me.

It was insane; it made no sense for her to feel this way. She should not want him in her hospital, should not trust her feelings toward him. He was the absolute wrong man for her.

She, like Albert, was a private person. She relied on herself and did not want the brand of attention Jon commandeered. Even out of uniform, other women in the shop were gazing at him, drawn to his presence. Jon's sleeves were pushed up, and the forearms beneath screamed, *Strong, capable guy here!* His jeans were loose and cut straight, not tight, but snug around his strong thighs.

She snapped her gaze down to her coffee. Forced her thoughts back to the recent surgery. Her legs had been cramped at her station, but she'd been unable to get up for a break. And somewhere in the middle of the procedure, hunger had crept in, but food wasn't allowed into the O.R. Even though many anesthesiologists discreetly smuggled in a granola bar here and there, she never did. Classical music had played over the speakers on her cart—Albert liked calming music. Some of the other surgeons were partial to heavy metal or even rousing show tunes or loud pop music, and that had always jarred her. But now, a haunting, old U2 song from her youth played. And she felt…like a hormone-ridden teenager, excited over a bad, completely inappropriate crush. Maybe it was time for that healthy rebellion she'd never allowed herself to undergo when she'd been younger—so terrified as she was of turning into her mother.

She looked back at Albert. If she were honest with herself, no matter how perfect he seemed for her logically, she didn't feel drawn to him and the safety he represented.

And that was too bad for her.

CHAPTER EIGHT

FINALLY THROUGH WITH her double shift, Elizabeth struggled to get into her condominium building with a bag of groceries under her arm, wondering if it was too late and she'd missed the baseball game.

The thin sliver of an October moon bathed the parking lot in a silvery glow. It had been a long time since Elizabeth had worked evening shifts like this, but Brandon's presence had wreaked havoc with her work schedule, and she'd been forced to make trades. The nighttime surgery she'd picked up had been emotionally draining—an organ recovery procedure from an accident victim. Elizabeth was drenched in sweat and feeling maudlin—cases where she didn't have to worry about waking the patient after the surgery was completed tended to do that to her. She wanted nothing more than to trudge upstairs, check that Brandon was okay, pay the babysitter and then collapse in front of her new TV.

Near the elevator, she called Mrs. Ham to let her know she was on her way.

"The game finished five minutes ago," her elderly neighbor informed her. "There's nothing on your TV but news. I was wondering when you were coming home."

Elizabeth sighed and pulled a folded check from her pocket. It was a bitter disappointment to Mrs. Ham that Elizabeth didn't get all the cable channels that Mrs. Ham received. Elizabeth needed to work to rectify that for her reluctant babysitter. *Add it to the list,* she thought. "How was Brandon?"

"Went right to sleep after dinner. Didn't hear a peep out of him."

Interesting. This was not Elizabeth's experience with her nephew. "Did you give him his gluten-free spaghetti?"

"Ate it all. That stuff doesn't taste half-bad. Did you know it's made out of corn flour? Who eats pasta made out of corn flour?"

People who are allergic to wheat, that's who. Elizabeth sighed again. "I'm leaving the elevator now. Why don't you meet me outside the apartment so we don't wake him up?"

"I'm already there. Left your TV on, though. Don't know how to shut the darn thing off. Your remote is different from mine."

"That's fine. I'll be right there." Elizabeth disconnected the call and stepped off the elevator.

She'd bought the new HD TV over the weekend, just so Mrs. Ham could be convinced to watch Brandon on nights that Elizabeth wasn't home. How Mrs. Ham had brought up two children was a mystery to Elizabeth. She suspected the woman's extroverted husband, who had passed last year, must have done most of the nurturing, because Mrs. Ham seemed to live for her television programs and sporting events.

"Gotta go," Mrs. Ham said after Elizabeth handed her the folded check she'd written. "It's past my bedtime." She hurried off down the hallway to the elevators.

Elizabeth entered her apartment, kicked off her shoes and put away the groceries, including some gluten-free cookies and a carton of ice cream. Brandon's last lab test had come in—Elizabeth had insisted on being thorough—and her nephew was officially cancer-free—not that Elizabeth had doubted he wasn't. She would give the good news to Brandon tomorrow night so they could celebrate. She'd already called her sister's counselor to inform him, but she wasn't allowed to speak to Ashley directly. The counselor had said he would relay the message as appropriate, and that her sister was doing well.

Elizabeth hoped so.

When she was finished unloading her groceries, she tiptoed over to her office, which she'd made into a makeshift bedroom for Brandon. Part of her longed to reclaim her haven. *Just a little over three more weeks,* she thought.

She peered inside and checked her nephew's sleeping form under the covers, then quickly withdrew. On the dining room table, she looked for his homework so she could check it for him but instead found a note to her, scrawled in Brandon's childish handwriting, which, she'd been shocked to learn, they didn't teach in school anymore. Everything was keyboarding. But her nephew had done his level best to keep his message neat and clear—no cursive, just simple printing:

Auntie, I hope you had a good night. Please wake me up if I am asleep when you come home. Love, Brandon.

Beside the note, he'd left a plastic footbath, along with two wrapped tablets of fizzy foot soak.

Aw. She put her hand over her heart. Maybe they really were forming a ritual together, she and her little nephew. He probably did this with his mom, too, because as a hairdresser, Ashley was often on her feet all day.

Elizabeth ran the tap water at its hottest, and when it was a soothing temperature, filled the tub and dropped the bath fizzies inside. She poured herself a glass of sparkling apple juice, sat on the couch and soaked her aching feet in the warm water, soft from essential oils and smelling like rosemary.

She closed her eyes and inhaled. Tears stabbed at the insides of her eyelids. Brandon was a sweet kid. It couldn't be easy dealing with his mom's absence.

Brandon's bedroom door squeaked open. Rubbing his eyes, he padded out in his pajamas. Apparently he was still young enough to snuggle into the couch beside her, his towhead resting against her shoulder.

Tentatively, she touched his hair. Soft, child's

hair. A bit crusty in places, because she suspected he wasn't always washing it at night, as he'd promised. Brandon was more of a morning child.

He yawned. "Auntie, did you get my note?"

"I did. My surgery went very late, and I'm sorry for that."

"Did you save the person's life?"

Her hand stilled on the crown of his head. "A little boy is getting a new kidney." That part was true. She just wasn't participating in that end of the procedure.

Brandon hugged her. "I'm proud of you, Auntie."

A lump formed in her throat. Nobody had ever been proud of her.

She patted his back in response. *Ashley has done well with him.* She hoped she could protect him like Ashley did.

"I might want to be a doctor, too," Brandon said.

"That's…" Elizabeth didn't know what to say. Her eyes were getting misty. "What kind of doctor?"

"A cancer doctor."

She almost gasped aloud. But maybe this was normal for kids who had survived cancer treatment, like Brandon had.

"A cancer doctor for *kids,*" Brandon specified. "That's what I want to be."

Elizabeth swallowed. This was getting to be too much for her. She was at the mercy of her emotions, and she didn't like or trust them. She took a sip of her apple juice.

"Auntie, can you help me?" Brandon's big blue eyes

gazed up at her. They were rich blue, like the seashore on a sunny day. For some reason she thought of Jon's eyes. They were a lighter blue—more shocking and bold, like hot fire. His were a man's eyes. Brandon's were still little boy's eyes.

Why was she thinking about Jon?

"I'm…" What were they talking about? Oh, yes. Brandon. A doctor.

She shook off her private doubt.

Brandon's teacher had told her that the boy was bright and clever, but he didn't apply himself to his lessons. He spent too much time "visiting his neighbors" and "helping them with their work." He was his mother's son, for sure.

But the intellectual ability was there. He was her nephew, too.

"I'm…thinking I can help you with your schoolwork," she said. "That's the only way to get accepted into the universities you'll need to attend in order to become a doctor."

She settled into the cushions, more sure of herself now. Yes, she could assist Brandon on the proper path to medical school, the steps he should be taking—

"Auntie, there's a program at the hospital, and I talked to the lady in charge today—she wants me to help. I need you to sign the forms so I can do it."

"What is the program?"

"It's with the Sunshine Club."

"The Sunshine Club?" Elizabeth looked at him.

She stared at her feet in the footbath. Was she being manipulated by a budding manipulator? "All of this?" She motioned to the water. "Were you softening me up?"

His eyes grew large. "I don't know what you mean, Auntie."

Elizabeth reconsidered. He was just an eight-year-old kid. He wasn't necessarily like her father. *Biological father,* she corrected herself. And Elizabeth wasn't naive, like she and Ashley's mother had been when they were children.

"Brandon," Elizabeth said, aiming to keep her voice calm. "You were at the hospital today only because you had no school due to a teachers' training session. Your district only schedules one or two of those per term. It's not a regular occurrence. Your schedule simply doesn't allow you to—"

"*I* can get a ride to the hospital." Brandon's lip protruded. "After school. Mrs. Ham can take me."

"Mrs. Ham has cataracts. She should not be driving herself, let alone a child."

"I'll find somebody else to drive me."

"Who?"

"I have friends," he said stubbornly.

She gave him a look. To have "friends" was to risk confiding. It was bad enough that Caitlin's son had told two other little school chums that Brandon's mom was in alcohol rehab. Elizabeth had suffered through the resulting meeting in the principal's office. She dreaded what Ashley would do when she found out.

"Brandon," she said softly. "Your mom loves you. And in order for her to heal, she has asked that what is happening with us—with our family—be kept private."

He bit his lip and looked down. She could tell he was trying not to cry.

"How is your school going?" she asked kindly. If he really was thinking about becoming a doctor, that was the best thing for him to concentrate on. "What are you working on in math? May I see your homework?"

He jutted out his chin. "We don't have homework. We're just little kids."

That wasn't entirely true. "How about your project on Scotland?" They were supposed to be doing a report on a country where somebody in their family had their roots. She'd been explaining *Braveheart* and the system of clans and kilts last weekend. She had rather enjoyed herself.

"I want to talk about the cancer program," he said between his teeth.

She sighed. "Was there an administrator involved? Do you have a name?"

"Susan Vanderbilt," he said without hesitation.

Elizabeth didn't know who she was. It was a big hospital; she would have to look her up. "I thought you were supposed to be in the day care doing your homework today?" she asked.

"They let me play with the kids in the cancer ward." He drew his finger around the Superman figure on his pajamas. She had a feeling he was fibbing.

"Did you wander off from day care again?" she asked.

"No." He shrugged. "The nurse said that I'm good with the kids because I know what it's like."

"Ah." Elizabeth settled back. What was she supposed to say to that? It was true he had a talent she would never have. Tonight, for example, her chief had asked her to speak to the mother of the organ donor she'd worked on. Elizabeth had deferred…she had no idea what to say. And she felt terrible. More so because her chief had shaken his head at her.

"I just don't see how it can work," she finished lamely. "I'm sorry. Maybe when your mom gets out—"

"My mom isn't here! You're here! Why do you have to be so *mean!*"

THE NEXT DAY during a break between cases, Elizabeth girded herself before heading upstairs to the children's cancer clinic she so rarely had reason to visit anymore.

On her way to the administrative offices, she bypassed the bright wall murals and whimsical activity centers in the children's outpatient waiting area. Brandon had spent several days a week here for over two years. Elizabeth had frequently met Ashley in these rooms while her sister sat with her sick child. It had been the hardest time of their lives. That Brandon wanted to help other kids in this position was a testament to his generosity of spirit, but, unfortunately, with his mother undergoing the crisis she was enduring, this was not the time for it.

Elizabeth walked the corridor until she found the nameplate for the administrator Brandon had spoken with: Susan Vanderbilt. Elizabeth waited outside her open office door while the woman finished up a telephone call on speakerphone. She sat on the edge of her desk, wearing a short skirt and a tight jacket, her fashionable shoe dangling from her toes as she laughed and chatted with her caller. So easy for her to express herself. Obviously hired for her public relations expertise, Susan was about Elizabeth's age and she seemed bubbly and dynamic, the opposite of Elizabeth's personality.

Elizabeth had brought her iPad with her by force of habit. She pressed it close to her chest, as if the barrier between machine and other people could magically protect her from awkwardness. She ought to know better.

"May I help you?" Susan asked, smiling, once she'd finished her call.

Elizabeth licked her lips and entered the bright office adorned with green plants, which felt natural given the sunlight streaming through the blinds. Such a different atmosphere from the windowless

O.R. where Elizabeth worked. Here, she was a fish out of water.

"I…understand you met my nephew yesterday. Brandon LaValley."

"I sure did," Susan said. "We're looking forward to working with him on the video we're producing." She reached over and pulled a form from her desk. "He said you were stopping by, so I got this ready for you." Her beautifully manicured nails with cinnamon-red polish shone as she offered the paper to Elizabeth. "All you need to do is sign and return it to me by the end of the week. If it's all right with his parents, we're set to go."

"That's just it," Elizabeth said softly. "It's *not* all right with his parents." She jerked her gaze from Susan and her trendy fingernails and fixed it on the wall, at a point above Susan's head, so she would not get disheartened or sent off track by any resistance Susan offered.

"Oh. I'm sorry to hear that." Susan paused. Elizabeth was just about to turn around and leave—because what more could she say?—when Susan asked, "Do you mind if I ask why?"

Elizabeth did mind her asking, very much. But unlike a tourist on the street, Elizabeth could hardly ignore a member of the hospital staff and hurry away. Elizabeth was responsible for maintaining a professional working relationship with everyone from janitor to Chief of Surgery. She nibbled her lip and weighed a response. "It's…just a bad time right now.

The situation is delicate. Everything I'm doing is for the child's best interests."

"I understand," Susan said in a small voice. "Is there anything I can do to help?"

"No!" Elizabeth suppressed the shudder. "Thank you."

"Okay. I mean, as long as I didn't offend you." Susan glanced at Elizabeth's name, embroidered on her lab coat. "Because I certainly don't want to offend a doctor from Anesthesiology."

"You didn't offend me. It's just..." Elizabeth was trying so hard not to be "prickly" anymore. "It really is a difficult time for us. And we're much too busy."

"You don't have to explain." Susan clasped Elizabeth's hand, still cradled around her iPad.

Elizabeth nodded, slowly exhaling, releasing herself from the woman's grip. She could leave now, go back to her job. The encounter had turned out... okay. She was still on track with her sister's wishes. All she had to figure out was a way to tell Brandon about her decision. Maybe during the drive home she could think of how to make it easier for him to accept. She turned—

And smacked right into Jon Farell.

She sucked in her breath. By error, she'd placed a hand against Jon's sternum. His chest was flat and broad, warm with his heartbeat and the hot blood that coursed beneath his skin.

Unable to move her hand, she stared at her plain, short-clipped fingernails pressed against the row of buttons on his collared shirt. Her pulse jittery, she lifted her gaze to his. Ever since she'd seen Jon in the cafeteria yesterday afternoon, she'd been thinking about him, hoping he would call. Wondering why he hadn't responded to the voice mail apology she'd sent him.

But of course, Jon wasn't interested in her anymore. She'd been too harsh to him the last time they'd spoken.

He stared down at her, not moving, his face impassive. But his ice-blue eyes seemed to bore into hers. "What 'best interests'?" From the inflection in his voice, he didn't sound happy to see her.

Dropping her hand, she stepped back. Clasped the tablet with both hands to her chest again. Of course, his concern was for Brandon. "Nothing," she said.

"Hi, Jon." Susan strolled around Elizabeth and smiled at him, showing off her dimples. "How are you today?"

Jon glanced at Susan, up and down, very quickly. "I'm fine." He returned his gaze to Elizabeth, but the damage was done. In her baggy scrubs, her scuffed and worn shoes, her distinct lack of makeup, she felt self-conscious in comparison to Susan.

"I talked with your agent this morning." Susan played with a dangling gold earring as she focused the glow of her attention on Jon. "She's excited about the commercial shoot. I told her we're ready to start filming on Monday."

"Yeah, I heard." But Jon hadn't stopped staring at

Elizabeth. She squirmed. His gaze pinned her as if blaming her for the decision with Brandon.

"Unfortunately," Susan nattered on, nodding her head toward Elizabeth, "Brandon won't be participating, so you'll be going it alone. But that should be okay. We can certainly work around it."

"Well. Everything's settled. I need to go." Elizabeth turned on her heel and escaped to safety out in the corridor.

Jon followed her. "What 'best interests'?" He spoke from close behind her ear. To her shock, he kept pace with every step she took down the hallway.

"Stop following me," she hissed.

"I want to know why you think I'm bad for Brandon."

Two passing residents turned to stare at them. Elizabeth cringed. "Please don't do this here."

"Choose your place, then, because we're having this out right now."

Feeling hot, she gripped her tablet tighter. "Fine," she said in a clipped voice. What did he care, it wasn't his hospital colleagues who were observing them. "Follow me."

Lengthening her stride, she headed as fast as she could for a quieter corridor, one that angled away from the children's clinic and led to a different wing of the vast hospital complex where she worked. Chairs and cubbyhole-type seating areas were tucked into various stops along the walkway. She would divert Jon into one of those, out of sight from passersby.

Jon followed her without a word, obeying for once. How could he possibly think she had something against him? Presumably, Jon had listened to her voice mail apology. If not, she would make him listen. It ate her up inside when he misunderstood her.

But all the chairs along the route were taken. There was no private spot at this time of day. Elizabeth hated to do this—it was her special place to hide, her sanctuary—but she diverted their path in the direction of the hospital chapel. Nearby were small, adjacent rooms with doors that closed, where surgeons often met to give news—usually bad news—to family members.

She chose a vacant room and closed the door behind Jon with a solid click. It was just the two of them, alone. And Jon was standing much too close to her, towering over her five-foot-eight frame, his gaze piercing her, forcing her to tilt back her head and look up at him.

Her bare neck was exposed. She felt so vulnerable to him. And so…aware of his presence. It made her sweat under her loose doctor jacket.

She should have thought ahead to the fact that closing the door not only gave them privacy from others, but it also gave them intimacy.

They stared at each other, both breathing heavily from the fast walk. His gaze went from her throat, to her lips, to her eyes, and back to her lips. His expression seemed to soften. His lips parted slightly.

Her nipples were tightening. She felt warm all

over. Never had she so wanted to be kissed. His smell just…drew her closer.

He lifted his hand to her, and she wanted to touch him. To run her hands through his hair beside his cheekbones. Such beautiful, masculine hair.

Longer than hers. The opposite of hers.

Abruptly, he crossed his arms and stepped back, exhaling heavily. He fixed his gaze at a point over her head. "Look, I understand that you and I are from completely different worlds, but that doesn't mean you shouldn't trust Brandon with me."

"Did I say that?" she whispered. "I never said that."

His gaze darted to her. "You're dead set against me. You always have been, Elizabeth."

She flinched at his harsh tone. And he was no longer calling her Lizzy, his old endearment. Maybe it was too late for them.

Disappointment coursing through her, she felt herself slumping. And here she had dared hope that Jon could see through her protective shell to understand she'd been *trying*. That she was willing to open herself up, a little bit.

She placed her tablet on a table and wiped her hands against her hospital scrubs. "My decision with Susan isn't about you. It's about Brandon."

"He's perfect for that program." Jon's voice was so rich and low it sent a shiver through her. "You should have seen him yesterday. He was great with those kids. And he was so excited to be there."

Jon's ice-blue eyes focused on hers, and he was

close to pleading. "Don't punish him for it. His presence in that ward had nothing to do with my influence. He deserves to be there more than I do."

"I know he wants to help kids with cancer." Did Jon think she didn't know her own nephew? "He told me that himself."

"Then why not let him do it?" Jon demanded. "Just because of me? What are you so afraid of, anyway?"

"Afraid?" She stepped back, furious. And she'd just wanted to *kiss* this man? "You really think this decision is all about *my* wishes?"

"Who else's wishes would they be?"

She felt her mouth widen in shock. "Jon, my conversation with Susan—which was *private,* by the way—was not about my wishes, or about any lack of trust in you. On the contrary, it was about respecting my *sister's* wishes. Because Brandon is not my child. He's not yours, either."

"Yeah, no kidding. So whose boy is he? Besides your sister's? Is Brandon in some kind of danger with his biological father? Because otherwise, I don't get your big urge to secrecy. I really don't."

"Wait." She put her hand to her head. "Are you asking about his biological father? Are you really going there?"

"Yes, I am." Jon leaned against the table where she'd set her tablet. "Brandon said he doesn't have a father. But everybody does—it's an inescapable fact. So tell me, Liz, who is he? Is he somebody dangerous? Is your sister in hiding from him?"

"No!" she sputtered. "Nobody is dangerous. Nobody is in hiding."

"Are you sure?"

"I…" She felt flabbergasted. And ashamed. Because she really didn't know. Ashley had never confided in anyone. Just like their own mother had never confided in them. Ashley had eventually figured out that Tony was their father, but not until she was about twelve or thirteen years of age, older than Brandon.

Elizabeth pressed her hand to her mouth.

She did know one thing: she felt protective of Ashley—as viscerally protective as she'd ever felt about wanting to keep their father's name a secret. It was nobody's business. A private, family matter.

"I'm sorry, Jon," she said as clearly as she could, "the bottom line is, I don't have the right to make this decision on my nephew's behalf. Brandon is an underage kid. I need you to understand that."

"Nope, doesn't make sense to me. Because if you don't have the right to make decisions on Brandon's behalf, then who does? Your sister?" He snorted. "She gave up her rights—at least in the short term—when she entered that treatment facility. You know I'm right about this."

"Why do you care?" she shot back. "And don't tell me it's for Brandon, because you've only known him for a week."

He stepped closer to her, nose to nose. "Why do you care about stopping him from doing what he was born to do? How does that threaten you?"

"It doesn't threaten *me*. You misunderstand."

"I think you're the one who doesn't want Brandon on television. I think it's personal to you. I think it would require you to get messy in ways that you don't want to. You might actually have to mingle with the rest of us lowly nondoctors. And I don't think you can stand that."

She gaped at him. She did not understand, in the least, where this was coming from. His gaze went from her eyes to her mouth to her...breasts. There was awareness between them, an interest, and he was fighting it, the same as she was. She got the feeling this wasn't all about the situation at hand. It was... something else. But she wasn't good at reading people. She was missing the point.

"Why do *you* want him so badly on this video project?" she asked. "How does it help you?" She clapped her hand to her mouth. "Oh, my gosh. The owner of your team sits on the board of the hospital...Mrs. Sharpe...Vivian Sharpe...she's chairperson of the Sunshine Club. You're doing this to impress Vivian, aren't you? And Brandon can make you look good."

He laughed sarcastically, but it was a false laugh— Elizabeth saw through it. "Right," he said. "Stop changing the subject. We're discussing you, Lizzy. If Brandon is at the hospital too much, being outspoken the way he naturally is, then he threatens your professional boundaries."

"It's about protecting him, not me," she pointed out yet again. "A television commercial is *very* public. It's as public as it gets. Much attention will be drawn to him, and I am not interested in exposure, of any kind. For me, or for anyone close to me. End of discussion." She turned for the door, but his voice stopped her.

"Exposure brings benefits to people, Elizabeth. To other people. It can help them. Isn't that worth it to you?"

"Not if it destroys the messenger in the process," she snapped.

"How? How would being public destroy Brandon? Destroy you?"

Elizabeth turned. "Are you blind? Look at my sister in rehab. As a kid, she focused on everyone else, drawn to the drama. She rarely focused on taking care of herself, and the result of that was chaos—out-of-control chaos. And do you know what results from *that?*" She sputtered. "Messes. There are messes to be cleaned up. Don't you see what happens? Don't you see where my sister is, and what I'm doing right now, taking care of Brandon? Don't you see that my way of living is *better?*"

There was a shocked silence. Elizabeth clapped her hand over her mouth. She needed to grab her tablet and get away. Away from Jon's shocked expression, away from his judgment. She pulled at the doorknob. Anything to get some air.

Jon's hand clasped her arm. Her first instinct was to go rigid, but his hand was warm, and her body—traitor—wanted him to touch her. Wanted his closeness.

"I know, Lizzy," he murmured. "I spent my early years cleaning up other people's messes, too, holding my family together." He spoke to her in that low voice that echoed through her bones and wrapped her in comfort. She shuddered, leaning into him, craving that warmth. "This commercial," he continued, "this video…it isn't one of those times. It's something that *heals*. Let it be healing for Brandon, too. Let it make him feel better about what he's going through."

Tears pricked at the inside of her eyelids. If only it was as easy as Jon made it sound. The publicity was just too big. At some point, ultimately, there would be consequences. It was only a matter of time.

"He's healing with *me*," she whispered.

And he was. She and Brandon had developed a routine together over these past days. They were getting closer. And he would be okay, once she broke the news to him and he got over his initial disappointment.

"I know he is healing with you," Jon said quietly. "He respects you. I see it."

Maybe Jon did understand. He wasn't fighting or angry with her anymore; he was letting her know that he was on her side, and he approved.

"Then let it go," she pleaded with him.

"I can't." He shook his head. "The kid got me involved. He sucked me in."

"That isn't good for you. It's not healthy."

He snorted. "You think I don't know that?" He pushed away from the wall. "But maybe I need to do this video with him the way you need your routines and your life. My job—being a Captains player—it's how I keep the bad stuff at bay, just like you do with being a doctor. I like how it enables me to help people. You…gave me a hard time about being too much of a white knight…maybe you were right, to a point. But that can be a good thing too, Liz. Because otherwise, why are we here? To be alone? I don't want to be alone."

She swallowed, knowing that this was probably more than he ever told anybody, maybe even more than he usually admitted to himself. She risked looking into his eyes. Oh God, he was so beautiful. So classically handsome, inside and out.

His hand moved from her arm to her waist and then to the small of her back. A proprietary touch.

See me, and be mine, it said.

But she could not allow this. Because he had been right about her—she was terrified of being part of somebody else's pain. And that included Brandon's pain and her sister's pain.

She needed to get back to her anesthesia. To her reading. To her studying. Watching the baseball playoffs at night on TV and cataloging what they were doing and understanding it…enjoying it. She needed to relax and to breathe in her home, in her private, protective shell. And as much as she would love for Jon—for this beautiful, feeling man—to be part of that inner shell with her, he just wanted too much. She could never be that public person with him.

"I need to go." She picked up her tablet from the table she'd set it on. Her hands were shaking uncontrollably. "I'm sorry."

She broke away from Jon. Let go of her connection with him, physically and otherwise. "If Brandon calls you upset this afternoon, could you please explain to him that the Captains don't want the liability of a child involved with the program? For me? Please?"

Jon's head tilted. "Don't, Lizzy." He looked directly into her eyes, pleading and, despite herself, she couldn't look away.

"Trust me," he said quietly. "Don't give up."

She closed her eyes. He was not going away easily. She hated to make this choice, to hurt him. But he had overstepped his boundaries by threatening her family's privacy, and she would protect what was hers.

"If you fight me on this, Jon, then I will file a complaint with…" She'd meant to say *Vivian,* but when push came to shove, she couldn't be that cruel. "With…with the hospital."

He stepped back from her. Physically stepped back. "No need," he said brusquely.

And when she left, he did not follow her through the doorway.

Everything was worse with him than before. And she'd done it in Brandon's name.

TWO HOURS LATER, she still felt terrible for the way she'd handled the situation with Jon.

She was not a person who threatened other people. This was not her vision of herself.

But she couldn't go back in time, and she didn't know what to do about it even if she could. So Elizabeth finished her last write-up on her last surgery and drove to Brandon's school to pick him up for the afternoon. Her nephew flew out of the building with all the pent up energy of an active little boy forced to sit still and behave all day.

Her heart went out to him. She smiled as he opened the door to her Prius, jumped inside and threw his knapsack on the floor as fast as he could talk. "Auntie! Hurry up, we're late, we have to get to the hospital!"

Her heart sank. How could she crush him? Before she could think of a response, several of his friends ran over to him, milling around the car, knocking on the windows and waving at him. Elizabeth felt herself shrinking back. *Ugh.* She was aching to be home already. But they were stuck in the Prius, idling in the school parking lot behind a string of cars waiting for the buses to pull out and leave. She really had no control over where they could go or how far they could advance or who could waylay them.

"Hello!" A pretty dark-haired woman knocked on the driver's side window. "Are you Brandon's aunt?" she called through the glass. "I'm Caitlin, Ashley's neighbor."

Elizabeth groaned. She had no choice but to flick the power switch and open the window. "Yes. Hello."

"It's so nice to meet you finally." Caitlin reached inside and clasped her hand. "We're really pulling for Ashley. Please give her our best."

"I'm sorry," Elizabeth said, "I don't know what you're—"

"I told them you're helping us, Auntie," Brandon piped in.

"And it's such good news about Brandon's tests being cancer-free," Caitlin continued, gushing. "Ashley will be so thrilled when she hears. How long will she be gone?"

It was a nightmare. An absolute nightmare.

"My mom will be back in a week or two," Brandon said to Caitlin. "I'll tell you when she's home."

And her nephew was in on it?

"Brandon, please put on your seat belt." Elizabeth closed the window to Caitlin and made a small wave.

"Goodbye, everybody!" Brandon shouted through the glass to his friends as the line of cars inched forward. Slowly but surely they made their escape from the school grounds.

As she stepped on the accelerator and merged with moving traffic, Elizabeth had no idea how to handle this new problem. Should she chide Brandon about keeping his mother's privacy? Or was that even healthy?

"Auntie, did you get the forms filled out?"

Elizabeth gripped the steering wheel. *Here we go,* she thought. She was so not handling this well. "Honey, I told you last night that it didn't look good, and not to get your hopes up."

"Did you talk to Susan?"

"Yes, I did. It turns out that for liability reasons, you're a kid and you can't work on the project." *Without a parent's permission, which Elizabeth was not going to give.*

"That's not what she told me yesterday." Brandon's look was murderous.

"Then she misspoke. I talked with her again and she said—"

"You *don't know,* Auntie."

"I work there with these people, Brandon," she said gently. "It's my job to know."

He leaned his forehead against the side window and said nothing more to her while they drove the remaining twenty minutes home, through the starts and stops of metro Boston traffic.

When at last she pulled into her parking spot at the condo building, Brandon opened the door as soon as it was safe, got out of the car and ran faster than she'd seen him run before.

"Brandon!" she called.

The wind had picked up, and some of the red and gold maple leaves were falling, swirling through the air. Elizabeth grabbed her purse and opened her car door. Standing there, watching Brandon run, she knew she was helpless to try to catch up. He sprinted across the parking lot and through the trees to an adjacent property. "Brandon!" she called again.

He kept on running. She had no choice but to toss her purse into the car and chase after him. Down a sidewalk, she struggled to catch up. But running wasn't her forte, and she didn't know her neighborhood well. She'd never once walked it. *Pathetic.*

Her heart pounding, she dashed up and down new-to-her side streets. She was wearing her hospital clogs, not exactly walking shoes, never mind running, and every now and then her ankle twisted slightly and she stumbled. But what could she do?

"Brandon!" she called out. "Brandon!"

She searched for him everywhere. There was a park two blocks over—who knew?—but he wasn't on the slides or the swings or in the sandboxes.

Standing beside a row of empty garbage bins, hunched over with her hands on her knees and out of breath, she had to admit defeat. Tears rolled down her cheeks. Her lungs hurt from running through the cool autumn air. Her hair was snarled and her doctor coat was tangled.

She had failed. She had disappointed Brandon, and then she had lost him. Elizabeth was just so…unequipped. So poorly handling a situation that was so simple, something every parent in Brandon's school could surely handle, no problem.

Yet again, there was that feeling of being a freak. A misfit. She could monitor a patient's vital signs and put in a breathing tube like nobody's business, but she had no idea how to relate to an eight-year-old kid.

Slumping, she walked back to her condominium building. She would have to call the police. It was making her panic, thinking it had gone this far. Ashley would be so upset. But the worst thing was that Brandon was gone, and Elizabeth had lost him.

What if he was kidnapped—snatched off the street? Or hurt? Or run over?

Oh, God.

She was wiping raw snot from her nose, fumbling inside her car for her purse where she kept her cell phone, but she couldn't find the phone. Her house keys were clipped to the outside of the bag—all she could think was that since she didn't have a landline of her own, she needed to get to Mrs. Ham's telephone as soon as possible. What if she had waited too long to call the police already?

But when she ran into the building, the door to Mrs. Ham's condo was open and the elderly lady stuck out her graying head. "Elizabeth? Please come here. There's someone inside who would like to speak to you."

Blindly, through her tears, Elizabeth saw Brandon. She'd never been so happy to see anybody in all her life. A raw sob tore through her as she rushed inside Mrs. Ham's condo and pulled her nephew into her arms.

"I'm sorry!" she cried. "I'm messing this up! Please don't run away from me again!"

Mrs. Ham looked at her with pity in her eyes. Elizabeth thought she might as well be stripped naked. But what could she do? She was responsible for this kid until his mom returned home. Three more weeks of life-altering, lack-of-privacy, no-instruction-manual torture, and all Elizabeth could do was navigate it day by day. Figure it out as she went.

She would just have to trust herself. Ashley already trusted her. Ashley had left her most precious thing, her son, with Elizabeth.

Jon was right. The only person who would be challenged by giving Brandon what he needed was *her*.

She clutched her nephew's shoulders. "If I get you into that program, will you be happy then?"

"Y-yes, Auntie."

"Explain to me exactly why you want to do it so I'm sure I understand."

"B-b-because I like Jon. I w-want to be like Jon. And I l-like helping those little kids." He put his arms around her. He felt warm and sweaty against her neck. "It's what I can do, Auntie. I'm good at it."

"Oh, Brandon." A lump in her throat, Elizabeth squeezed him tightly. She wanted to help him. She would help him.

"Please get me in the program, Auntie," Brandon whispered.

If he was in the program, then maybe she could

have a little bit more time to relax, too. Yeah, that was a positive way to look at it.

"All right." Before she could talk herself out of it, she smiled at him, said goodbye to Mrs. Ham and plunged up the stairs, leading Brandon along beside her. "I'll need you to come into the condo with me so we can call the hospital and get you started."

His face broke into an earsplitting grin. "I can do that."

She would repair the bridge she'd burned. It was still her hospital, her home turf. "But in the future, you have to promise to work with me, not against me. Do you hear me, Brandon?"

His eyes were huge. He nodded at her, sniffling, his lashes still wet. The poor kid—she didn't blame him, she was scaring herself. She would just have to take this step-by-step. Like the grown adult that she was.

Brandon clung to her as she unlocked her condo door. When they got inside, he waited on the couch and watched cartoons while she found her phone inside her purse and brought it into her bedroom. She shut the door and called Ashley's treatment center.

"Please," she said, once she had Ashley's counselor on the line, "I know you prefer I don't talk with my sister, but this is important."

"Ashley's doing well," her counselor replied. "She's very brave, and she's making progress. But I'm sorry, I can't have her talk with anyone on the outside just yet. It's best for her treatment and her progress."

"I see. When will I be able to talk with her?"

"Unsupervised? The Sunday night we send her home."

Three weeks from this weekend. Elizabeth swallowed.

"Is there anything else?" the counselor asked.

"No. Just…tell her I love her. Take good care of my sister, please."

When she hung up, Brandon stood in the doorway. "Can we go to the hospital now?" he asked plaintively.

"Not yet, sweetheart. Let me call them and ask first, okay?"

With her back to him, she called the switchboard and asked for Susan's number. Susan picked up right away and Elizabeth immediately launched into her apologetic speech.

"I'm sorry, Dr. LaValley," Susan said. "We found another former member of the Sunshine Club for the program, a college student. He's a baseball player. Jon Farell found him, actually."

Jon Farell. Great. For once, he had listened to Elizabeth and followed her wishes.

But Brandon was standing in her bedroom, looking at her, his lips trembling.

Elizabeth disconnected the call and took his hands in hers. "Sweetie, I have to see Jon, first. There's… paperwork to be discussed."

The look on Brandon's face was of pure gratitude. And love. He clasped her around the waist and gave her a huge hug. "Thank you, Auntie," he said in a small, muffled voice.

That meant more than if he'd begged and pleaded and cried.

And struck her just as forcefully.

JON WAS SITTING in the college trainer's office watching video with Coach Duffy when, from across the room, the sound of tinny guitar music and finger snapping erupted, muffled inside his gear bag.

"Do you have a Spanish girlfriend?" Coach Duffy asked.

"No. Why?"

"Because that's a ring tone. It sounds like a flamenco dancer is summoning you."

Jon scratched his head. He didn't use ring tones like that with his phone. Odd. But he was watching his fastball mechanics in slow motion on the video monitor, so he ignored the call. All he cared about was that Coach Duffy and he were pitching together again. Finally.

It wasn't until Jon got home and, checking his missed calls, saw an entry for BRANDON!, all in caps.

The kid must have programmed his phone number into Jon's phone. Jon stared at it lying in his palm. Thinking back, he recalled that there had been a few minutes yesterday when he'd asked Brandon to hold the phone for him while he signed a few autographs.

But there was no way he was calling Brandon back.

Because there was no way to salvage this…relationship, if it could be called that, with the kid's aunt. She was simply too closed off. Afraid to take a risk.

Worse—what Elizabeth had said to him in her parting shot?

It was irretrievable. He would not, could not, forget.

CHAPTER NINE

SHE LOOKED LIKE a hooker. At best, a lounge singer.

Elizabeth stared at her reflection and cringed. A bright red wrap dress gaped low on her bosom, tied tight around her waist. When she turned her back to the mirror, the spandex in the material clung tightly to her booty.

Ugh. She was even calling her derriere a "booty," because that's what her eight-year-old, cartoon-watching nephew called it.

Whatever the name for her overcurvaceous backside, it was the bane of her existence. She simply sat too much. Even the two ballet classes a week she took at work, in the hospital exercise studio, did not help. If anything, they made her "booty" even "bootier."

"You look beautiful." Brandon glanced up from playing with her cell phone long enough to give her a kid's missing-tooth grin.

"Sweetie, thank you for saying so."

"That red is the same color as is in the Captains uniform. Jon's going to love it."

She bit her lip to stop from laughing and glanced over her nephew's shoulder at Mrs. Ham. The blasé babysitter stood in the doorway to Elizabeth's bedroom, a turkey sandwich in her hand, and shrugged. "If you want to catch the attention of a professional athlete, that's the way you need to dress."

"So you said." There were three other dresses tossed across Elizabeth's bed—dresses already tried on and rejected by Elizabeth's two beauty consultants. "Looks like a funeral outfit," Mrs. Ham had said regarding the first dress. "I wouldn't let my cat wear that one," she'd said to the second. And "You should check out my mom's closet. She has lots of dresses," Brandon had replied to the third.

This red dress, the last in Elizabeth's closet, had, in fact, been a gift from Ashley. And the tags were still attached to prove it.

"I don't know," Elizabeth mused, thinking of Susan Vanderbilt. "Maybe I need some nail polish, too." Cinnamon-colored. She turned to Mrs. Ham. "Do you have any red nail polish?"

"Do I look like I own red nail polish?" Mrs. Ham took a bite from the turkey sandwich. Gluten-free bread, but Elizabeth didn't have the heart to tell her. "Honey," Mrs. Ham said, "stick with the dress. I brought up two sons—trust me, they're not looking at your fingers."

Elizabeth turned to the mirror and sighed. "I don't have shoes to go with this outfit."

"My mom does," Brandon shouted from the bed where he was sprawled, checking Elizabeth's cell phone once again for a potential voice mail from Jon. By the frown on his face, it seemed there were none.

"I don't see why Jon doesn't answer my text messages. He must really be mad at you, Auntie."

Brandon had sent Jon *text* messages from her phone? Elizabeth confiscated the phone from the boy and buried it in her purse. "Honey, why don't you go to the bathroom and pick out a lipstick for me? Any color you want. They're in my drawer by the sink."

Brandon brightened. "Okay." He trotted off to the bathroom, and Elizabeth thanked her lucky stars that she'd had a nurse anesthetist colleague who was also a Mary Kay sales consultant. Elizabeth didn't normally wear makeup, but she liked her anesthetist, and her anesthetist was right, the makeup had come in handy. At some point in her life, no matter her occupation, every woman needed to put on the bling.

It was even sort of fun. Maybe. Okay, Elizabeth had no choice. She needed to convince a man to pay attention to her. To give her a second chance. And since he hadn't been answering her phone calls all morning, and apparently was not interested in returning the voice message she'd left him, this was her last hope.

Elizabeth opened her jewelry box and pulled out her lucky diamond-chip earrings. Again, a gift from Ashley when she'd graduated from med school. She made a mental note to stop by Ashley's house to pick out a pair of shoes from her closet. If there was ever a time she desperately needed her big sister to help her, this was it. An eight-year-old boy and a cranky neighbor didn't make the greatest fairy godmothers. Then again, Elizabeth made a terrible Cinderella.

She looked in the mirror again. And winced at her reflection.

"Should I take Brandon with me?" she asked Mrs. Ham. "Jon relates better to Brandon than he does to me."

"I doubt that. And did you know that every time Jon Farell gets a message from your phone number, it has Brandon's name on it? He said he programmed it into Jon's phone."

"He did?"

"Jon Farell doesn't want to talk to Brandon." Mrs. Ham nodded at Elizabeth's tight dress. "You'll have to go in alone and change his mind. If you get my drift."

That's what Elizabeth had been hoping to avoid. "What do you think the odds are that a professional athlete is home, alone, awake and dressed at eleven o'clock on a Saturday morning?"

"He's single?" Mrs. Ham asked. "And it's the off-season?" She didn't look hopeful.

Please, may Jon Farell be home, alone, awake and dressed at eleven o'clock on Saturday morning.

Regardless, at the rate Brandon was moping and complaining, Elizabeth couldn't put off the visit much longer.

A half hour later, she was programming the GPS in her Prius for the Back Bay Towers, which is where Brandon told her Jon lived. She tried not to laugh hysterically. What was she going to do once there?

Ask the doorman to call up to Jon's apartment for her, and then beg him to let her in when Jon said no?

But Jon didn't say no. Twenty minutes later, still shivering with cold from her lack of a coat, Elizabeth stared when the doorman in Jon's lobby hung up the phone and pointed her to the elevator that served Jon's penthouse apartment.

Upstairs, Elizabeth stepped out of the elevator to find a young man, exceedingly handsome and in his early twenties, waiting for her in the corridor beside Jon's door. He smiled widely at her, his hands in his jeans pockets. "Hi. I'm Bobby."

"I'm...Elizabeth."

"Great to meet you." He indicated the open door. "Come on in. My brother is getting changed."

"Uh..." This obviously was a bad time. But if she left, she would have to go home and face Brandon's disappointment. No, thanks. She followed Bobby inside the apartment...and immediately stumbled in the low kitten heels she'd borrowed from Ashley.

Holy cow, Jon's place was awe inspiring. High ceilings with a solid glass wall that led to a balcony and a magnificent view of the Boston skyline and harbor in the distance. *This* was where Jon Farell lived?

"I know. Impressive, isn't it?" Bobby said.

She nodded.

"I live in a new dorm over at B.U. We've got great views, too, but nothing close to this."

Elizabeth turned from the windows and smiled nervously at the second man in the living room. He appeared to be in his late twenties, stocky and some-what balding. Also, cranky. He tipped a green plastic soda bottle to his mouth and lifted his hand to her in a silent greeting.

"Hello," she said. "I'm Elizabeth."

The man nodded and placed the bottle on a coffee table littered with a jumble of notebooks, pens and a laptop computer, not to mention the man's crossed feet, wearing construction boots. The television was playing before him, some kind of sports talk show, but he kept his gaze glued to her dress. She tugged on it self-consciously.

"That's our middle brother, Frank," Bobby ex-plained.

"Nobody told me Jon had a girlfriend." A rough, smoker's voice seemed to come from out of nowhere.

Elizabeth glanced around, confused. Frank hadn't spoken and neither had Bobby.

"Turn me around and let me see her," the voice insisted.

Bobby grinned at her. "That's our dad. He's here by videoconference." Bobby reached for the laptop and turned it so Elizabeth could see the screen.

The glare from the sun made her squint. She could just make out a handsome man, an older version of Jon, but with very short dark hair. "Pleased to meet you," Elizabeth said.

"Likewise," he grunted.

And then everyone looked up, so Elizabeth turned,

too. Jon had walked in wearing white baseball pants and not a stitch of clothing otherwise.

Oh, my. He had the most drool-worthy chest she'd seen in a long time—which was not saying much, since the only bare male chests she saw regularly were on the operating table, and even those were typically covered with drapes by the time she saw them.

She stared at Jon, slack jawed. Beneath a thin gold medallion on his neck, he had a fine sprinkling of chest hair, then a flat stomach, and then more sprinkling of hair below his belly button and into his... waistband. Embarrassed, she jerked her gaze to his face.

He was staring at her, too. Up and down. He looked like he'd been whacked by a baseball in the head, slightly dazed. *Thank you, Ashley, for the sexy dress.*

"Um, Elizabeth?" Bobby said. "We're going for lunch at Legal Sea Foods. You're welcome to join us."

"No," Jon said. "She is not."

She felt herself deflate. Jon's face had hardened, and he didn't look likely to change his mind. He was angry with her, and for good reason.

This was all a mistake. She really should leave.

"Elizabeth, what do you think about the scandal with the pitching staff?" Frank asked. This was the first he'd spoken, and his voice was richer and deeper than she would have guessed. So similar to Jon's voice, it was eerie.

"Um..." She faced the TV. The men were watching one of those sports discussion programs where the sportswriters analyzed players and teams. Jon looked distinctly uncomfortable by it, but his brothers were hanging on to every word.

"Don't," Jon said through his teeth. He picked up the remote control and turned off the television.

"Hey, I was watching that," his father said from the videoconference.

"Don't listen to them," Jon said to her. "They don't know anything."

"Elizabeth, do you want something to drink?" Bobby asked her. He was obviously the polite one.

"Um…"

"She doesn't," Jon said. "She was just leaving."

If only she could. She felt crushed by the way Jon was treating her. She longed to head for the door, but Brandon was counting on her. She pictured his little face, filled with hope, and then crushed with defeat if she came home empty-handed.

"No, I'm afraid I can't leave just yet," she murmured. "I…really need to speak with you, Jon."

He raised one tired brow. And good grief, her hormones went into overdrive. But he…didn't care about her. Not anymore, because she had blown it. Per usual, she had pushed away somebody who'd wanted to get close to her, even somebody kind. It was as if she couldn't trust kind people. She always figured there had to be an angle. And, oh, it was just so much easier being alone, wasn't it?

But she wasn't alone, not for the next three weeks until Ashley returned home.

"Fine," Jon said. "I need to take a shower and change clothes first." He looked pointedly at her. "You can come with me and talk, or you can stay out here and wait."

"I'll, uh, stay out here."

"Exactly what I thought," he said. With his face unreadable, he pointed to his brothers and his father. "Entertain Dr. LaValley until I get back. And keep the damn TV off for the duration."

Elizabeth sucked in her breath. "It's okay. I'll wait outside—"

"No," Jon said.

And while she watched, incredulous, he stalked across the hardwood floors and into another room. A door slammed shut. Faintly, she heard a shower running.

There was dead silence in the room. She shifted from high heel to high heel and glanced to the youngest brother, Bobby. He was still standing beside her, smiling. "Do you want to sit down?" he asked. He pushed Frank's feet to the carpet and moved some papers, making a spot for Elizabeth on the couch between him and Frank, and facing their father on the video screen.

"Certainly." She exhaled. As gracefully as she could, she stepped over Bobby's feet and wiggled into the space between him and Frank. Immediately, she sank into the big comfortable cushions. All three men were doing their level best not to look at her legs but were failing. Her dress was inching up over her knees, so she tugged at it, unsuccessfully. This was the last time she was listening to an eight-year-old and a geriatric for fashion advice.

"I'm sorry I interrupted," she said to the men. "It really will only take a few minutes to talk to Jon and then I'll leave."

"How do you know him?" Frank asked in that deep, Jon-like voice. And like Jon, he had a scowl on his face. "Are you really a doctor?"

"I… Yes. Of course I am." Should she be insulted? "I was Jon's anesthesiologist."

The three of them let that sink in. They glanced from one another, then to her. Their father asked, "Is his hand okay? Or is it gonna be a career-ender?"

"Um…" She got the impression that Jon didn't share much with them. This was interesting, considering she had thought him so eager to please. "I'm not his surgeon or his primary care doctor, so I really can't say." In fact, she couldn't discuss his case with them at all. There were laws against it.

Changing the subject, she asked, "What was the topic on television just now?"

"Are you a baseball fan?" Bobby asked.

"I…" Oh, what the heck. "Yes, I am," she said softly.

"Who's your favorite player?" Frank demanded.

Was this a test? She could say *Jon,* but that would be seen as sucking up. She could mention Rico Martinez, her favorite pitcher in the playoffs, because she really did admire him. But that might insult Jon.

"I like catchers," she said. This also was true. She admired them as tough, strong leaders who seemed to run the game equally with the pitchers, but under less fanfare and scrutiny. Sort of like how she felt as the anesthesiologist on a surgical team sometimes.

"Catchers?" Frank made a guffaw. "Does Jon know that?"

"Some of his best friends have been catchers," Bobby reminded them. He turned his eyes on hers. A light baby-blue, similar to Jon's but without the sharpness. "Which catcher do you like best?"

There was one catcher she remembered...what was his name? "Gioni," she said. A name from her child-hood. She remembered that she'd liked that it rhymed with *pony*. "He wore his hair long, like Jon does, and he had the same dark, tanned skin. I always cheered when he was up to bat."

"Carl Gioni." The father shook his head on the videoconference screen. "Wow, that name is a blast from the past. I loved him, too."

"He made it into Cooperstown," Bobby said.

Cooperstown, New York—that was the site of the national baseball museum.

"Made it on the first ballot," Frank remarked.

"That would be awesome if we could get Jon in there." Bobby picked up his soda bottle.

"Not a chance," their father said.

They all three looked into their drinks.

Elizabeth looked at her hands splayed on her lap.

Their silence made her uncomfortable. And a little angry.

"I don't see why not," she said.

Three heads jerked up. They stared at her.

"Jon is…working on a new pitch for the new season." Brandon had told her that, too. "And…and he's doing community service for the team charity." The reason she was here.

"Yeah, but Jon is too old to begin work on the Cooperstown dream," Frank said.

"And I was too young to begin work on the medical school dream," she snapped. "I don't see what difference that makes."

"Rose-colored glasses," the father muttered.

"Pardon me?" she said to the screen.

"You're just like Jon. Wearing those rose-colored glasses. Seeing the world as better than it is."

"That's a laugh." She leaned her face closer to the screen, so she could see him more clearly. He had a beaten expression and downcast eyes. "I'm the most practical person I know. And Jon is extremely down-to-earth, as well. Don't you believe that he can accomplish anything he sets his mind to?"

JON STOOD BEHIND the bathroom door, cracked open an inch, just enough for him to eavesdrop.

His heart was in his throat. Standing in that thick field of steam, naked except for a towel around his waist and a bandage on his finger.

He hadn't wanted to like Lizzy again. Damn, but

he didn't need the heartache. He needed an unrequited, hard-on crush for another man's woman like he needed a second tumor on his finger—but here it was, anyway.

This lady had made it clear to him, on more than one occasion, that he was nothing to her. That he was a means to an end, and Jon was tired of being other people's means to an end. He was trying to be selfish and to think of himself for a change. But it was so damn difficult for him—not who he was at all.

He was the pack mule of his family. The guy who kept up Dad's spirits, who showed Frank and Bobby what was possible in life, if a person didn't lie down and just quit trying. And it worked for Jon—or, it usually did.

Until he'd met Lizzy. The one woman in Boston who wasn't charmed or impressed by him, not at all.

He knew she didn't like him. She'd shown him so many times. So why was she sitting in his living room *sticking up* for him? Saying the same things to his dad that he would have said had he been there, too.

Jon had gone into the bathroom to shower, fully expecting her to walk away. No way had he expected Dr. LaValley—antisocial, awkward Dr. LaValley— to sit down with three male baseball fans, all gloom and doom over the impending end to Jon's career.

They were mourning his career without even trusting him to turn it around, for cripes sake.

He silently stalked to his bedroom, opened a drawer and took out a pair of clean underwear, a

T-shirt and a pair of jeans, and put them on. Barefoot, his hair combed but still wet, he went back to the living room.

He still didn't know what he was going to say to her. Originally, he'd vowed to have nothing to do with her or her problem with Brandon, whatever it was.

Now…she'd given him hope. And it was the worst, damn thing, because in his view of the world, leopards didn't change their spots, and neither did people. People were who they were.

Except, Lizzy's eyes lit up this time when she saw him. He stopped dead in his tracks. What. The. Hell. What had happened to her threats to report him to the hospital? She hated him, didn't she? As a man, she had no respect for him. He'd reached out to her, told her something true about himself and she had stomped his heart into the ground.

She stood. "Jon…" She visibly swallowed. Looked him up and down. And blushed as red as her dress.

He froze, not knowing what to do. Like a green kid, he looked her up and down, too. Under her loose, boxy hospital scrubs—and even under her boxy at-home weekend sweatpants—he'd had no idea of the body she was rocking. He had imagined, many times, but even his imagination wasn't this good. That hot, red dress clung to all her curves. What man wouldn't imagine picking it up by the hem, peeling it over her long, bare legs and tugging off that belt at her waist? His heart hammering, his gaze tripped over hers and then met it. The tip of her tongue came out slightly, but her lip bit it back. She gazed down to the toes of her sexy shoes, embarrassed.

He shook his head. Damn. A medical doctor who had a whole other side to her. And when she turned to glance back at his brothers, struck dumb with silence as they sat on the couch just staring up at her rear view... Holy shit, he had to get her out of here.

"Elizabeth," he said, striding forward. "Can I talk to you in private?"

She looked relieved. Smoothing her dress, she crossed the room to him as Bobby, Francis and his dad looked on, still mesmerized.

Jon loved his apartment. Usually, he thought it was a great space. But the floor plan was open, and the only room with a door, giving them privacy was... his bedroom.

"No." She turned away once she saw his bed. In a low voice, she said, "Maybe, um, we can talk in the hallway."

Right. He was beginning to realize it was pretty obvious why she had come. "You want to talk about Brandon, don't you?"

She nodded.

Feeling irritable, he motioned her to the balcony off the living room. With a view over the Boston skyline, it was the main reason he'd leased the place. Normally, he enjoyed the floor-to-ceiling panorama, but not when his family could sit on the couch and watch him and Elizabeth through the window like a front-row seat to a floor show.

Unfortunately, once outside, Elizabeth pressed against the windbreak, taking a position on the balcony with her back to his family. Great. He faced them, which at least allowed him to keep his expression neutral. Even with his bare feet cold from the cement slab, he didn't move a muscle. No way was he showing anyone that he cared what this woman thought, rocking body or not.

Resist her. He had to. Because in no universe was the refined Dr. Elizabeth LaValley ever going to consider falling for a guy like him.

JON LOOKED LIKE he just wanted her gone. And she was so pathetic...dazzled by his presence and not even minding the cool air outside.

He had to be colder than her. His hair was damp. His arms were bare in his short-sleeved T-shirt as he stared at her, his face stony.

She tugged on her dress again, willing it to cover her better. "I'm sorry I bothered you at home over this, but I didn't see any other options."

He clenched his jaw. "What do you want, Elizabeth? Spit it out."

Not even *Lizzy?* Had she pushed him too hard? She swallowed. "Brandon is...more upset than I've ever seen him. He really wants to be part of your program at the hospital. He idolizes you."

"He shouldn't idolize me. I'm no hero."

Why was he saying that? "Is this about...whatever is playing on that television program your family was watching?" She hooked her thumb toward the living room.

"No," he said flatly. "It is not."

Drop the subject. That's what he was telling her. Though she didn't understand what baseball players typically went through in the off-season, she could see that whatever it was, it seemed to be taking its toll on him, because he lacked his characteristic patience. She needed to get straight to the point.

But it was a scary point. What if he said no? Curling her windblown hair over her ears, she stared at the ocean in the distance, hoping he would cooperate. "Will you *please* let Brandon back into the program?"

"And here I thought you were so dead set against it," Jon drawled.

Did he want her to apologize? Fine. She walked to the railing. "I...was wrong." She bit her lip. "I made the decision from my point of view, not from Brandon's."

"You can't even look at me when you speak."

She inhaled and dared to gaze into Jon's beautiful blue eyes. He seemed hurt. Well, she was, too.

She wished he understood that she wasn't like other people. She would love to be naturally feminine: adept at handling children and chatting with charming men. Ashley could do that so well. Susan Vanderbilt, too. But Elizabeth was just...an outsider. Being with Jon like this brought it all to the forefront...the pain, the awkwardness.

"You can't look at me without making a face," he said.

If only he could step inside her shoes. "I'm frightened, okay? I'm…frightened for Brandon, and I'm frightened for me. I don't know how I'm going to survive another three weeks of this."

"And *I* make you feel frightened?"

"Don't sound so surprised," she said.

"You're a *doctor,* Lizzy. You're way out of my league."

She gaped at him. "Everybody loves you. You're so comfortable with people. I only know how to keep to myself."

Jon looked her up and down. "Why did you come wearing that red dress today?"

She made a small laugh. "Brandon found it in the back of my closet. I've never worn it before. But he really wants to be in the Sunshine Club program. He foolishly thought this getup might help." She sighed at him. "Can't you *please* get him back in? Don't let my mistakes and insecurities hurt him."

He smiled widely at her. "You look nice in that dress."

He wasn't making fun of her. At least, she didn't think so….

"Why was the dress in your closet?" he pressed. "Did some guy buy it for you?"

She laughed out loud at that one. "No!"

"What did you buy it for, then? A big event? A date?"

Yeah, right. She snickered. "*I* did not buy it. Ashley did. I was helping her with Brandon, finding the best doctors to treat his illness, and she wanted me to celebrate with her when his chemo was completed. And we were all set to. Until…" She looked down.

"What happened?"

Why was she even telling Jon this? She shivered, a rogue gust of wind sweeping past them. "His cancer came back." She tried not to think about it but failed. "We thought he wouldn't make it."

She squeezed her eyes shut. Poor Ashley. Maybe she still couldn't trust that Brandon might be well for the rest of his life. Brandon was small for his age. His growth had been stunted. Jon was sweet to spend time with the boy and talk with him about baseball, even though it was obvious that Brandon had little chance of ever playing at Jon's level, no matter how much he practiced. Brandon would always show the effects of the cancer he'd fought and survived.

"I really do love that little boy. Please, Jon. Let him be part of your Sunshine Club program."

Jon looked at her with a careful, hard poker face, and it scared her. It crushed her to think of going home and having to say "no" to Brandon again. And it hurt her that Jon didn't care for her anymore. He may have once, but she'd scared him away, too. She had secretly hoped upon hope that maybe Jon could be the one guy she wouldn't scare away. That there was a crazy possibility that he had seen beneath her prickly mask, her skin of protection, to the vulnerable, frightened…human…person beneath the doctor's scrubs. "Please help Brandon, Jon. Please."

"I DON'T WANT to help Brandon. I want to help you."

Jon watched her reaction. Lizzy blinked at him, shocked. Well, he was shocked too. Lizzy had been the one who'd accused him of helping people too much, that first night he'd met her at her condo.

"How do you want to help me?" she asked.

He rocked back on his bare heels and let himself leisurely look her up and down. He let his gaze linger on her belt, tied at the waist of a red, wraparound dress that she had apparently only worn this once. "Do you *ever* go out?" he asked her. "Do you ever do anything fun for yourself?"

"Yes," she insisted. "Of course I do!"

"Really?" He gazed into her big brown eyes. "When was the last time you went out in Boston?"

Her mouth opened and then closed. She had answered him without saying a word.

"You live in a world-class city," he said, "with so much to offer." He spread his arms to the city below them.

"I'm not here for me," she said in a confident voice. "This request isn't about me."

"To me it is. I want to take you out—on a date."

She blinked at him and shook her head. "No. Please just say yes to Brandon."

He turned for the living room. Saw through the window to his family sitting on the couch, watch-

ing him, every movement he made. Jon just felt so…
tired. Tired of always striving. Always walking on
eggshells.

Lizzy was just another person in the long line of
people who wanted something from him.

He opened the sliding door to his apartment. Away
from the privacy and the wind, and into the warmth
of his living room. Prepared to usher Lizzy out.

But she gripped his bare arm, stopping him. A
firm, insistent grip on his biceps from a small, cool
hand.

He hadn't expected her touch. It felt…good.

"One afternoon," she said in a faint voice. "Saturday. I can go out next Saturday." Her hand gripping
his arm was shaking.

"I want three Saturdays," he said. "Three weekends, until Brandon goes back to his mother. Then
I'm cutting you loose."

"Three is too many!"

"Three or nothing," he insisted.

"You…might not like it."

"Oh, I will, sweet cheeks. Bet on it."

She gasped. Her eyes widened, darting from his
family on the couch, to him. But her hand was still
latched onto his arm. She licked her lips. "Brandon
goes with us."

"Nope," he was about to reply, but then he realized
he actually did need Brandon, at least for the first
outing. He knew so little about this woman. "Fine,
he can come with us the first Saturday."

"The first *two* Saturdays," she said.

That would give Jon one last Saturday without the eight-year-old in tow. "Done," he said.

"Oh, my...." She put her hand to her shiny brown hair. She looked good with her hair done up and then windblown like that. And mascara stroked on her long lashes. It gave him some hope that she thought enough of him to try to impress him. "You don't know anything about me, Jon. You don't know what you're getting into."

Maybe not. But he ushered her inside. And as if his family were patients, she politely said goodbye to them.

When at last the door was shut behind her, and all eyes were on him, even his dad's, over the laptop screen, Jon spoke. "What? She's seeing someone. Another doctor, not me."

"You don't stand a chance," his father said.

"Why?" Frank said to his father. "Jon's a pro ball player."

Sure. And Lizzy was the one person in Boston who wasn't impressed by that.

"I don't know," his father said. "Didn't you hear them on the baseball shows? The way things are going, Jon might not have his job much longer. It's worse than I thought."

"Don't worry," Frank said to Jon. "Bobby and I will kill for you if we have to." He nudged Bobby. "Isn't that so, brother?"

"It won't come to that," Jon said. Because over

his dead body would he lose his job—he was doing everything in his power to keep it.

This thing with Lizzy? It wouldn't get in his way.

CHAPTER TEN

ELIZABETH HAD VOWED to stay away, but two days later on a rainy Monday afternoon she picked Brandon up from school and ferried him to the hospital for his video shoot. And like a moth to a flame, she found herself staring again at Jon.

She wasn't the only female doing so. Three other hospital employees—a receptionist, a nurse and a volunteer—gawked from the doorway to the Sunshine Club conference room.

At least Elizabeth had an excuse for hanging around—it was her nephew that Susan Vanderbilt helped onto one of two interviewer's stools. Jon stood beside the other.

"Did you know that Jon Farell is going to be in the bachelor auction for the Sunshine Club fund-raiser?" the receptionist whispered to the volunteer. "I saw the paperwork."

"If I had the money, I would bid on him in a heartbeat," the nurse murmured back.

The fact that other women would pledge money—presumably big money—to go on a date with Jon Farell, while Elizabeth had to be dragged kicking and screaming, was not lost on her.

She clutched at the lapel of her doctor jacket. What would she and Jon even talk about this weekend? They were from such different worlds, how could either of them spend a day with the other without staring at each other in perplexed silence?

Brandon padded over to her and retrieved the water bottle Elizabeth held for him. "You don't have to stay if you don't want to, Auntie," Brandon said, unscrewing the cap and taking a gulp. "I'm good."

"I'm so proud of you for helping the Sunshine Club, and for showing me what a good thing this is for you to do. Will you be okay here without me?"

"I'm not alone." Brandon wiped his mouth and thrust the bottle back at her. "I get to sit with Jon." He smiled and trotted back to his idol.

Susan settled Brandon's stool closer to Jon's, while a camera assistant clipped a small microphone to the neck of Brandon's T-shirt. Elizabeth had no doubt that her budding media-savant nephew would handle Susan's instructions like a pro.

Certainly, he was safe and happy and in his element. Elizabeth could leave without worry. She glanced at her watch. Her department meeting was in five minutes, and Susan had already promised to walk Brandon back to her once they were finished.

She nibbled her lip and took one last look at Jon. He was sitting cross-armed on the stool, not saying much. On the surface, he appeared his normal, easygoing, happy-baseball-player self. But Elizabeth had long practice at observing people, figuring out what was happening on the inside. She knew what a tightened jaw meant. Jon didn't like Susan directing the stylist to comb his hair. His lips pressed together in distaste at the offered makeup application.

Susan bent over Jon, her cleavage stuck in his face, and Elizabeth felt a stabbing inside her. *That* was jealousy. The nurse next to Elizabeth just sighed in appreciation.

Wonderful. First Elizabeth couldn't tear herself away from Jon, now she was envious of another woman's attention. She was treading on dangerous ground. She just had to remember that it was only a silly fantasy fueled by her attraction to Jon's pheromones.

How was she going to protect herself come Saturday?

Meanwhile, Susan touched Jon's arm and murmured something into his ear. Jon flashed a half-hearted smile. Elizabeth squirmed.

Didn't everyone see Jon was only going through the motions?

She wasn't the only observer to the video shoot. Besides the three women hovering in the doorway, there was a cameraman and a makeup and hair stylist. Another young man held what appeared to be a script. Susan orchestrated the activity, and Brandon was along for the ride.

Jon, of course, was the heart and center of everyone's attention.

"Jon, I like how you dressed today," Susan said, gazing through the camera lens at him. The women beside Elizabeth tittered because, yes, Jon did look like he'd stepped out of a male modeling shoot, wearing a deep blue collared shirt and a navy suit jacket with tan chinos.

The colors would pop on camera, while the suit showed his seriousness for the subject matter. And selfishly, to Elizabeth—though maybe not to everybody else—the blue in his shirt collar brought out a depth and richness to his eyes she hadn't noticed before.

It warmed her. It settled in the core of her and radiated outward. She felt deliciously shaky between her legs.

"Unfortunately," Susan said, strolling back to stand too close to Jon again. "We need you to wear your Captains uniform for this segment. Did you bring it with you?"

Jon frowned and sat back with his arms crossed. "Yeah. Sure."

Because of course he was Captains property. Brandon gave Jon a funny look. Even her nephew wore his Captains cap.

A shadow crossed Jon's face, but just as quickly, it was gone. He stood and, for first time since Elizabeth had been watching from the corner, he noticed her.

His eyes seemed to spark. One side of his mouth lifted, as if smiling to her in secret. She smiled back, her hand pressed to her lips.

He winked at her and snagged a duffel bag before heading into the restroom, closing the door behind him. When he came out again, he wore his Captains shirt, number 13, over his chinos. Susan made a fuss of adjusting his posture on the stool, of taking her time leaning over and pinning the microphone to his collar.

Through it all, Jon's gaze darted discreetly to Elizabeth, while Elizabeth stood, her hand clasped on her scrubs over her heart, allowing her gaze to tangle with his.

She was still breathing heavily when she felt a tap on her shoulder. She knew whose tap that was and stiffened, as if caught doing something wrong. Across the room, Jon bent, reaching for his water bottle, oblivious to her dilemma.

Elizabeth stepped into the corridor outside. "Yes, Albert?" she asked as calmly as she could.

The cardiac surgeon wore his street clothes—chino slacks and a smart sweater. His hair combed but damp, fresh from the gym shower, she assumed, he appeared ready to drive home for the day. "I volunteered to find you. Dr. Fine is ready for your meeting."

Elizabeth thought of her beeper and her phone, both turned off and stowed downstairs in her locker. "Tell him I'm on my way."

"Is...your nephew's schedule settled?" Albert asked.

"Yes. Thank you." She smiled tightly and headed for the elevator to avoid any more questions. If this wasn't a wake-up call, she didn't know what was.

She needed to get her act together and stop fantasizing over what wasn't good for her.

Unfortunately, the only person who could assist her in getting her head clear for the weekend was an eight-year-old. And he was unduly biased.

JON FELT HIS temporary good mood evaporate. He had glanced down for just a moment. When he'd glanced back, he'd caught Lizzy—red cheeked and lips glistening from the looks they'd been flashing at one another—leaving the room behind the doctor he'd seen her with last week.

Hell. The videographer adjusted the tripod while Jon ground his teeth, wondering what to do about it.

"We're putting together this video," Susan explained to Brandon, "so that financial donors will see the good work we do for children with cancer." She took turns flashing her smile between Jon and Brandon as if they were both at her beck and call. "So. Are we ready to begin?"

Brandon nodded enthusiastically. Jon fought the urge to get up and follow Lizzy. But it wasn't his place. The only things keeping him from snapping at Susan to knock it off were one, Brandon sitting beside him, and two, the fact that the whole dog-and-pony show was for a really good cause. Doubly so, because the resulting video could help Jon get his contract signed for next season.

Lizzy was his problem. He was consumed with her. He'd been fantasizing about wanting to bring her out from her customary position, always on the sidelines, observing life instead of participating.

What could he do to get her to take a big bite out of life with him? Open her up to new experiences, beyond Wellness Hospital and the doctors inside?

Saturday was his first opportunity. He needed to think of someplace worthy to take her. He was lucky she was interested in him, too. Every time he'd glanced at her, her focus had been on him. Not Brandon. *Him.*

He wanted it to be for the person he was inside. For the man he was beneath the Captains uniform.

A photographer's studio light suddenly turned on, flooding the space with heat.

"Brandon," Susan said from behind the camera, "why don't we start with you. As a cancer survivor, can you tell us about the treatment you received at Wellness Hospital?"

Jon focused on the flesh-and-blood kid sitting so close to him that their knees were touching.

"I don't remember too much," Brandon said, tilting his head up to the camera. "I was a little kid, you know."

Susan bit her lip, trying unsuccessfully to keep a straight face. She addressed Jon. "When we're finished with Brandon, we'll ask you some questions on camera as well, such as how you got interested in helping children, and what it means to you as a Captains player to participate in the Sunshine Club."

Jon shifted uncomfortably. This was where it got

dicey. He'd always operated on the belief that what he *felt*—about these kids, about their illness—was nobody's business but his own.

But he nodded at Susan, because he'd had media training, too. He'd spent years on a big-market team, and he could talk to the press with a smile on his face—without saying anything of note—as long as the day was long. "Sure," he said.

His glance flicked to Brandon. Besides, the kids and their families were the heroes here, not him. If Jon could bring a smile to someone having a lousy day—and in a sickbed, there were many lousy days—then he'd done his job.

"Jon, if you could look over here—"

Crash. "Damn it!" said a high-pitched female voice.

The assistant had knocked over the camera tripod. The noise sounded suspiciously like a lens shattering.

Susan hovered over a group of people picking at the camera, assessing it. Her expression was doubtful. "Why don't you take your break while we find another camera?" she said to Jon. "We'll give it a half hour, okay?"

"Sounds good." She didn't have to ask him twice. Jon grabbed his suit jacket from the chair he'd left it on and tossed it on over his Captains shirt. "You want to get a Coke?" he asked Brandon.

"Yes!" Brandon jumped off the stool and curled his hand inside Jon's pitching hand.

Jon left it there, small and warm. He led Brandon out of the conference room and to the elevator bank.

While they waited, Brandon held up a baseball, arranging his fingers over the seams in the way Jon had shown him. "See, it's a four-seam fastball," Brandon said.

"You've been practicing your grip. Good job."

"It's hard for me because my fingers aren't as big as yours."

"You'll grow," Jon reassured him. "Plus, if you practice, your fingers will get looser, more flexible, and it will start to feel easier."

Brandon looked up hopefully at him. "Will you catch with me?"

"No, sorry, bud, I really can't. But I can show you some throwing mechanics, and you can practice them with your team coach."

"I'm not on the team, yet," Brandon said glumly.

"Do you have neighborhood buddies to play with you?"

"Not while I'm at Auntie's." Brandon sighed. "I can't wait to go home."

Not a comment for Jon to pursue. It also wouldn't be smart to ask the kid how his mom was doing. "Well," Jon said, "I could get you a pitch-back. That way you can practice with yourself. Get the ball into the strike zone as often as you can."

"*Then* will you teach me the curveball grip?" Brandon begged.

"What's the rush? You have years for that. Even

when I entered the big leagues, I only had three pitches that I had solid control over."

"If I had a really great fastball," Brandon mused, "then nobody would be able to hit off me."

"Yep," Jon agreed. "You've got that right."

Maybe this would be something to help occupy the kid's considerable energy, for the next few weeks that Lizzy had him, at least. "Is there a yard outside your aunt's building, a space where we can set up a pitch-back for you?"

Brandon thought a minute. "We could set one up on the curb beside the parking lot."

A true city kid, like himself. "On Saturday, we'll check with your aunt to make sure the area is safe, and that there are no windows that can be broken by a flying baseball."

Something to discuss with her on Saturday. The other consideration was to suggest bringing Brandon to a training center, but that might tick Lizzy off. She was already committed to carting the kid to and from Susan's sessions with the videographer, and that was probably enough for now.

The elevator arrived. Jon followed Brandon into the—thankfully—empty car.

"Push the button for the roof café," Brandon said. "It's on the top floor."

When they got to the roof café, Jon saw a glassed-in view that overlooked Boston.

In the distance was the new Rose Kennedy Greenway, built over land where years ago, the Big Dig had taken place. Which brought Jon to his dilemma: where in Boston to take Lizzy on Saturday? What did she like? What did they both like that would show the brown-eyed brunette he wasn't just a big-league curiosity that people gawked at and sucked up to?

"Did your aunt say anything about next weekend?" he asked Brandon, who was already at the order counter, talking to an ice-cream scooper dressed in a white apron.

"She said we're going on a family fun day with you," Brandon said, pulling napkins from an automated machine.

"A…what?"

"You, me and her. Together. Like to the movies or something."

The last place Jon wanted to take Lizzy was someplace where she'd have another excuse not to talk to anybody.

"Anything for you, sir?" the café attendant asked.

"A can of Coke, please." He pulled his wallet from his back pocket, which still hurt his sore finger a bit. The attendant handed Brandon the dish of ice cream he'd ordered because Jon hadn't been paying attention. Bubble-gum flavor. *Good grief.*

"So your aunt told you about Saturday?" Jon sat down at a table and faced the kid with his oversize, dripping bowl. Not smart, considering they were going to be filming again in twenty minutes. "Why are you calling it family fun day?"

"Because my friend Derrick has a mom and a dad

and a brother and a little sister, and every Saturday they do something with everybody in the family all together, and my mom calls it their family fun day. So we started doing it, too." Brandon stuffed a spoon into his mouth contentedly. "Last time we saw the dinosaur movie on IMAX. We went to the candy store, and I got gummy worms."

"What, no bubble gum?"

Brandon blinked, the vanilla ice cream with the streaks of blue and pink in it halfway to his mouth. "Gum isn't allowed in movie theaters. Don't you know that?"

No. Because he didn't go to movies, or to family fun days.

"I want to take—I want us to take—your aunt someplace that she'll really like." Jon spoke in a low voice, angled away from the door, because there was a woman who'd entered the café and she was staring at him with that look he knew too well. He didn't want to be recognized—not right now. He wanted to think about Lizzy and what he could do with her on Saturday. He was so out of his league on this. "She's a doctor. She's smart. She reads a lot." He'd been in her apartment; he'd seen the bookcases and the piles of magazines on her coffee table.

"You read a lot, too." Brandon rolled his eyes. "I got the books you sent over yesterday."

Yeah, Jon had read a lot as a kid, together with his mom. Then after she'd died, pitching had substituted for books. He'd boxed up the books and kept them, though.

"You'll keep them in good shape for me, right?" Jon asked. "I'm going to want them back once you move home."

"What are you going to do with them then?"

"Keep them for when I have kids," he said gruffly. "After my baseball career is over."

"*That* is going to be in a long time."

"It is." Speaking of which, Jon glanced at his watch—their break was almost over. He needed to figure out a way to ask Brandon to help him understand his aunt. She confused and befuddled him. She challenged him and...

She really didn't need him. She was the first person he'd met who was aloof and self-directed on that count. He liked that. But now that he had a chance with her, he wasn't sure what to do with it.

"So...I saw some magazines on your aunt's coffee table. A bunch were from the Smithsonian. That's the big museum complex in Washington, D.C. It has buildings dedicated to art, space travel, dinosaurs, geology, American history. There has to be something specific she likes about it."

Brandon took his mouth off the lump of ice cream he'd stuck in his mouth like a banana. "She likes to read me books that show how people used to live a long time ago." He swept his arm to make an arc.

"How long ago?" Were they talking cowboys, World War II, or ancients? To a kid like Brandon, a long time ago could be back when Jon had been in college in Arizona.

"Well, one book has pictures of a castle and knights."

"She likes castles and knights?" Dr. Elizabeth La-Valley, a closet romantic?

"…and there was one with a town in it, with different kinds of shops and houses where you could see how families lived in olden times. The scientists dug it up, and saw how it used to be, all dirty and broken. But then you put the clear sheet over the page—" he pantomimed with his hands "—and then another sheet, and the book shows how the houses used to look like—where the mom and the dad slept, and where the kids played, and where they ate, and the garden they kept…"

"Wait, so…like an archaeologist would do?" He was thoroughly confused.

"Someday, Auntie is going to take a boat trip, and stop in all kinds of places like that, but for now, she's too busy and she has to work, so she reads about it in books and imagines how it was back then. That's what she told me." Brandon resumed licking his spoon.

Baloney, Lizzy was too busy. She just didn't want to break out of her routine.

Jon put down his drink. He needed to find a museum exhibit that cataloged an archaeology dig of some sort. Boston was swimming in museums.

Museum of Fine Arts, Museum of Science, Isabella Stewart Gardner Museum…

"I want to make sure we're doing something unique," he said to Brandon. "We need to go someplace your aunt hasn't been to before. Where else has she gone on other…family fun days?"

Brandon shrugged, slurping down the last of his melting ice cream straight from the dish. "She doesn't go with me and Mom and Sharma when we go bowling or to the movies."

Lizzy would hate to know Brandon was telling him this. Still… "Does she, uh…go with any other families?"

"No. My mom says that Auntie wants a family of her own, but she doesn't know how."

Wow, that was… It made him sad.

"When I was little and sick, my mom says I survived cancer because of Auntie. She knows doctor things. But I'm supposed to help her with…people things."

"Well, you're doing a good job," Jon said in a low voice.

Brandon brightened. "I could spy for you. If you call me tonight, before bedtime, I'll tell you what she's reading."

Jon was creating a monster. "No. You've helped me a lot already, buddy. I think I can take it from here."

Lizzy was just so complicated. He felt like a sixteen-year-old again, completely ignorant when it came to women.

"Let's head back," he said to Brandon.

But they were too late. Two young women came tripping into the café, and when they saw Jon, one of them gave a squeal of recognition. "You're Jon Farell, aren't you?" She clapped and gave him a flirtatious smile. "I'd recognize your hair anywhere."

"Omigod, we *love* your hair," the second girl said.

The first girl held up her iPhone. "Can we take a picture with you? *Pleeease?*"

Jon smiled, but he was feeling irritated. He was suddenly tired of being public property. The season was over.

"You're *so* in the news," the second girl said. "But don't worry, we believe in you. We don't believe a word they're saying."

"I'll give you a photo, but over there, away from the kid." Jon steered them to an adjoining table. He was enough of a professional that he stood with a frozen smile while each girl took turns snapping a photo with him. It would be uploaded to Facebook within ten minutes. Such was life in this century.

"Thanks," he said to the girls. But his heart wasn't in it. Brandon looked forlorn. Jon felt…

Not grateful. Not at all like he was making somebody happy.

Not in control.

The opposite of everything he usually felt when fans recognized him and wanted to pose with him.

Oh, Lizzy, what are you doing to me?

"I can't let that happen on Saturday," he said aloud.

"I don't like when people take pictures of you," Brandon agreed. "You're supposed to be with me today."

"Sorry, buddy." But Jon didn't see what he could do about it.

An hour later, in front of the camera, Jon still felt rattled. Susan spent the remaining time interviewing Brandon about his thoughts on visiting kids who were in the cancer ward and how it felt from the point of view of a cancer survivor. Brandon did a great job answering her. Jon was grateful he could push off his part of the interview until the next session, because he had nothing genuine he cared to share about how he felt at the moment.

He ushered Brandon back to the child care facility. Lizzy had left a note—she was in an emergency appendectomy surgery and would be back for Brandon in another hour or so, if all went well. Jon was glad he wouldn't bump into her. He needed time to think.

He retrieved his SUV from the hospital garage and then drove to meet Coach Duffy for a scheduled workout with his college team.

After a bullpen session, he stretched and cooled down with ice to his elbow. And a couple hours later he was back in his SUV, following crawling traffic northbound when his phone rang. It was Brooke, his agent.

"I was gonna call you tonight," he said into the phone. "Some fans said something that bothered me today. They said that I was 'so in the news'—what would they have meant by that? Is there something I should be concerned about?"

"Not a thing," Brooke said lightly. "Just keep doing what you're doing. I'll worry about your contract. How are you pitching?"

"Fine." Better than he'd expected.

"Good. I talked with my contact on the hospital board, and they've penciled you in for the bachelor auction in two weeks."

Wait, what? "I told you I'm not doing the bachelor auction."

"Jon, you don't have a wife, or even a girlfriend. Vivian knows this. There is no excuse for you not to participate."

"Who told her?"

"Does it matter? What's so bad about raising money for your owner's pet cause? She'll be there for the event. It'll get you major brownie points."

"I thought I was getting brownie points by doing the video."

Brooke sighed. "So, worst-case scenario, you go on a date with a wealthy cougar—or her wealthy daughter—who lusts after you. So what?"

"Is that all?" he said sarcastically. If Brooke wasn't seeing it, he couldn't explain to her. "Sounds like I'm expected to put out, too. You wouldn't be singing this tune if it was you being auctioned off."

Brooked laughed. His teeth went on edge. "Oh, come on," she said. "I know you, Jon. Don't play coy."

His hands gripped the steering wheel. She had crossed the line.

"Look, my phone is ringing," Brooke said. "We'll talk about this later, okay?"

"You bet we will," he said to dead air. There wasn't a doubt in his mind what he was doing next. He turned the SUV toward his apartment, where he'd stashed the business card for the hair-donation cancer charity that Susan had given him. Jon was cutting off his hair—every damn bit of it—and going incognito. If no one in Boston recognized him until spring training, life could only be better.

Because being a spectacle for baseball wasn't what he'd signed on for, and until now—until *Lizzy*—he'd forgotten that truth.

And if anyone on Vivian's team gave him a hard time, he would remind them that he'd donated his damn hair for the cause.

It didn't get more personal than that.

CHAPTER ELEVEN

WHEN ELIZABETH OPENED the door to her apartment that Saturday morning, she gasped and put her hand to her mouth. Jon had cut his hair! His beautiful hair!

By reflex, she reached out and touched it. Silky in her fingers, and short. Cut above his ears, it took away the mystical quality the long brown hair with the white streak had given him. Jon seemed more human now, just a man. His jawline appeared stronger, his nose more pronounced.

Jon's ice-blue eyes regarded her, and she realized her fingers were brushing his scalp, caressing him like a lover. Embarrassed, she jerked her hand back. "I can't believe I did that. I'm…sorry."

Jon chuckled, deep in his throat. "If I'd known you liked my long hair that much, I would have reconsidered."

"Oh." She pressed her hand into the pocket of her jeans, up to the knuckle. "You cut it for charity, didn't you?"

"No." He shifted on his feet, hesitating. "Turns out they need at least eight inches of hair to make a wig for the kids who are fighting cancer. They couldn't use mine because it was too short."

"So you decided to cut it, anyway?"

He said nothing. She was reminded of how uncomfortable he'd looked that afternoon in the Sunshine Club, with Susan fussing over him and the women tittering and gawking at his presence before the camera. "In any event, no one will recognize you now," she said brightly.

"That's the plan." His voice was quiet. He seemed different from the man who'd come to her house weeks ago, determined to connect with her life as if it was inevitable. Back then, she had criticized and attacked him unfairly. Then she had gone begging to him on Brandon's behalf. Now…

Her plan for the day was up in smoke already. She'd intended to remain neutral and treat him like any other man. But he had upended her.

"Are you going to let me in, Lizzy?"

"You've surprised me." And she couldn't stop staring at his haircut. He looked like a completely different person. "I thought you enjoyed being public."

"Not everything I do has to be public."

"But your hair was your trademark."

He looked her up and down. "Your scrubs are your trademark, and yet here you are, in street clothes, just like me."

Standing in the corridor of her humble condominium building, and dressed in jeans and a light jacket, Jon did look like he could be anybody. Maybe he was trying to be normal, to be seen as a man and not an icon. He blended in, like the men she worked with at the hospital.

But he could never be just anybody to her. Shaken, she opened the door wider to him. He stepped past her with a sidelong glance, that strong arm brushing against her breast.

She inhaled as tingles went through her. Her body always responded to Jon. Where was Brandon? He was supposed to be here as her shield and her chaperone. She looked in the hallway outside her condo. One of her neighbors had decorated their door with a Halloween scarecrow overnight, but other than that, they were alone.

Leaving her door open, she followed Jon into her kitchen. She was just…unnerved. Jon did that to her. Whenever they were in the same room, he distracted her. Took over her imagination with thoughts of what it would feel like if she pressed herself to him, from chest to thigh….

Presently he kept his distance, checking out the pumpkin she and Brandon had been carving on the kitchen table. She'd been able to use her scalpel skills, and that was fun. But when Brandon had noticed Jon's SUV drive up, he'd bolted downstairs to meet him. So where was he…?

"Brandon went downstairs to meet you. Do you know where he is or what he's doing?" she asked Jon.

"Oh, yeah, he's setting up his—"

"Jon!" Brandon came bursting in the door. "That pitch-back net is so awesome!"

He stopped short. "Wow. You cut your hair off."

A smile played on Jon's lips. "You noticed, buddy."

"People won't take your picture today." Brandon grinned, showing the gap in his mouth from his missing tooth. "Good."

"That's why I did it. It's our time today."

Brandon turned to Elizabeth. He carried his baseball glove and wore his Captains cap. "Are you ready to go, Auntie? It's family fun day."

Oh, that term of Ashley's. It drilled a bittersweet core straight through Elizabeth's heart. What did she and Ashley know of family fun?

She started to protest, but caught Jon and Brandon sharing a look. "What's going on between you two?"

"We collaborated." Jon winked at Brandon and tilted his head. Brandon took a moment to process whatever it was that was being shared, then ran for his bedroom door. He came back with a homemade card.

"This is for you, from me. It's a thank-you for taking care of me. I made it at the hospital."

Elizabeth glanced at Jon. This was his idea. And it was so sweet and unexpected, her eyes felt moist. She was not the type of person that people gave spontaneous gifts to.

"I…" She put her hands to her heart and knelt to her nephew's height. "I'll treasure it very much. Thank you."

Brandon beamed. He glanced up at Jon. "Now can I tell her where we're going for family fun day?"

"No," Jon said. "Not yet."

She stood, gazing between them, from one to the other. They really were in cahoots. Brandon really was great at dealing with this...baseball player who was so different from her. She was only good with people if they were in a hospital gown and had an IV attached. An IV where she could add some sedating drugs, if necessary.

She pulled on her short boots with the two-inch heels and drew her leather jacket off the wooden hanger in her coat closet. "Am I dressed appropriately for...wherever it is we're going?"

"Yes!" Brandon said, tugging at her arm. "Let's go, Auntie."

Nodding, she opened a kitchen cabinet. Having learned to prepare when it came to Brandon, she opened her purse and loaded a few gluten-free snack bars inside. Gluten-free snacks weren't easy to find in public places.

Jon held the door for her and, careful not to look into his eyes, she brushed past him on the way out. On the way down the elevator, Brandon leaned close to Jon, crowding him. The space was so tight she felt light-headed. To relax, she gripped her car keys in her hand.

Outside, she walked ahead of them to her Prius.

She heard a quiet chuckle behind her, and she turned. Jon was shaking his head. "You want to take your car?" He nodded to her Prius.

"Yes, of course. What's wrong with it?"

"It's only big enough for one person, Lizzy."

Well, that was an exaggeration, but maybe it was a bit small for Jon. He had long legs and wide shoulders and very big hands…

She glanced away. Great. Did she always have to be so physically aware of him?

"Come on," he said. "We'll take my SUV." He stood beside his behemoth monstrosity of a truck that looked like it could hold a baseball team and all their equipment.

She smiled despite herself. "Typical. You carry the world around with you, and I travel by myself."

"You're my entourage today, Lizzy." He opened the passenger door for her. "Climb in." She felt his palm on the small of her back.

Her heart pounding, she stepped up slowly. His hand stayed on her back until she settled into the seat. The interior of his truck was comfortable, with worn leather seats and clean windows. On the dashboard was a pair of athlete's sunglasses, and wedged on the console between them was a parking tag that read "Captains."

But it was the air inside that got to her. The scent that made her heart ache. She closed her eyes and inhaled. Jon. All Jon. That same, male, distinctive… whatever it was…aura, presence, pheromones…that had so gotten to her on the day she had met him.

Outside, Brandon was chattering at Jon, whining about wanting to sit up front, too, but Jon was firm. Then a rear passenger door opened, and Brandon was escorted inside. "Put on your seat belt, buddy." And then Jon slid inside, beside her.

She opened her eyes and he was regarding her with a calm, small smile on his face. "Brandon is really looking forward to this," he said in a low voice.

Brandon pulled on the back of her seat, in case she hadn't gotten the message. "Guess where we're going?"

Hmm. What did Brandon like? "The ballpark," she said. Which was exactly why she hadn't worn her sneakers, because she was not participating in any kind of sport activity, no way, no how. "Somewhere to hit balls and play catch with Brandon."

Jon turned to her and raised his brow. "No," he said flatly.

"Guess again," Brandon yelled.

"Um." She was kind of sorry she'd insisted that Brandon come with them. What else did he like? "The zoo."

"Strike two, Auntie."

"Fine," she said. "I give up."

"Don't tell her yet," Jon commanded Brandon. Her nephew sighed and settled back in the seat with his electronic game.

Jon started the engine and drove out of her condominium parking lot. Elizabeth peered at him from her peripheral vision. He glanced sidelong at her as well. She just couldn't get over him with short hair. She decided she liked it.

He could almost be someone she worked with. But

her colleagues didn't smell so good. They didn't set her senses on edge. She closed her eyes and breathed in again. This would not do, to feel so aroused sexually. What had she gotten herself into? Jon was probably going to take them someplace with other baseball people. Their wives, their children. Normal families, not like hers. She'd been dreading this day all week. Meanwhile, Brandon hummed along to a song that played only in his head.

It could be worse. Her nephew could be homesick for his mom, and so far, she'd avoided that difficulty.

She was lucky. They'd had a few bumpy days, but as long as he got to see Jon at the hospital every other day after school, he was placated.

She owed Jon so much. Surely Jon knew it, too.

That was the problem.

The SUV slowed, and Jon pulled into a parking garage by the Charles River. Elizabeth peered out the side window. She hadn't been paying attention to their surroundings, so lost was she in her crazy, mixed-up thoughts. Jon pulled a ticket from an automatic dispenser and tossed it on the console, before roaring up the slope to find an open parking space.

Elizabeth picked up the ticket. *The Museum of Science?*

Jon was taking her to the Museum of Science?

Her hand shook and she put the ticket down. Was he pandering to her? Was the jock trying to impress the doctor freak? Because what could Jon possibly find interesting about a museum of *science?* Brandon was no student, either. His interest in anything remotely intellectual was nil. It was all she could do to get him to sit still and read a storybook to her before bed.

Actually, he'd been getting better at reading aloud. He liked Jon's selection of books. A lot of sports stories geared toward young boys.

"Are you okay?" Jon asked her as he shut off the engine.

"I...don't think I've ever been here," Elizabeth said, unbuckling her seat belt and stepping into the garage. She smelled the exhaust from cars and saw groups of children herded by adults. "Maybe once when I was a kid on a school field trip, but that was so long ago I can't remember."

"I used to come here all the time." Jon held open the SUV door for her nephew, and then shut it and activated the lock. "My mother taught seventh grade science. She used to bring us into Boston on the weekends. Even though my brothers were little, they loved the hands-on stuff."

This was the first time he'd spoken of them to her. He hadn't even introduced his brothers to her the day she'd intruded upon them at his apartment.

She fell into step beside him, following the line of people straggling to the elevator. "I met your two brothers and your father at your apartment last week. Your father is in...Arizona now, right?"

"On vacation." Jon raked back his hair, frowning, as if he still wasn't used to the blunt edges. "He works construction on big projects in Boston, or he used to before he retired this summer. He met my mother when she came to Boston as a college student from California. They were an unlikely pair. But, she married him and moved here."

"I..." Jon was walking fast, so Elizabeth hurried to keep up with him.

He blocked the elevator door until she and Brandon were inside. "Sorry I'm rushing, but we have timed tickets."

"For...?"

"You'll see." And he still didn't tell her, even when they were inside the hustle and bustle of the museum itself. He led her and Brandon without consulting a map, so he obviously knew where he was going. So much was happening around them. Elizabeth glanced from side to side, taking it all in. Everything she gazed at, Jon watched, too. She was almost ready to believe that he hadn't pandered to her, that he genuinely enjoyed the place. Why hadn't she ever come here on her own? The museum was interesting. Yes, crowded with families and children, but she could overlook that because they were her kind of crowds: science lovers.

And through the winding trek, no one stopped them to ask for an autograph from Jon or to take a photo with him. The haircut had done its job.

She felt herself relaxing.

"Here we are," Jon said.

The exhibit sign read Pompeii.

Elizabeth gasped. "There's an exhibit on the Pompeii excavation, here, in Boston?"

And, indeed, there it was, everything about the nearly two-thousand-year-old city—buried beneath the ash of the volcano Vesuvius and not found again for nearly seventeen hundred years—that she'd been reading about since she was a child.

She drank it all in, unable to contain her excitement, darting from exhibit to exhibit: the Roman frescoes, the statues, the dinnerware, the plaster casts of the food on their plates. And more fascinating, and terrible: the plaster and resin casts made from the impressions in ash of the people caught up in the eruption, huddled, their faces covered with their hands. She stopped before a plaster cast of a small dog, its collar clearly visible.

"He looks just like Oliver," Brandon marveled beside her, referring to his and Ashley's little dog. "Can we go visit him at Sharma's house sometime?"

"Of course." Elizabeth smiled at Brandon, understanding that not everyone was such a nerd as to enjoy the fruits of an archaeological dig. To be able to use one's imagination to see clearly how these ancient, doomed people had lived, so long ago, didn't come easily to everyone. But it did to her. Vividly, she could imagine their pain and their fright at the overflowing volcano as viscerally as if she'd been there herself.

She felt, rather than heard, Jon step behind her. His face was reflected in the glass of the artifact case before her. She put her hand on his image. She'd had no idea this exhibit was coming to her home city. "How did you know I would like this?"

"Brandon," he said softly.

Her nephew held Jon's hand and beamed at her. She knew better. Brandon may have told Jon about the books and brochures scattered over her house, but Brandon didn't understand the significance and would not have known about this exhibit, or this museum.

She met Jon's gaze. *He* was the one who understood. Maybe if she showed him what she felt, he would understand that, too.

She lowered her eyes. "I…had been thinking about taking a cruise that stopped in Naples so I could visit Pompeii in person. And now…I don't think I need to go."

"A cruise still sounds good," Jon said.

It did. But not with Albert as her partner, or anybody else who didn't care or understand what it meant to her. She turned back to the exhibit.

"I knew you would like family fun day, Auntie," Brandon whispered by her side.

Yes. Yes, she did.

JON STOOD NEAR a live animal exhibit, one eye on Brandon, while Lizzy stood beside him. There were similarities between them he hadn't realized until now. Lizzy had escaped from the pain of her childhood by diving into history books. He had escaped by hurling himself at the science and mechanics of baseball pitching.

"How did you develop an interest in archaeology?" he asked her.

"From books I picked up in the library as a kid." Even now, she was thumbing through a book she'd picked up in the museum gift shop. "Then, when I was in college, even though I was a premed major, we were allowed one elective per semester on anything we wanted. I chose courses from the archaeology program, because I loved the thought of digging to see ancient civilizations."

Her cheeks were pink, and she looked...excited. She was also standing close to him, her arm brushing his. He didn't move, just watched her enthusiasm. It was like seeing a flower open and bloom for him.

"One year," she continued, flipping to another page, "I got to assist on a dig in Jamestown, Virginia. It's one of the most important archaeological sites in our country, and it was...amazing. I got to unearth a prehistoric Native arrowhead, along with pottery shards and some pipe remnants."

She grinned at him, looking more excited and natural than when she performed her surgery, he'd bet.

"Why didn't you become a historian?" he asked.

"No way," she said, tucking the book into her purse. "What I'm doing at the hospital is practical. There's never any worry that I won't be able to pay my bills or have to rely on somebody that I don't want to rely on." Her jaw set. "No, history is just my hobby, and that's fine by me."

Still, her face clouded over. If only she could see how personally powerful she was. He figured this woman could pretty much handle anything she set her mind to.

A teen came rushing by, almost knocking Lizzy over, and she grimaced. He stepped in front of her and deflected a second kid following behind. But Liz's face was pale. She really disliked crowds. On the other hand, crowds exhilarated him. He got energy just from being near them, and pitching for the Captains, in a ballpark with tens of thousands of people, was a rush unlike any other.

Brandon barreled over and grabbed Lizzy's hand, then hopped up and down. Jon would bet that the kid felt the same way he did; he reveled in the noise and the stimulation. No wonder Lizzy doubted herself when it came to Brandon.

"Do you want to move on?" Jon asked her. "I read there's a butterfly exhibition. It's probably quieter. Butterflies don't make much noise."

She smiled tremulously at him. "I don't want to be so one-sided. What do you want to look at?"

You, Lizzy, he thought. *I like looking at you.*

They started following after Brandon, who was meandering from kiosk to kiosk. "I guess I just like watching people's reactions—people watching," he said.

"Did you have any interest in the Pompeii exhibit?"

"Sure, when you explained what the different pieces meant in context." He thought for a moment. "You know, you're talented like that. You're an awful lot like my mom was."

"Was?"

He shook his head. *Don't go there,* he told himself. "It's a compliment. I'm used to scientific-minded women." He'd missed it, actually. Too much.

"Do you date many doctors?" she teased.

"I don't *date* anybody."

"Too busy?"

"The travel."

She nodded. "From April to October, right?"

"Yeah. Spring training starts mid-February in Florida and lasts until Opening Day in April. Then we play 162 games over 180 days. Eighty-one of those games are on the road, all over the U.S. and Toronto, Canada." He paused, but she was listening closely. She understood what he was telling her, that he was unavailable for relationships. Real ones, anything that went beyond "fun days" or fleeting one-nighters.

"And if you're Rico Martinez," she mused, "you also have playoffs and the World Series to contend with."

"Got a crush on the pitcher, do you?" He grinned at her. "Yeah, with the postseason, the schedule can last until almost November. So that leaves us with just November, December and January to ourselves, pretty much."

They were in the main part of the museum now,

and the feeling was airy with the cavernous ceiling and wide-open lack of walls. Lizzy looked up and squinted into the light.

"That's a heavier schedule than I thought," she said in a small voice.

Maybe he'd thrown a cloud over what had been, until now, a pretty good day. Mentally, he kicked himself.

But she stopped and picked up his right hand, the scar still healing, and traced her finger over it. "It sounds like you're totally focused on your goals, the same as I am."

He liked the feeling of her hand on his. He intertwined his fingers in hers. His hand seemed to swallow hers up. "Is that okay with you?"

"It's a relief, actually." She gave him a dazzling smile that lit up her whole face.

He looked into her big brown eyes, and he felt his body stir. The curvy brunette just…gave him an instant hard-on. He'd been walking beside her, behind her—enjoying her amazing round ass and her root-beer-colored eyes. The thought of her spending the night with anyone besides him made him feel antsy.

"Are you seeing anyone?" he asked point-blank.

Her cheeks flushed pink. "No. Of course not."

He felt relief, though maybe he shouldn't. That doctor in the coffee shop had been interested in her. "Your sister says you want a family one day."

She pulled her hand away and resumed walking. "Brandon should not have said that to you."

He caught up with her in two seconds. "It's not a big deal, Lizzy. I do, too. Just not until baseball is over for me."

She glanced across the room at Brandon, jumping up and down like a human pogo stick. "What happened to your mom?" she asked. "You started to tell me. Then you stopped."

"It doesn't matter."

"It does to me."

He paused. But she wouldn't use it against him. She wouldn't tell anyone—she was so ridiculously private. "She died when I was...Brandon's age."

Her eyes widened and her mouth opened. "So... you grew up without a mom?"

He shoved his hands in his pockets and moved ahead. This wasn't something they needed to talk about.

She caught up with him and tugged his hand. "I grew up without a dad. But you already know that from Brandon."

"I do."

She swallowed and nodded. Maybe it was too much. Maybe he'd lost her. Dating, hanging out with a woman, whatever you wanted to call it—it was supposed to be casual and fun. A distraction from all the stress on the road. Usually an escape from a difficult loss or bickering teammates or media people whose probing questions were a pain in the butt.

But not...this. This...fascination mixed with aching and wonder. And the constant, buzzing attraction. She rested her hand against his belt loop and bumped her hip into his. And then his good hand—his pitching hand—had her small hand intertwining with his again.

His groin tightened. They locked gazes. Man, what he wouldn't give to gather up Brandon, toss him in the SUV and drop him off at the babysitter's house while he drove Lizzy—sexy Lizzy, enigmatic Lizzy—back to his apartment for a fun day of their own, family be damned.

Brandon chose that moment to come running over. "Can we see the electricity display?" He turned and pointed. "It's that way."

But there was already mad electricity where Jon was standing.

Lizzy dropped her hand from his and stepped back. "Yes. Good idea."

Aw, what the hell. Nothing was going to happen between him and Liz, anyway. He had too much to lose to let himself get distracted, and she had her own plans. "Sure. Let's go."

He kept lots of space between them for the remainder of the afternoon. Brandon was good for that.

It was going to have to be enough to watch Lizzy come out of her shell and enjoy that. Nothing more.

AT THE END of the day, when it was just turning dark outside, and Brandon was yawning and there was nothing left but to bring them both home, Jon parked the SUV and walked them to Elizabeth's condo.

"Jon, that was awesome!" Her nephew threw his arms around Jon in an exuberant hug that only an eight-year-old could manage. "We did pretty good with her, didn't we?" he whispered.

Elizabeth smiled to herself. She heard every word, and Jon knew it before he answered the boy.

"Yeah, I think we did, buddy."

"And you'll bring me those baseballs you promised?" Brandon asked him.

"Will do." Jon glanced over Brandon's head at her and in the lamplight, met her gaze.

She held her breath. She wanted him. But did she dare?

Brandon ran ahead down the pathway and scooted inside the door to the brick condo building. Jon put his hand on the doorjamb as if to follow Brandon upstairs. But at the last moment, he turned. With a sigh, Elizabeth made her decision, and let herself melt closer to him.

His face was shadowed from the light in the hallway behind him. She couldn't see his expression, but…she could feel his heat. His chin was tilted toward her, close enough to feel the warmth of his breath. And his smell. His hand went to the back of her head, his palm just skimming the back of her neck.

Yes, she trusted him not to crowd her, not to lean on her, not to direct her. He would let her be who she was. And he wasn't scared away, either. "Come here," she whispered.

His face came closer to hers. Their mouths were nearly touching, but not quite. Her lips were just a whisper from his.

She licked her lips, and he made a soft noise.

"Auntie?"

Jon stepped away from her and smoothly yielded to Brandon at the same time. In the darkness, her nephew saw nothing.

"Good night," Jon said to her, his hands at his sides.

"Are you leaving?" she asked stupidly.

"Yes." He patted Brandon on the head. "I'll see you Monday at the hospital, kid."

"Okay!"

"Brandon, please go upstairs and brush your teeth," Elizabeth said. "I'll be up in a minute."

Her nephew left. The door slammed behind him and she didn't move a muscle. Jon stared at her. "Do you know what you're doing?" he asked in a low voice.

"You said…three dates."

"Yeah, but I didn't expect…"

"What?" she challenged him.

"This." He leaned in and kissed her. With hunger, with firmness, with desire. Mouth to mouth. And she kissed him back, with everything she had. For a brief second, their tongues touched, stroked.

"Jon!" Brandon poked his head outside the door again, oblivious. "I forgot my baseball glove in your truck."

Jon groaned and pulled back, and Elizabeth put her

hand to her mouth. She couldn't help it; she smiled at him, feeling silly and punch-drunk and…delicious. "You were right," she murmured. "I did like it…very much."

Jon sucked in his breath. He looked stunned.

"I'll call you," she said breezily. And then she strolled into the building.

CHAPTER TWELVE

LIZZY DID CALL HIM, on Monday, during his lunch hour, when Jon least expected it.

"I can't make it this Saturday," she said. "Can you come over on Thursday for dinner at six, instead? That's the day after Halloween. Also, the day after game seven of the World Series. Thankfully, I'm not on call that evening."

He would chuckle if he wasn't so irritated with her. What was this, family fun day number two? A pizza dinner with her and Brandon on a school night was not what Jon had in mind, not after that kiss they'd shared.

But the time and location of the next date was not his choice.

"Fine," he said. "Dinner it is."

Maybe, Jon thought as he tossed down his phone, staring at the remnants of his brown-bag lunch on the desk in Coach Duffy's office, Lizzy was dialing down the intensity. Maybe she'd thought it over and had changed her mind. There was nothing but complications involved in getting too hot and heavy, and they both knew it.

Jon wadded up the empty bag from his lunch and tossed it in the trash. He felt like crap.

Still, he would be seeing Lizzy. Plus, he'd be getting away from shoptalk for the evening. He was sick of thinking about his contract problems and the escalating criticism on sports radio.

Maybe he should treat the dinner as a night of hanging out with an old friend. Just show up and be a good guy to her and the kid and attempt to enjoy himself.

"What kind of flowers does your aunt like?" he asked Brandon on Monday afternoon at the hospital.

"Don't know." Brandon wiped his nose. "But I need some baseballs to practice for tryouts. And I need a new glove, too."

The trek to Dan's Sporting Goods later that day was easy. Jon bought the baseballs, but he ignored the glove request for now. He wasn't going to spoil the kid—the glove Brandon owned already suited him fine.

On the flower question, though, Jon decided to phone Brooke.

"Hi, Jon," Brooke said when she picked up. "I was thinking about you. I have a meeting set up with the front office next week."

"Good. Keep me posted." He paused for effect. "What kind of flowers do women like?"

Brooke giggled. "Are you asking me what my favorite flowers are?"

"No. I'm asking because I'm meeting someone

tonight." Which brought him to his main point. "Tell Vivian I can't be one of her bachelors at the charity auction, because I'm seeing someone."

There was a long silence on the other end. Then a terse, "Who is she?"

"She wishes to remain private."

"Fine. Roses always work."

So on Thursday Jon stopped by a combination farm stand/florist place he knew in the suburbs. But the long rows of flowers and bouquet options overwhelmed him. Lizzy didn't seem like a flower sort of woman, anyway. When he saw the bags of locally picked apples, big and ripe, he knew they fit the bill. It was a family supper he was attending, not a seduction.

At exactly six o'clock he knocked on her door, a bag of apples under his arm and two regulation youth-league baseballs for Brandon in each back pocket.

He expected the kid to answer the door, his energy bouncing off the walls as usual.

What he got instead was Lizzy. In a sexy black dress.

Whoa. His gaze skimmed from her neckline, to her hips, to her bare legs and back up again. She wore shiny pink gloss on those usually naked bow lips. And all he wanted to do was draw them inside his mouth and kiss it all off.

His elbow loosed on the bag of apples propped on his hip, and one by one, the apples slipped and dropped to the hardwood floor. *Plunk, plunk, plunk.*

She straightened the bag from him and then knelt to pick up the fallen apples.

"Lizzy, what's going on?" he asked.

She looked up at him with a small, secret smile. And he could see straight down her cleavage. She was wearing a black lace bra.

Whoa again.

"Brandon is staying with a schoolmate tonight." She stood with the apples he'd dropped. "Thanks for these, by the way. They're Cortlands—cooking apples—I think I'll use them to bake a pie."

"You…cooked?" was all he could think to say. The house smelled like roasting chicken with great-smelling autumn herbs in the oven.

"Come inside." She took him by the hand, and he followed like a baby duckling. "There are lots of things you don't know about me, Jon. There are two or three dishes I'm pretty good at."

He would just bet. "You set this up so we would be alone?"

"I know, it's crazy. We are a completely mis-matched couple." She rolled her eyes. "But I couldn't help it. I could no longer deny the attraction." And then her gaze roamed over his body.

He wasn't getting the greatest feeling, as if he was standing in another charity bachelor auction of sorts. "So, to be clear. Is this a date, or is it just a meeting for sex?"

Her cheeks turned pink. "Why can't it be both? I

mean, you're married to baseball. And that's good, because…it's safe. In the end, you'll always choose baseball."

"You're afraid I'll fall in love with you?"

"No! I would never presume that. I just…don't want you to expect too much from me."

He removed the baseballs from his pockets and set them on the couch. Brandon would know what to do. Jon sure as hell didn't.

"Look," Lizzy said, "I'm being practical. I know this isn't long-term between us. You travel. You have a very public baseball career. And I work in Boston. I have a very private hospital career. In the reality of making anything work longer than that, we are an impossible couple. Anyway, you said…back that day in your apartment…that you were going to cut me loose after three dates. And I thought…if I didn't act soon enough…" She blushed. "I can't stop thinking about you, Jon. I need you, but not in the way that you think."

"How do I think?"

She sighed. "Everybody else cares about you because of baseball. They want your status to rub off on them. But I don't want that. I want…*you*." She looked at him, seemingly shy.

Anybody else would have stopped there and taken her. He wanted to. Man, he wanted to. But he couldn't help messing with fire. Because he needed to *know*.

"So, to be clear, my job tonight is to be some kind of stud to you?"

"What? No!" Her eyes darted as if panicked. "I don't *know* why I'm attracted to you. I don't know why I see myself in bed with you. It has to be... chemical. And temporary. But I don't want anything more than that."

"Neither do I," he said.

She drew back, confused. "You don't?"

He had news for her: he didn't fall in love. Never had. Maybe it was because of his mom's early death. Maybe it was because he didn't tend to bond that way—he'd been accused of that more than once. "So, let's talk about ground rules," he said.

"Is that a baseball thing?" she asked nervously.

"It's a human thing, Liz."

Her brow scrunched. "I don't understand."

Of course she didn't. She was so cocooned in her own world, separate from everyone else. What an irony that she worked in a big, public, healing profession.

"It means that we're setting the boundaries for what we expect of each other so there'll be no problems later," he said.

She hugged herself. He understood he was making the discussion cold, almost transactional. But it was for the best this way.

And yet, he wanted her so damn bad. Wanted to strip off her shell, get inside her head. See that expression of happiness when she saw how good he could make her feel—

She nodded. "You're absolutely right. This is for one night only. After that, there is no reason for sexual contact."

He nearly laughed aloud, but he kept control. "That's just it," he patiently explained. He couldn't tell her that he wanted something different from what was normal for him…he was out of his comfort zone, too. Maybe he *was* falling for her. But if he told her that, she'd run screaming. "I want a rule that it's something we'll decide afterward. We'll see how it goes tonight."

Very smart, and very safe. Maybe it wouldn't work. Maybe *they* wouldn't work.

She frowned. "Why would this go beyond a night?"

She really was a babe in the woods. He stared at her, his tone blunt. "You might like it, Liz."

WAS HE SERIOUS? Elizabeth wondered. She'd assumed this was for one-time only, just to sate a silly curiosity she had. It really was clinical.

It was also crazy. Yes, she'd had fun with him on Saturday, but really, they were simply too different as people to have any sort of relationship.

But the way Jon was looking at her, those ice-blue eyes…he made her shiver. He always made her shiver.

"I don't like your rule," she said. "It's too open for me."

"And that terrifies you." He said it as a statement.

"It's not practical. What more could you want from me?"

He gave her a sad smile. "I told my agent today that I'm seeing somebody. Somebody private, and I won't divulge her name. I was thinking of you when I said it—don't make a liar out of me, Liz."

"Why in God's name would you do that?" she wailed. "Now they'll be trying to find me—"

"No. This is a private arrangement." He said it in that low, mystical-sounding voice. God, she ached for him. His kiss on Saturday night had kept her up for hours, tossing and turning, wondering how she could get through this physical attraction that burned like she'd never been burned. It had to be because she'd met Jon when she'd been at her most vulnerable, upset over Brandon, and worried for Ashley.

Brushing her hands over her dress, she turned to the calendar on her kitchen wall, filled in with all the dates and times and commitments for Brandon's schedule. Ten more nights, that's all she had to survive until Ashley was home and her routine was back to normal. Jon's proposal needed to work with her life, too.

She pointed to the calendar. "Until next Sunday, when Ashley comes home. Ten more days. But that's my absolute limit. Those are the only parameters I can promise you. And during that time, I have Brandon to care for. He's my first priority."

He nodded. "Sounds like the rules are set then."

"Any others?"

"Just a question." He cocked his head. "Have you ever done this before?"

She sputtered in anger. "Of course! I am an experienced medical professional. This is a natural bodily function."

His mouth curved on one side. "You've done it clinically?"

"What does *that* mean? That I've done it in the hospital, on an overnight on-call session? Of course not!"

"What I mean, Liz, is have you ever been in a relationship?"

"Me? Are you *serious?* And don't look at me like that, Mr. Married-to-Baseball, because you haven't, either. You're just like me. I researched you on the internet, I know!" she said a little too loudly.

He grinned at her. "Oh, Lizzy, you are too much fun for me."

"Is that an insult?"

"Sweetheart, it's my highest compliment."

Something in his tone made her pause. He wasn't laughing at her. He was looking at her as if he was in pain and he was longing for her. It was the oddest sense, as if he was showing her something of his true feelings. The part of him that he not only covered up and hid from the world but denied was even there.

Her heart squeezed. "I'm sorry for yelling at you. I just…don't know what's happening to me."

He gave her a small smile. "Me, neither, if it's any consolation."

She shifted, glanced at the stirring spoon she

was still holding in her hand. "We should probably eat now."

"Yes." But he didn't move a muscle. Just continued drinking her in with his eyes.

"Jon…?"

His smile flatlined. He crooked his finger to her.

"What?" she asked tentatively.

He crooked his finger again. Locked his gaze on her eyes. She felt the full force of his burning intensity and nearly dropped the spoon.

"Wh-what about dinner?" she asked.

"You're dinner." He reached over to the stove and turned off the burner. "Save it. We'll both be hungry later."

Her breath sucked in and she drifted toward him, the hand holding the spoon dropping to her side. Her other hand she curled around his neck, drew him to her, though he didn't offer any resistance; he followed his body and let himself be drawn to her.

When their lips touched, he gently drew her bottom lip inside and nipped it. She made a little moan and pushed closer, enjoying the feel of his breath mingling with hers, and the fact that he did not release her. Instead he angled his mouth and kissed her like she'd wanted him to.

She didn't need to be nervous, because *all* he did was kiss her. Tenderly lavishing attention on her as if he was fascinated by her mouth, leisurely taking his time as if he enjoyed kissing her. His hand fell away so that only their mouths touched. She felt achy and full of yearning. She would give anything to brush against his chest.

He drew his thumb along her cheek. "Lizzy, you drive me crazy, do you know that?"

That pleased her. She tossed the spoon to the table and wrapped both arms around his neck. "I can't stop thinking about you. I try, but I just can't."

He smiled and picked her up, as easily as if she were weightless, his hands beneath her bottom. The hem of her dress rode up, while the top of it gaped down. She was up high, looking over him. "I want you so badly," she said.

His mouth went to the gaping neck of her dress. Nudged aside the fabric. And his lips drew down on her budded nipple. Through the lace bra, he gently suckled.

She bucked in his arms. She hadn't expected that at all: nobody had ever done this to her. She felt wild and wet and…she needed more. "Jon…please…"

But he didn't give her more. Just spent all his intensity and attention on that one breast.

This was more than she had bargained for, or expected. He was only making her need grow. She whimpered again. "Please?"

"Have you had enough?" he murmured, his mouth still on her breast, his breath hot against her skin.

She squirmed. "No. Don't tease me. Please. I can't stand it."

"Do you want me to stay and give you more?"

"Yes." She glanced to her bedroom. "I do."

He strode with long paces, Elizabeth still in his arms, to her bedroom. And when they got there, he gently placed her on the bed. She pulled him down on top of her, but he withdrew, leaning back and placing his palms on either side of the pillow cradling her head.

"Lizzy, I'm warning you. My hands and my mouth are going to be all over your body tonight. Tell me now if you need to back out."

She couldn't speak. He'd put incredible visions in her head. "I don't want to back out."

His eyes burned into hers. "There is nothing halfway or easy or pretty about me, darling. Once we start, you're getting my full intensity. Do you have condoms?"

"Yes…in…my medical bag…" She reached over, straining, and yanked at the drawer on her night table. "Please, Jon…"

He lay down beside her and pulled her on top of him, and he started kissing her all over again, true to his word.

"THAT WAS…THE MOST amazing…thing…I've ever been through." Elizabeth reached up and cupped Jon's cheek with her palm. The sex had made her completely inarticulate. It felt like…a soulful experience she had never imagined possible. "I cannot believe you don't have some lucky woman tied to you for life."

He gave her a languid smile. They were both entirely naked. He was beside her, idly tracing her face as if she was the most amazing person. She stretched like a pleased cat, her toes curling and uncurling.

"I've decided that I like your ground rules," she said. "I would indeed like to do this again." She glanced at him. "How about you?"

He lazily curled a lock of her hair around his thumb. "I decided before we even started."

"Honestly?"

He smiled. "Yep."

She sat up. "Is there somebody else you're running from?"

His brow furrowed. "What do you mean?"

"You had to tell your agent you're seeing someone. Why? Did you need to get out of a messy situation brought on by another one-night stand?"

He laughed. "No." But there was something about his expression that discomforted her.

"Your dating life is complicated, isn't it? We should have discussed this in the ground rules, shouldn't we?"

His blue eyes met hers. "Do you want to know the truth?"

"I do."

He rolled to the pillow and put his hands behind his head. He glanced over her, to a spot on the wall. "The Captains asked me to do a charity bachelor auction."

That must have been what she'd heard those two nurses talking about last week. She pictured it now. Jon up onstage. A line of women screaming out dollar figures for him. How much money they were willing to bid.

"Oh. That is terrible," she said.

A week ago, she would have guessed he would love the attention. But she knew him better now. "They think you'll do anything for baseball, don't they?"

He turned his head and his gaze met hers. He knew she understood. "I'm not a slab of meat, Lizzy."

No. He was so much more important than that. But lots of people thought he was just a commodity. In a sense, hadn't she tonight? Expecting he would hop into the sack with her just because she'd asked? What if the gender roles were reversed?

Elizabeth swallowed. There was a tight line between them, and she felt she was feeling his pain, too. Seeing what he'd really longed for.

She kissed him softly on the lips. "I don't think of you as an athlete, or anything like that. I think of you as a person who didn't run away once he saw what I'm really made of."

The breath seemed to leave him. He rolled over and wove her fingers through his.

She felt herself shaking. There was just something about him. Something that drew her to him, and she couldn't fool herself that it was only physical. It was an emotional need, too. She felt as if a drape had fallen away and he saw all the damage that had been done to her, the imperfect person that she was. And yet, he understood and cared for her in spite of it.

She sat up. She had to stop this closeness—it was

frightening her. "You were right about establishing ground rules. I've made a new decision. I don't need to do this again."

"Nope," he said, grinning at her. "Me, neither."

And as she fought her disappointment, he winked at her. "I'm teasing. I want to. But whether you decide to again or not, remember the agreement. For ten more days—until the bachelor auction—you're my secret girlfriend. Sleep with me again or don't, but either way, you've got to ditch that doctor I keep seeing you with at the hospital."

"Albert?" She'd already "ditched" him, at least in her mind, but Jon didn't need to know that.

"Whoever he is," he said, "I don't want to see him around you."

"Well, I don't want to see you with any women, either."

"Done. Anything else, or are we good now?" He was settling under her comforter. Fluffing the pillow.

She looked at him with alarm. "You're staying tonight?"

"Hell, yeah."

"What if I told you to leave?"

"I'd say you were being prickly. Besides…" He shook the condom box on the bedside table. "If I leave, we won't get the pleasure of deciding if we want morning sex, will we?"

Oh. She leaned back on the pillows, visualizing. She definitely wanted to try that with him, very much.

He turned off the light and pulled her naked body

close to him, so he was spooning her. "Good night, Lizzy baby."

She had never known how much she would like a man's strong arms—and warm, broad chest—wrapping her close to his heart.

BUT ELIZABETH DIDN'T get a chance to see if there would be morning sex or not, because the call came in. Loud. Buzzing.

Elizabeth moaned, rolling over. "Is that your phone or mine?"

Jon rolled over and pulled her to him. He had an erection. Oh, God, she wanted to stay in bed so much. "I turned my phone off, Lizzy," he said, nuzzling the back of her neck.

"I can't turn mine off. I'm a doctor." She reached over him and grabbed for it on the table.

Crap. It was from her sister's counselor. "I have to take this." She got up and reached for her robe. "You can take a shower if you want," she told him.

He pressed a kiss to her forehead, and her heart welled up. If her life wasn't so on edge at the moment, she would ask him to stay longer.

She went into the kitchen and took the call. "This is Dr. Elizabeth LaValley."

"I'm sorry I called you so early," her sister's counselor said, "but I figured you have an early shift. I needed to check with you because you haven't responded to my email."

No, Elizabeth hadn't checked her personal account in a while. "I'm sorry. Is my sister okay?"

"Yes, she's doing quite well. The reason I'm calling is to inform you of a planned family counseling session next Friday. Your mother has confirmed her attendance, and I was wondering about yours."

Her breath hitched in. "I'm afraid not. I think it's best that Ashley speak with our mother alone."

"Dr. LaValley—"

"Will you be requiring Brandon's presence?" she asked.

"No. We only allow children when they're over twelve years of age."

"Very good. Now if you'll excuse me, I'm late for work." She hung up her phone.

Jon met her in the living room. His shirt was unbuttoned and he was still zipping his jeans, but he looked like the sexiest guy to do the walk of shame to his car, ever.

He grinned sheepishly at her. "I'm late, and we overslept."

She stood on tiptoe and kissed him. "I want to do that again."

He lifted his hand in a mock salute. "Any time, just call me."

It made her problems with Ashley and her mom hurt a little bit less.

CHAPTER THIRTEEN

JON WAS STILL feeling the rush from being with Lizzy when he stopped at a convenience mart near her house and ordered a take-out coffee and an egg sandwich. The local newspapers were on a rack by the cash register, so while Jon waited for his egg to cook, he idly scanned the headlines.

To his shock, his name and headshot were printed on the front-page sidebar.

Jon nearly choked on his coffee.

No way was he buying a newspaper to support those bloodsucker sportswriters, so instead, he scanned the seating area to find a discarded sports section left behind from an earlier patron. He unsnapped the section of newspaper. Right there, above the fold, was the headline: Farell Named as Trouble-maker in Captains' Clubhouse.

He sat heavily at the empty table, feeling sick to his stomach. The reporter in the byline was a guy Jon knew well, a man he personally liked, and who Jon had thought liked him back. Jon had given the bastard more quotes than he knew what to do with in the past, but this time, he hadn't given Jon the courtesy of a heads-up? Not a single call for a quote?

What the hell? Gritting his teeth, forcing himself to scan the article—which went against everything he believed in—Jon caught the gist of it pretty quickly.

The Captains had lost all those games in September and had failed to make the playoffs specifically because the pitching staff had a bad attitude, sources said, and the ringleader of those pitchers was the local guy. *Him*.

Jon crumpled the newspaper and threw it in the trash. Then he retrieved his order and went out to his SUV, slammed the door and rested his head on the steering wheel.

More than anything, it stung. He got along with everybody, the ultimate team player. He'd thought they'd all liked him. He always did everything he could for them. And yet, here he sat, staring a railroad job in the face.

Somebody on the team had dropped his name to the reporter, obviously. Of all the pitchers on the staff, someone wanted rid of him the most. They had scapegoated him. Jon wasn't an ace, but he wasn't small potatoes, either.

This was writing on the wall he couldn't ignore. He could do everything perfectly from here on out, but if management and ownership were looking for an excuse to make the scandal go away, they could easily do so by dropping him from the roster.

Boston was a big-market sports town. Once a scandal erupted, the explosion could linger for weeks, months, years. Hell, there were still people who whined about losses from twenty years earlier, as if they'd happened only yesterday. The carping, moaning and complaining was fed by wall-to-wall sports shows: radio programs and cable television talk fests that broadcasted in a loop over and over, 24/7. Dozens of people made good livings doing nothing but criticizing Captains games, dissecting each and every play, each and every day.

Normally, Jon ignored it. Thought of it as a game he was pretty good at managing. But this...this...

Was his own damn fault.

He closed his eyes and leaned back against the seat. There was no decision. Nothing else he could do except call his agent.

"Yes, Jon," Brooke said when she picked up. "You weren't home this morning. Your phone was turned off and you weren't home last night, either."

"Nope," he said. He owed Brooke no explanation as to how he spent his time.

"Anything you care to tell me?" she asked.

He held the phone to his ear and watched as a guy his age pulled open the door to the convenience mart, followed by three towheaded little kids. "Yeah. What can I do to get my life back?"

"That depends. Were you drinking in the clubhouse? Did you participate in that?"

Oh, shit. He hadn't read the article that carefully. "Is that what the newspaper says?"

"It does. And I'm getting nervous because you're not answering my question."

Jon was silent. What could he say?

He wanted to say nothing. He needed to think. Needed to find a way to counter this, to fix it…

Get serious.

"Jon?"

"I'm here." He ran his hand through his shorn hair. Tried to knock some of the cobwebs out of his brain. What could he do? Ask Brooke to arrange a sit-down with a reporter? That would make it worse, because he couldn't lie, and he couldn't explain his way out of this. Even to him, it made no sense.

Brooke sighed audibly. "All right. Here's where we stand. Management and ownership told me that they're behind you. Vivian is aware of what you're doing with the Sunshine Club, and that can only help you. I also told them you're working on improving your changeup pitch, and that you've been conducting daily workouts you'll be continuing until spring training. As far as that goes, you're doing everything right."

Jon knocked his fist against the steering wheel. Watched the guy his age with the three boys come tumbling back outside to their minivan. "What about a media day?" Jon asked. "Will they be setting something up?"

"That's just the thing I wanted to talk about, Jon. The entire pitching staff is forbidden to talk to media. Management isn't budging on this."

"Yeah, well, somebody has been leaking." Jon

thought of all the guys he worked with. Who could have talked? Who would want to blame him?

He'd thought he was the one guy on the team that everybody liked, that nobody had a problem with.

"Take my advice," Brooke said. "Don't go on the record with any reporters. That can only backfire."

He had a splitting headache coming on. There was nothing in his experience or background that had prepared him for this. He didn't see a way out.

"What does your dad say?" he asked.

There was a silence. "Max is in the ICU," Brooke said softly.

The intensive care unit. Shit. "Oh, God, I'm so sorry. Will he be okay? What's going on, Brooke?"

"He's…fine. Just a…setback with the heart surgery."

"*Heart surgery?* Brooke, you should've told me."

"You know Max." She sighed again. "He doesn't want anyone to know. Jon, you're the only one I've told, so please keep it under wraps for him, okay?"

"Are *you* okay?" Jon asked.

"Yes. Thank you for asking." Her voice broke. "You're the…only one who has."

A lot of good it did him. Jon hung up the phone. *Get serious.*

He did the only thing he could do: he went to his morning workout with Coach Duffy. One great thing about Coach Duffy was that he didn't ask questions, and Jon didn't volunteer answers. They just pitched.

Videotaped. Broke down the mechanics. Videotaped again. One of the young players volunteered to catch for Jon, and he appreciated it, even though the young guy threw it back hard enough to sting Jon's healing finger. Jon had to tell him a couple times to lighten up.

The afternoon did not go as smoothly, though. Jon toyed with skipping the team conditioning exercises but, ultimately, ruled out raising Coach Duffy's ire. This wasn't like fielding practice with the pros—no joking around, no hanging out. These were college students and Coach treated them that way. He didn't let them look sideways at someone.

So there were whispers and stares that came Jon's way. Most of the guys looked too frightened or in awe of him to say anything to his face, and Jon was glad that he'd set the precedence where he wasn't their buddy, wasn't their pal. He hadn't ingratiated himself to them, told jokes or tried to be that easygoing, fun, good guy that everybody liked.

For once, Jon had acted like an ace.

It had been smart. It was serving him well now, because no one felt familiar enough to rib or question him.

When his job was finished—when Jon had run the last wind sprint and stretched in the final lunge—he gathered his gear and headed to his SUV before anyone could waylay him. There were no reporters staked out, because reporters didn't know about his workouts at the college.

Coach Duffy had probably threatened the players with death—or worse, losing their scholarships—if they said one word.

After Jon was back on the highway, rolling with traffic in the slow lane, he drove up one exit and then turned into a McDonald's where he could park anonymously at the far end of the lot and check his messages.

With the engine idling, he turned on his phone. As he'd expected, his message inboxes were over-loaded. He didn't dare go on Twitter. He wasn't big on using the social media service, but he did have an account, and it would be…chaos. He dreaded look-ing at it. Should probably just delete the whole thing.

He scanned his phone's text messages: Francis's and Bobby's were on top of the list. Jon called Francis first. His middle brother sounded ready to explode.

"Francis, hang tight," Jon said. "Seriously, I'm beg-ging you. Do not make this worse than it is."

"I just want to call those guys and tell them off," Francis sputtered. "They're such blowhards. They don't know us at all. We gotta do something!"

Us. There it was again. He'd never really noticed how Francis used "us" and "we" until Lizzy had pointed out his patterns, making Jon take a hard look at his history and his relationships with his family.

"Don't worry, I'll fix it," Jon said, "with the team

and behind the scenes. And once my contract is inked, I'll fix it with the fans, too."

"The fans love you, Jon! You're the only one on pitching staff who won games in September and October!"

"Francis, I said I will fix it."

"But I can't take it! What if those bastards get you railroaded out? Then what will we do?"

Jon sucked in his breath. He felt like he was a kid again and Mom had just died, and everything was a mess. Everyone was at wit's end. Dad had withdrawn, and...

Whoa. Dad hadn't texted him. Jon was sure of that.

"Jonny?" That was Bobby's voice on the line with Francis.

"Why are you out of class? For what I'm paying for your tuition bills, you shouldn't miss a minute of school."

"I called him over to my place," Francis said. "Family has to stick together."

Jon held the bridge of his nose in his fingers. There was that headache again. "Listen," he said very quietly to his two younger brothers, "everything's gonna be okay. I'll take care of it. You trust me, don't you?"

"Keep us posted," Francis said.

Jon hung up and tossed the phone into his duffel bag. Then he threw his SUV into gear and steered back to the highway. Just as dusk was settling over the city and streetlights were turning on, Jon came to the stoplight in front of his apartment building.

Two television vans were parked out front.

He stared. But maybe the news trucks weren't for him. This was Boston, a big city with a lot of stories and people a thousand times more important than him.

Still, it was too coincidental to risk.

When the light turned green, Jon swung a left turn and headed toward the inner suburbs and Lizzy's condo. Once in her familiar parking lot, he backed into her guest spot and grabbed his duffel bag. For the first time in his life, Jon was grateful to know a woman so private he would bet she hadn't told anyone she knew him, never mind that he'd spent the night with her. Her nephew wouldn't have a clue he had been here either.

Brandon.

Oh, hell, Brandon.

Jon's pulse plummeted. The kid was a huge baseball fan—he would have heard everything in the article by now, and he would be upset. So disappointed in Jon. And after what the kid was going through with his mom in alcohol rehab...

He had to find him. Jon climbed out of the truck, tired, sweaty...and with a massive headache. He had no idea what he could possibly tell the boy once he did sit him down.

But Jon had little time to consider, because as soon as his sneakers hit the sidewalk he saw Brandon on the strip of sparse lawn beside the condo building.

The boy made a pitiful windup at the pitch-back

net Jon had brought him. While Jon watched, Brandon doggedly hurled the ball at the strike zone Jon had outlined for him with black electrical tape. The baseball bounced off and veered wildly. Again and again the kid pitched, but the ball went everywhere but where it was supposed to go—back inside Brandon's glove. Instead, it careened off the PVC piping and rolled onto the asphalt. But no matter what crazy throw he made, the kid didn't quit.

Years ago, that would have been Jon, too. He felt choked up, seeing up close again how baseball had meant everything to him at that age. In a sense, it still did. It was the greatest game; it connected him to family, to tradition…to himself.

"Brandon," he said quietly. When the boy's face turned, Jon saw in the streetlight that tears were streaming down his face.

Jon dropped his duffel bag and went to the kid. As far as Jon was concerned, it was a misconception that boys didn't cry. He'd known girls in his neighborhood growing up who'd never shed a tear. Then, there were Bobby and Francis, who were the complete opposite—there was a time when they cried almost every night. Big, heaving sobs into their pillows in the dark, when they thought nobody was awake or listening. It had ripped Jon's heart out. He'd wanted nothing more than to make them feel better, every day of his life, as long as he had breath.

When Jon had been a kid, he'd talked his brothers out of their down moods, charmed them into feeling happy, made up crazy games, told stories, laughed, gathered people around them. Anything, to make them not think about what was happening to their family. And for all these years, it had worked for Jon, too…or so he'd thought.

But this time, with Brandon, there were no words. Jon had disappointed the boy. The kid's hero had come crashing down, in a way that was personal to him. Jon had laughingly abused the same substance that had taken Brandon's mother away.

Jon could never undo that.

He got down on both knees and hugged the kid to him. Brandon put his arms around Jon's neck. He choked out sobs, sweaty and hot and with snot dripping from his nose onto Jon's practice shirt. But Jon held on to him tight.

A car pulled into a spot behind them, illuminating them in bright halogen headlights.

"Come inside," Jon said to Brandon in a low voice. "Let's go upstairs to your aunt."

"Sh-she doesn't know," Brandon said, wiping his eyes with his fist. "Sh-she was in surgery all day. Mrs. H-Ham saw the article and picked me up from school."

Good, that would make it easier for Jon. "Then I'll tell your aunt everything now, so she knows, too." He didn't want to, but he had to. It was the only decent thing to do.

He picked up Brandon and carried him to the elevator, his pitching arm be damned. Even soaking wet, the kid didn't weigh a third of what Jon routinely bench-pressed. And Brandon wasn't deadweight—he clung to Jon's neck. The poor kid had never known a father of his own, and it was a shame. Say what Jon would about his sad childhood, at least he'd always had a dad, and for the first seven years of his life, a mom—a great one. That meant something.

Jon knocked, and Liz opened her door wearing yoga pants and a cotton T-shirt that clung in all the right places. But now wasn't the time for appreciating Lizzy's beautiful body.

She saw Brandon's tears, and her eyes widened. She slung the dish towel she was carrying over her shoulder and held out her arms to the boy. "Are you okay, honey? Did you fall and hurt your knee?"

Jon shook his head and set Brandon down. "Physically, he's fine."

"Thank you for bringing him upstairs," she said to Jon. She ushered Brandon inside and got him some tissues. It struck Jon how much of an effort Lizzy was making. She had come a long way in a short time with the boy. It made what Jon was about to tell her so much harder.

Lizzy trusted Jon. Or, she was beginning to. And he was going to stomp that trust into the floor.

"Brandon," Jon asked quietly, "will you please play quietly in your room while I tell your aunt the news?"

Brandon nodded without looking at either of them, and headed for his room.

"What news?" Lizzy perched on the arm of a chair, rubbing her arms and looking worried.

Jon sat on the couch and girded himself. "I know you don't read the sports pages, but there's an article about me that's pretty high profile."

"Really?" She smiled slightly, trying to make the situation lighter. "Which is exactly why there will never be anything long-term between us. Because publicity isn't my strong suit."

He ignored the message he didn't want to hear. It was the wrong time to bring it up, and it irked him. "Brandon is pretty upset about it."

"Oh, all right." She stood. "Let's look at the article then."

As if he would ever carry around that newspaper with him or even let it into his house or car. He snorted. "I don't read the stuff written about me, good or bad. What other people think of me has no bearing on how I act or think." He paced the small living room. Shit. Who was he kidding? "Actually, that's not true. I do care what you think of me."

She looked at him for a long time, silently nibbling her lip. It brought to mind the fact that he'd been here last night, and they'd made love in her bedroom. How had everything gone so wrong, so fast?

Finally she walked to the kitchen table and, from a pile of mail on the table, picked up a rolled-up newspaper secured by an elastic band.

"Great," he said. "You get home delivery."

"In my mailbox. I don't always have time to read it,

though." She pulled off the elastic band and flattened the newspaper on the table. He caught a whiff of printer's ink. She flipped through the sections—the front-page news, the national news, the local news, the living section, the business section…the sports pages.

Upside down, Jon saw the headline, Farell Named as Troublemaker in Captains' Clubhouse, alongside a photo he hadn't noticed earlier, of himself in street clothes, long hair and a five-o'clock shadow. He looked like a criminal.

Yeah, the bastards in the media had nailed him good.

Lizzy hesitated. She glanced from the article to him, as if afraid to proceed. "Do you mind if I read it?"

"By all means," he said sarcastically. "I'll wait while you do."

She lowered her head. From his peripheral vision, he saw Brandon enter the room and flop into a chair beside the sofa.

Icing on the cake.

Jon paced the length and width of the tiny apartment. Waiting for Lizzy to finish reading and render a verdict in the lengthening silence was torture. Just a few years ago, he would've told her that the article was garbage, and that if she didn't take his side, then they were finished. Most of the guys he played with would've said the same thing: *take a stand.* But Jon couldn't. With Lizzy, he had to pace, saying nothing, letting her read the lies and hyperbole written about him. It was hell.

Her face fell. Not only was his career dying in front of his eyes, but so was Lizzy's good opinion of him.

She glanced up from the newspaper, distress reading clearly in her big brown eyes. "You drank shots of alcohol in the clubhouse? Before every game?"

"No," he said quietly, "it was beer. Never hard liquor. And it wasn't before every game, just our home games."

"And that makes it okay?" She stood, staring him directly in the face. "Jon, I have to ask, do you have a problem with alcohol?"

"You know that I don't," he scoffed. "I've spent hours and hours with you. Have I had so much as a drop of alcohol in your presence?"

Brandon whimpered. Oh, hell. Jon had forgotten about him. He raked his hand through his hair—his short hair—that he still wasn't used to. He crossed the room and took Lizzy by the hands. "This isn't what it appears to be," he said in a low voice. "Believe *me,* not them."

She pulled away. "This isn't…harmless to me." She wiped her hand over her mouth. "It's personal." Her voice cracked.

"Lizzy," he said gently, "I didn't know you or Brandon back when this happened."

"Of course I know that." She glanced over at her nephew. "Brandon, honey, you shouldn't be listening."

The kid looked scared. He was only eight, and

his world already had a big crack in it, even without Jon's help.

Jon went over and led Brandon to his temporary bedroom. "Don't worry," he murmured, smoothing the boy's hair. "Everything's going to be okay."

"It doesn't look okay," Brandon whispered.

"Trust me to fix it. I promise you, I will fix it." He sat on the bed and put his arm around the boy for comfort. After a few minutes, he got up to leave.

Lizzy watched from the doorway, her face in shadows. But a tissue was pressed to her nose, and that told Jon how she was feeling about him at that moment.

Outside the boy's bedroom, he reached for her. "Lizzy, honey…"

She shook her head. Her arms wrapped around herself, she walked back to the kitchen, back to that damn newspaper.

"My sister…Brandon's mother…is in rehab for drinking," she said in a strangled voice. "For binge drinking. Social drinking—like this." She tapped the newspaper. "I know it might sound silly to you, but I shared her childhood, too. We had so many alcoholics in our family. I don't…I can't…touch the stuff, partly because I don't trust myself." She covered her mouth with her hand. "It's in my genes."

"Lizzy…" He walked over to her and stood close, close enough to feel the heat from her distress, but he didn't touch her. She didn't want him to.

"It's not in *my* genes," he murmured, keeping his

voice down in case Brandon was listening. "I don't remotely have a problem with alcohol, not even close. But as long as we're together, since it bothers you that much, I won't drink when I'm with you. It's not a big deal to me. I'll respect that of you and Brandon."

She seemed to be wavering. He touched her shoulder, felt the soft cotton, warm from her body heat. Suddenly, the thought of losing her—of her telling him to leave—was making him feel desperate. He had to make her understand why he'd made the choices he had.

"Lizzy…you're on a team, right? A team of doctors and nurses. Let me make an analogy. Let's say your top surgeon—your big guy, the one who's famous, who has the great skill—is a real, excuse the French, ass of a person. He gets along with nobody. He has a bad attitude. A chip on his shoulder. And let's say that his bad mood is infecting other people on the team, especially the new kids who have come up from the minors…from med school, I mean." He coughed.

"And then let's say," he continued, "that the whole pitching staff—the doctors—are being affected. They're botching surgeries. People are noticing. So how can you fix it, since the hospital isn't going to fire the star? What if you, as a middleweight doctor on the team—not a star, not a newbie, either—had a talent for calming the big dog? And this particular big dog likes the idea of sticking it to the team, of breaking the rules on a game-by-game basis. So you take a few swigs of beer from a communal six-pack before the game with him. It makes him feel like a rebel. It makes the team feel like there's cohesiveness in having a secret group ritual before every game."

"But, Jon, that ritual made you lose most of your games," she pointed out. "You had a lead in the standings until the last few weeks of the season."

"That's just it, Lizzy…it *didn't* make us lose. We followed the ritual throughout the spring and summer. We stopped right about the time our slump started. The big guy, our ace, was having shoulder problems, I suspect, though it was—is—pretty hush-hush. But it wouldn't have taken a genius to figure it out. I mean, the speed on his fastball dropped from 98 to 94 miles per hour. And he lost every game he started in September. His bad attitude came back. The younger guys caught it, too.

"If you ask me, Lizzy, that ritual had helped us. Yes, alcohol is bad—drinking in the park on game days is against the rules and we're horrible role models for having done it. I get that. In retrospect, it was a mistake. But, Lizzy, it didn't go down like this reporter wrote that it did." He pointed to the newspaper. "It's just irresponsible that he used anonymous sources and didn't even speak to me. I'm unavailable? Give me a break. And now, I'm not supposed to defend myself because I'm under a gag order from my team management. I wasn't even supposed to talk to you about it."

She moved her hands from her mouth, and he could

see the fresh distress on her face. "You always have to help other people, even when it hurts you, don't you? Even to your detriment."

"What?" *That's* what she'd taken away from his confession?

"When are you going to look out for yourself, Jon, first and foremost?"

"I *was* looking out for myself. But it's what team players do."

"Yes, but the rest of them weren't looking out for you, were they?"

No. No, they were not. On the contrary, someone had thrown him to the wolf pack.

"I've watched you these weeks," she said. "You look out for your brothers. You look out for me and for Brandon. You even look out for your teammates. But you don't think about yourself, not enough."

It sounded suspiciously like she was forgiving him. He grinned at her. "That's why I like you, Lizzy, you care."

"I *do* care about you, Jon."

He leaned over and kissed her. "I care about you, too." He stroked his thumb along her cheek. "Can I stay tonight on your couch? There are two news vans outside my apartment building."

"Did they follow you here?"

"No, and I won't ever let them. You're not going to be involved in this." He paused, glancing to the partially open bedroom door. "I need to talk to Brandon now."

She reached her arms around him, and it felt great. "Put yourself first. I mean it."

"Don't worry about me."

"I have to." She rubbed his shoulder. "You're growing on me. I don't want you to get hurt."

He was flattered. "I won't."

"What are you going to do?" she asked.

"Appeal to Vivian's better nature. It's the only way."

Lizzy tilted her head at him. "Are you talking about the Sunshine Club?"

"I am."

"So…is that the reason you were so gung-ho about doing community service for the team?" A realization seemed to be dawning on her face. "Jon, were you *expecting* the scandal to come out?"

He wasn't sure what she was getting at, but her eyes were wide.

He took her hand and wove his fingers through hers. "It wasn't as mercenary as that."

"Yes, but you chose Brandon," she reminded him. "You came and visited me from the very first night."

"I visited you because I wanted to see you, Lizzy. Not because of any scandal I was covering."

"Then why didn't you tell me about the drinking until now?"

Because he was public, and she wanted to stay private, and they were back to the problem that always plagued them. He sighed. "I was protecting you from it," he confessed.

"Well, don't do that anymore." She swatted him, but in a playful way that told him that while she was serious, she still forgave him. "I mean it."

In future, Jon knew that it could get far worse for her if sportswriters knew she was important to him. He could never let that happen. "Lizzy, I wasn't using you."

"I know, but do you see how it could appear that you used Brandon? Isn't it convenient that he's a cancer survivor with the Sunshine Club?"

"That's not how it was. I had my own issues with cancer in my family. I didn't even want to go into that damn kids' cancer ward. Brandon happened to be there that day, and he's the one who talked me through it—"

Damn. She had fooled him again. She had an expression on her face as if she was looking right into him, seeing all his problems. As if she was studying him the way she studied her archaeology magazines and her medical job.

"Look," he said, pushing away from her. "Let me talk with Brandon. He probably didn't wash up yet, so I'll help with that. Then I'll sit with him until he's feeling better."

"Please do not nurture us." She put her hands on her hips. "Jon, I see you. You're deflecting from what we're really talking about."

Great. Talking with her was like living with a shrink. "I just explained to you what's going on with me. If you're not interested, there's nothing more I can do here." He headed for the door.

But she wasn't following. She just stood with her arms crossed, a bemused look on her face, studying him.

He could go to Coach Duffy's place or even Brooke's condo. Scratch that, both were terrible ideas. Staying at Brooke's would be the wrong move for obvious reasons. And Coach Duffy...

Would lecture him. Just like in high school. About getting serious. About overcoming his family problems. *"Everybody has family problems. You got dealt a tough break. We all get tough breaks, some of us sooner rather than later. But the mark of a man is how you pick yourself up and overcome them."*

Jon closed his hand around the doorknob. If he was going to have to face hard truths about making poor choices and allowing himself to get sucked into a scandal and throwing everything away that he'd worked so hard for, then he would much rather face those truths with Lizzy. There was always the hope that he could sweet-talk her into bed and cover her mouth with kisses....

"Jon?" Her tone was gentle. "You told me last weekend that your mom died when you were young. Did she die of cancer?"

He had expected many things, but not that question. Jon turned to look at her.

She wasn't saying anything. Just studying him. Quietly compassionate.

"Yeah," he said, exhaling. "But don't tell that to any of the Sunshine Club people."

"I won't," she said quietly.

He trusted her. His Liz was a locked vault. Other people…Susan, if she knew…

"I don't want to be exploited like that," he said.

"I understand." She leaned her forehead into his shirt—his sweaty shirt, reminding him that he hadn't changed yet. "And now you understand why I didn't initially want my nephew involved in that hospital charity, because I don't want him exploited like that, either."

He stroked his hand over her head, making her sigh. "I won't let him be exploited. I promise you that."

SHE BELIEVED HIM.

Elizabeth pressed her hands around Jon's waist, her forehead to his chest. She was overcome with feeling for this outwardly tough, masculine man who hid his inner vulnerability about his past. Unable to stop herself, she'd crossed the gulf that separated them and pulled him close to her. She'd known as soon as he'd shown up at her front door that something was seriously wrong, because he was still in his workout clothes. He had razor stubble on his chin and jaw, and his hair was tousled. Grass streaks were on both knees of his close-fitting gray baseball pants, and his white shirt with the navy blue sleeves smelled of his scent.

She didn't care. She loved it, in fact.

She slid her hands beneath his shirt and over his chest. She loved that she was getting to know him more and more, inside and out. She could see now that it bothered him to have people fail to appreciate him, just as she desired so desperately to keep her self-reliance.

"I see you," she whispered. She ran her fingers over the sprinkling of chest hair over his pecs, over his heart. This man was constantly getting in trouble because it was his natural bent to look at the people around him, to observe what they needed, and to do what he could to help everybody out. It was what Jon did; it kept his demons at bay. And she would no more change that about him than she could change her own studious nature.

It calmed her to see this.

"Let me help you," she said. "I'll drive to your apartment and pick up some clothes. You can stay here with us as long as you like."

"You want me to stay?" he asked in that low, mystical voice.

She nodded, not trusting herself to speak.

CHAPTER FOURTEEN

WITH A LOW MOAN, Jon lowered his mouth to Elizabeth and kissed her, slow and deep, as if he never wanted the kiss to end…or her to leave. She felt his hunger and his desire, his hand that cradled her head and his tongue that swept inside her mouth, mingling with hers. She felt dizzy, standing on tiptoe to press closer to him. Her body melted against his, the full length of her torso to his. He felt so nice. She dragged her hand through his shorn hair. Over his strong, capable, bulky shoulders and around his neck.

He sighed, breaking the kiss, leaning his forehead to hers.

"Auntie?"

Elizabeth jumped. She'd forgotten about Brandon.

Jon gave her an amused, secret wink with those remarkable blue eyes. He squeezed her hand and then stepped around her to her nephew. "I'm staying for dinner tonight, buddy. It looks like we're having… uh…" He checked the counter by the stove where she'd been interrupted preparing their dinner. "Hot dogs with gluten-free buns." He made a grimace.

"Are the Captains going to kick you off the team?" Brandon asked.

"Brandon!" Elizabeth said. "That's not a nice question."

"It's okay, Lizzy," Jon said, kneeling to face her nephew. "I'm not going anywhere. You've got nothing to worry about. I told you, I'll fix this."

"How?" Brandon asked, echoing her concern. "You're not a free agent yet. And you're not a 10-5 man yet, so you can't veto a trade."

"What is he talking about?" Elizabeth asked Jon. "What's a 10-5 man?"

"It's inside baseball talk," Jon answered. "Like knowing how hot dogs are made. You're better off not knowing."

"I *like* knowing how things are made," she said.

He smiled at her. "Yeah, Lizzy, you would."

"I'll explain it, Auntie," Brandon said, picking up his baseball from the table and tossing it into the air. "It means that Jon isn't under contract, so the Captains don't have to keep him on the roster for next year if they don't want to, because he hasn't been with the team for seven years. But, if Jon had ten years in the major leagues, and five years with the Captains, then he would be a 10-5 man, and that means he'd be under contract and could veto a trade to another team." He tilted his head to Elizabeth. "Did you get all that?"

Not really. "More or less," she said.

But when Brandon's back was turned, Elizabeth whispered to Jon, "How are you going to get the Captains to keep you?"

"Do you want to help me?" Jon said. "Because there's that Sunshine Club fund-raiser event at the hospital coming up. Vivian Sharpe will be there. You could go with me as my date."

Go out in public with Jon like that? "I...don't think I can do that."

"Yeah, I didn't think so." Jon laughed, teasing her. He spoke close to her ear. "Then come to me tonight when Brandon is asleep. We'll lock the bathroom and take a shower together."

She gasped at him. "Jon!"

"What? Your door has a lock, doesn't it? We'll be quiet."

She felt breathless. Daring. Alive.

After dinner, she climbed into her Prius and drove the fifteen minutes into Boston to Jon's apartment tower. Once inside his lobby, she kept her head low and headed for the elevator. When she got to Jon's penthouse, she took the key he'd given her and let herself in.

She turned on the light, and immediately pressed her hand to her chest. His home was truly gorgeous. Huge and airy. In the dark of the night, she could see all the lights of Boston beyond his balcony windows. It was a beautiful place, for a beautiful guy.

But she had work to do. Jon had given her a list of things to gather and an empty duffel bag. She went into his bathroom first. There was so much intimacy in this simple errand. She snapped on the light and marveled at the walk-in shower, the big Jacuzzi tub and the clean, open space. From his list, he wanted her to gather his toothbrush and his own soap and shampoo.

"No offense, Lizzy," he'd said, "but if I smell like a flower in the locker room, I'll never hear the end of it." She used products with essential oils of frangipani flowers, her current favorite. Jon had insisted he liked it on her, but she could see where it would be too much for a man.

She found a travel case sitting open on the counter. Jon said he traveled so often that he still hadn't unpacked all his things. She zipped the travel case closed and placed it in the duffel bag she carried. Then she went into Jon's bedroom.

Everywhere, it smelled like him. Feeling lightheaded, she sat on his bed. King-size, with a thick comforter and firm pillows, as if he liked spending time sleeping comfortably. The sad thing was, she could picture herself sleeping here peacefully, too. She picked up his pillow and inhaled deeply, feeling contented with the desire that just couldn't seem to be extinguished, no matter how many times she saw him.

She carefully placed the pillow back on the bed. Of course, the arrangement between her and Jon was still just for the short term, wasn't it? When Jon had his contract signed and Brandon was returned to his mother, weren't they going back to their own separate lives again?

Truthfully, she wasn't sure she wanted that anymore. She wasn't sure *what* she wanted.

Feeling unsettled, she turned to leave. On the bureau at the end of the bedroom, near the windows, was a framed photo. This was the only photo or piece of artwork she'd seen in Jon's apartment, and it was of his family, grouped in a studio shot. His father, about Jon's age now, looked proud and happy. Very faintly, Elizabeth could see Jon in him—in the color of his hair and the shape of his eyes and chin. A woman sat in the photo—Jon's mom—and Elizabeth could see that Jon was definitely her son, too. She had the same easy smile, intelligent eyes and lines around her mouth.

Elizabeth felt sad all of a sudden. She came across people with sick family members all the time in the course of her job. Sometimes the stories didn't have happy endings but, always, Elizabeth had felt a layer removed from it. She'd had her barrier, her distance.

And she was losing that with Jon.

She tilted the photograph and studied the young Jon, and felt her heart cracking open. That was the only way to describe it. In the course of knowing him, he was opening her up. She wasn't sure she liked that.

She set the photo back on the bureau. Took note of the other two small boys. One, an infant, was posed on his mother's lap. The middle boy, closer in age to

Jon, stood with his hand gripped on his older brother's elbow.

This told her everything she needed to know. Jon was the glue in his family. His family needed him, and he needed them to need him.

She would never need him. Because she didn't *need* anybody. She was...an island of competence.

Jerking open the drawer in front of her, she found T-shirts and a few pairs of jeans, professionally folded, as if he used a service. She grabbed one of each. Just one, because Jon was staying at her place for only one night. That's what he'd specified.

A single item remained on his list. Underwear. He'd teased her about it—"I know you'll get your jollies going through my underwear drawer, Liz"—but after spending two weeks doing laundry for a little boy—a messy little boy—the novelty of handling male undergarments was lost. She'd never grown up in a house with a male, after all, but now it was getting to be old habit.

Still, her fingers lingered in the drawer. Soft underwear. Gray. The pair had fit Jon so well. She remembered him, standing in her apartment. How his erection had looked in them. The way he'd peeled them off.

She squeezed her eyes shut. And her phone rang, causing her to jump.

She dug it out of her purse. "What is it, Jon?"

"Just checking that you got there okay."

"I'm perfectly capable."

"Yup. You're also the type who won't ask directions if she's lost."

She sighed. "I am not lost. Actually, I have my hands in your underwear drawer at the moment."

He laughed. "Exactly what I'm dealing with here. Brandon was, uh, dancing around with your bra on his head until I rescued it. Word to the wise, Lizzy—don't leave unmentionables to dry where there are eight-year-old boys roaming around."

"That's great," she said, rolling her eyes. "Thanks for telling me."

"Is that what you doctors wear under your scrubs? Black lace bra and panties? Because I've always wondered."

"Is there anything else you need?" She shut his bureau drawer with her hip. "I'm on my way out."

"Yeah. Could you grab an energy drink from the fridge? And bring the loaf of bread. I know you think it tastes the same, but this gluten-free stuff just doesn't do it for me. Something I'm not willing to compromise on."

So he'd compromised on big stuff, but the little stuff tripped him up. "Got it. I'll be back in half an hour." She hesitated. "Wait…"

This "being domesticated" with another human—especially a guy—was a new experience for her. This was not the vision she'd ever had of herself. Sure, she had hoped for it someday—had sometimes enviously watched normal families on the street, but had assumed that she didn't have what it took to be part of that world.

This, though, she could handle. Jon let her be herself. He was always present—not absent, like her father—but not suffocating her, either.

It was nice, actually.

"Um, is Brandon okay?" she asked him.

"Yeah. My plan is to wear him out now so he'll sleep for us. Do you have any pharmaceutical-grade sleeping potions in that doctor bag of yours?"

She shivered. "Don't even joke about that."

Hanging up the phone, she went to his refrigerator. A nicer refrigerator than hers, and stocked. The sink was clean, too. She glanced back in the refrigerator, dipped her head and saw that the bottom shelf was lined with energy drinks. And beer.

She paused. No, no, no. She would never have beer in her house. It was just too dangerous.

Quickly, she grabbed two cans of the popular energy drink, and then took the loaf of bread from the center shelf.

Before she left, she glanced around his apartment one last time. She had to admit, for a guy who traveled a lot, the place was surprisingly homey.

She was heading toward the door when it opened. She froze, her heart in her throat. A man with his back to her was busy pulling his key from the lock. Not a big set of keys, like a maintenance man with a passkey, but someone Jon knew, whom he'd given his key to.

The man turned, and when he saw her, he jumped. "Whoa! You scared the shit out of me!"

Elizabeth gripped the duffel bag and squinted at him. "Francis? Is that you?"

"Yeah, I'm Frank," he said in that low voice so like Jon's. "Jon's brother."

"I met you," she said calmly. "The other day. Right here." She pointed to the couch.

He nodded slowly. "You were wearing that red dress."

"Yes, I'm Elizabeth."

Frank's gaze narrowed. "Jon doesn't have time for a girlfriend."

"Nor do I have time for a boyfriend," she said hurriedly. "Don't get the wrong impression. I'm just here picking up a few things for him." She lifted the duffel bag, but he didn't seem impressed. "Are the news vans still outside?"

"No." Frank shoved his keys into his front pocket. "But I don't like it. It's a bad time to be dealing with press. We don't have a contract for next season."

"We?"

Frank narrowed his gaze at her again. "Jon. You know what I mean."

No, she wasn't sure that she did. "Shouldn't Jon be the one to worry about that?"

"You don't understand how we are," he said defensively.

"I think I do understand," she said softly. "I also think you must have things in your own life that are yours alone. That aren't part of Jon's or anybody else's life. Those are the things you should treasure."

"Treasure?" He lifted his chin and scoffed at her. "What do you know about me? What did Jon say?"

"Nothing." She shrugged. "I just know Jon, and I know that he's going to be okay. He's a strong person and he'll find his way out of this."

"You really believe that?"

"Yes," she said. "I do."

Frank nodded. "In that case then, why don't you deliver this message to him?"

"Okay, what message?"

Frank scowled and crossed his arms. "Tell Jon that Dad called me. He's getting married in Arizona, and he doesn't want us there for it."

CHAPTER FIFTEEN

His FATHER WAS getting *married?*

Jon hadn't moved from where he sat on Lizzy's couch since she'd given him the news. His world was being upended. It was all he could process.

"Are you okay?" she asked him.

"No." Maybe he should go to Mr. Yanopoulis's house so he could grill his old neighbor for more information about his father's supposed bride.

But as Lizzy gazed at him, Jon realized he needed to go directly to the source. He took out his phone and stood. "I'm going to make a call."

"You can do it here," she offered.

"I don't want to wake Brandon."

She peered at him as if not believing him. Jon just…needed to be alone. He couldn't bear to see Lizzy's sympathetic eyes studying him as old wounds opened up and bled. So he threw on a sweatshirt and headed outside. Walked into the dark where he could have space to think, beside Brandon's pitch-back net on the quiet, lamp-lit lawn.

So many memories of similar times from his childhood. He sat on the curb and made the call to his father. Everything was changing, and he wasn't sure what he was going to do about it.

"Hi, Dad," he said quietly when his father picked up. "Frank told me you're getting married."

"Ah, hell. It's just a casual thing we're throwing together. I told him not to say anything."

"Why, Dad?" Jon stood and walked from the sidewalk to the pitch-back net. It pained him to have to ask this. "Who is she?"

"You know Mary Angela."

"Mary Angela Curtin?" That was the sister of the guy whose town house his dad was staying with in Phoenix. She was Jean Yanopoulis's friend.

He tried to remember if his mother knew her, but he couldn't be sure.

Shit. "Dad, isn't she the woman with all those poodles? You hate poodles. You're a cat guy."

"Eh. She only has two. The dogs drove with us in the RV. They're not bad, Tiger won't mind them."

Jon held the phone at arm's length. Was he in the Twilight Zone? "Where did this decision even come from?"

"Aw, come on." His dad sighed. "Look, she's a great lady. We like it in Arizona together."

"Wait—do you mean that not only are you getting married in Arizona, but you're gonna move there, too?"

"Why not? You like Phoenix," he said defensively. "Remember the good times we had watching you play out here in the minors?"

"Yeah." Jon had loved his time there between college and the majors. As far as he knew, though, his father hadn't been interested in their neighbor back then.

He hoped not, because Mary Angela's husband had been alive in those days. A big, barrel-chested cop who'd died of a heart attack in the line of duty. The funeral had been huge.

She was a widow, like his dad was a widower. Jon couldn't help asking: "Do you love her, Dad?"

"She ain't your mother." His dad's voice was faint and sad. "But I like it here with her. Besides, you three are settled now. You've got Bobby set up with his college. Frank has the house, and it's time he had it all to himself. You're fine—you've always been able to take care of yourself. Nobody has ever had to worry about you, no sir."

Jon gritted his teeth. "You weren't going to tell me? You were just going to get married and move to Arizona and then surprise us all?"

"Why not? I don't want you to make a fuss. You always make a fuss."

"Not this time, Pop." Jon thought about hanging up the phone, but he wasn't that dramatic.

"You have your own problems. Frank called me today, but I already knew about that article. I read it on the computer. Mary Angela has a subscription to both Boston papers. She knows how to set up these things." His voice filled with pride.

Jon closed his eyes. "Great."

"Be careful you don't lose everything you worked for over this drinking thing," his father warned.

There was no "drinking thing." And there was nothing more to say. Jon muttered a goodbye to his dad and then ended the call. He trudged back upstairs to Lizzy's place. He found her dressed in a silky green bathrobe with a gigantic Chinese dragon embroidered on it. She was looking at him thoughtfully.

He reached into her refrigerator and grabbed one of the energy drinks she'd brought over from his place.

"Is everything okay?" she asked softly.

No. My life is frigging falling apart. But he smiled at her. "Yeah. I've got one more phone call to make. A short one."

"Okay. Feel free to make it here. Brandon is asleep. He won't wake up."

"Are you sure?" he asked in a low voice.

"Take your time." She smiled and rubbed her arms. Then she went into her bedroom and closed the door. Jon had never felt more grateful to her. This was a woman who understood privacy.

He picked up his phone again and called Bobby. Broke the news in as neutral a manner as possible.

"Wow, that's awesome," his kid brother said. "It's about time Dad got remarried."

Jon's hand involuntarily tightened on the phone. Bobby *would* feel that way. He'd been an infant when their mom had gotten sick. He'd confessed to Jon once that he couldn't even remember what their mother's voice had sounded like.

"I like Mary Angela," Bobby said. "She has hot daughters, too. Have you ever met the twins?"

Jon remembered them as two ponytailed rug rats about Bobby's age who liked to switch identities. Probably interesting as college girls, but he wasn't a cradle robber. "No," Jon said. "But it sounds as if you knew Dad was seeing her. Am I the only one who didn't?"

"I knew it was her he went to Vegas with, but he asked me not to tell you and Frank about it. Jeez, Jon, quit hating on him, it's a good thing. Wish him well."

Stung, Jon hung up the phone. Long after the call ended, he sat staring into space.

His father was getting married and moving away. Their dad didn't need the memory of their mom anymore. That meant he didn't need Jon anymore, either.

Jon took a long drink from the can. Rationally, his father acting happy and getting on with his life was a good thing. A positive for everybody in the family. But why couldn't he feel it?

"Jon?" Elizabeth stood in the doorway.

He started. He hadn't known she was still awake.

"Do you want to talk?" she asked.

He shook his head. Really, he felt weary. It had been a long, lousy day. The worst day he could remember in a long time. The newspaper article, people blaming him, the team scapegoating him—that was crappy enough.

But his dad getting married…that had just sucker

punched him. He felt eight years old again, alone, and with a hole the size of Arizona in his heart.

She nodded and left him alone. He heard a door close, and then after a time, the running water.

Lizzy...I need Lizzy.

Of everybody he'd pushed away tonight, she was the only one he really, truly wanted to be with.

He got up and tried the bathroom door. It was open, so he went inside. A layer of steam fogged the mirror and warmed his face. Lizzy's back was to him, adjusting the spray of the shower, and she was still wearing that silky Chinese dragon robe with the embroidered orange fire. The belt cinched her waist tight, and beneath that was smooth silk covering the most beautiful, rounded ass he'd ever seen in his life.

He went from zero to hard in two seconds. When he closed and locked the door behind them, she turned.

"Jon?"

He put his finger to his lips. Then he put his lips beside her ear. "We can't talk. Brandon's asleep."

She shivered, and he wrapped his arms around her from behind, pressing her bottom against his erection. She stirred beneath him and he nearly groaned, but he suppressed the noise.

She turned her head, planting a soft kiss on his jaw. "I'm glad you're here," she whispered.

His heart seemed to break open. "I want you," he murmured back. "You're the only person who makes me feel better."

She sighed, her big brown eyes gazing at him. Kissing her beautiful long neck, exposed by her short hair, he nudged her robe open and ran his hands up, between her thighs and over her belly to her breasts, caressing the weight of them. She gasped, rubbing her bottom against him, and he thought he might lose it at that moment. He gently spun her so she was facing him, and kissed her, deeply.

God, he needed this woman. Needed her arms around his neck, the flesh of her hips in his hands, her long leg, curving around his backside.

"I didn't…expect…this…" she whispered.

He hadn't, either. Not really. Not this feeling.

With the splash of the shower in the background, a constant drumming of water spray on the tub, he intertwined his tongue with hers, tasting the peppermint toothpaste still on her breath.

She sighed and broke his kiss. "Your shower would work so much better for this."

Lazily, he smiled at her. He'd forgotten she'd been in his apartment tonight. Obviously, she'd looked around and liked what she saw. That gave him a sense of masculine pride.

Never had a woman fit so well with him. "As long as we're taking the risk of conversing, are you on birth control? Or do we need the doctor kit with your condoms again?"

She gave him a secret smile. "Until I met you, I didn't need birth control. The condoms are in the drawer beside the tub." She indicated with her chin.

"There." He glanced, and saw that the placement was perfect. He could reach for the drawer when he was ready.

But it appeared she was more ready than he was.

She tugged at the button on his pants. He peeled off his T-shirt and obediently stripped down his pants and his boxer briefs.

And then with her smile gazing into his eyes, she parted the shower curtain and led him inside. And inside that pitiful little shower tub, she soaped him up from head to toe, taking her time lavishing care and attention on every part of him. She shampooed his hair, a long, gentle massage using his shampoo. He felt the stress of the day, all the pain, leaching out and running down the drain. And when all the soap and shampoo was washed out and he felt better, he took his time with her, too. Bathed her with that exotic, Hawaiian girly-smelling soap she used. Rubbed the bath sponge over every inch of skin.

But then he could no longer stand it. He let the sponge drop and, instead, caressed her with his bare fingers. With his thumbs. With his mouth. She was wet and stretched for him, her breathing getting harder. He found the condom, pulled it on and she guided him inside her. Standing in the shower with the water, now cool, raining down on both of them. Her legs were long compared to his, and their height worked together. *They* just worked.

She was exactly what he needed after a day in which everyone had seemed against him.

AFTERWARD, THEY TIPTOED from the bathroom, as quietly as possible. "Do you want to sleep in my room?" Elizabeth whispered to Jon.

"Not with Brandon here, I don't," he murmured.

"You're right. I almost forgot, I'm so used to whispering."

Elizabeth prepared a makeshift bed on the couch for Jon. She smoothed fresh sheets over the cushions, plumped a clean pillowcase onto her spare pillow and found him a warm blanket.

Alone in her own bed, she thought about Jon sleeping in her home—wonderful, happy thoughts—until she fell asleep herself.

The next morning, Jon was gone before Elizabeth woke. She found the pillow, sheets and blanket folded at the end of her couch. His clothes that she'd brought back from his apartment were gone. She looked for a note but didn't see one.

Being a Saturday, she drove Brandon to play with Caitlin's son for the day, and then headed to the hospital for her work shift, feeling strangely bereft.

She was shaky inside. The lovemaking last night had been different from before. Her boundaries toward Jon were shredded, it seemed. The physical intimacy was deeper. There were emotions in her heart she had shared—about her mom and sister, about her fears with alcohol—that were new to her. She had let Jon deeper into her world over these past weeks than she'd let anyone before. It was exhilarating. And yet, terrifying.

As open as Jon was with her—physically, at least—he didn't once share how he felt about what was going on with his family. Yes, he had expressed it through his lovemaking but, under pretext of needing to keep quiet for Brandon, they hadn't discussed it. It made her feel left out and a bit empty. She hadn't realized the extent of it until she'd been struck by his empty bed and folded sheets that morning.

Did she even have a right to ask Jon about how he felt? They had an agreement, after all. An end to their time: just eight more days, by her calendar. Nine, if she counted tonight, but he hadn't mentioned anything about wanting to get together later.

Things *were* becoming confusing between them. This wasn't just a controlled fling anymore; last night, after she had come home from meeting Frank, it had spun out of her control and gone beyond her reach.

How could she go back to the prudent person she had been before meeting Jon, and life without him in it, after what she was feeling for him now?

She pulled into the parking garage at her hospital, not thrilled about the weekend shift she'd had to pick up, and the fresh day of emergency cases ahead. She hurried toward the elevators, pulling her long sweater tighter around her in the cool morning air—so suddenly colder overnight that she could see her breath hanging in the air before her—when her cell phone rang.

Her pulse leaped, but no, it wasn't Jon, it was her mother. The call Elizabeth had been dreading. "Hi,

Lisbeth, this is Mother. I booked a flight into Boston this Friday, arriving at twelve-thirty."

Elizabeth pulled her sweater even tighter. "That's good, Mom, but I haven't checked my schedule yet. If I'm working, you'll have to take a taxi."

"Well. I was hoping to see my grandson before I checked into my hotel."

Elizabeth swallowed. "You need to discuss that with Ashley and her counselor when you see them. Brandon won't be part of your session because, according to their rules, he's too young."

"Lisbeth. The only reason I'm going up there in the first place is because Ashley needs me." Her mother sounded huffy and self-righteous. But that was typical.

Elizabeth fought the urge to hang up and flee, but she stayed on the line. Jon would stay on the line. "I'm glad you'll be present for her, Mom. She wants you to see her."

"The counselor said you're invited to meet with us, too."

He should not have said that. Elizabeth gripped her phone. "It was agreed that it's best for you and Ashley to spend the day together. You'll help her by being there."

"Well, I just don't know."

"I need to go, Mom." Elizabeth checked her watch. "I'm at work now, my shift is starting. Good luck with your travel next Friday."

She hung up the phone and hurried through the

automatic doors to the hospital. Her pulse was racing. If she let her mother close, her mother would consume her. She needed to stay free.

Heading into the coffee shop, intent on a large, double-shot latte to make her feel better, she almost bumped into Albert.

He smiled at her from his position waiting in line. "Hello, Elizabeth. I see you're on my team this morning."

"Am I?" She gazed at the muffin selection inside a display case. Just another person she did not want to see or talk to.

"I was going to call you this weekend," he said from behind her.

It was hard to believe she had ever considered him a potential boyfriend. Elizabeth made her muffin selection—it would be a long time in surgery—and then turned to face him. "Thank you, Albert, but I don't think that's a good idea. You and I are best as work friends. Professional colleagues."

He shrank back. "Of course." He didn't say another word, and as soon as he could, he hurried from the café.

She stared after him. No, she did not want to be with Albert. But she did feel better after their brief exchange. More like a person who coped rather than a person who avoided the difficult conversations.

Feeling thoughtful, she went to her first case of the morning. As usual, she monitored the digital readings on the screen in front of her, and her shift passed quickly. The wonderful thing about her job was that it occupied her. While she worked, she rarely had time to consider what was missing in the rest of her life.

But once her case was over, her mind returned to thinking of Jon again. She thought of the way he made love to her. The look on his face during that last moment before he came inside her.

Shaken, she closed her eyes. This would not do…

And then, without much notice, Jon strolled into her work space. Her department seemed to go quiet as he walked toward her. All the nurses and orderlies and medical patients watched him. A more recent photo of him had been in the newspaper this morning, and people recognized him now.

This time, Jon was a curiosity. There were whisperings and comments behind the backs of hands. Nobody asked him for his autograph, though Jon didn't seem to notice or care.

Her heart swelled. His courage in the face of his public humiliation made him even more compelling to her. She ached.

Jon held his head high, as if he respected himself no matter what anyone else thought. But she knew the truth. Oh, she knew. She'd never met a man who cared more about pleasing people than Jon did. Now that she knew about his family, she could understand why.

"Lizzy, babe." Jon leaned over and kissed her cheek. His face lit up to see her.

She felt her bones melting. "What are you doing here?"

"I made a decision." Jon pulled her aside so no one could hear them. "I'm flying to Arizona this Friday for my father's wedding."

"That's…good. Really good."

He nodded. "I don't like having things weird with my family. I needed to settle it."

She thought briefly of her mom, and silently agreed with him. "I think that's a wise idea."

"Yeah. And if the wedding sucks, Arizona is always great to visit, anyway."

"Right." She nodded, knowing she would miss him. But that was crazy of her, wasn't it? Where had the old Elizabeth LaValley gone?

"I haven't told you the best part." Jon gave her a grin, showing off those dimples. "I know you can't leave Brandon alone, so I bought three seats together in first class. I hope the name on your ticket matches the name on your driver's license."

"What are you talking about?" she asked, dumbfounded.

He gave her an innocent look. "You won't be able to fly otherwise, Lizzy. Homeland security rules."

"Let me see that." Her hand shaking, she took the printout and studied the passenger names on the airline itinerary: Jon Farell, Elizabeth LaValley, Brandon LaValley.

She felt a funny feeling in the pit of her stomach.

"The tickets are refundable," Jon said. "But I really would like you to go."

"You want *me?*" she whispered. "And Brandon… to go to your family's wedding?"

"Yeah." He waited until an orderly with a rattling cart of dirty lunch trays passed by, and then Jon stepped closer, smoothing her hair with his thumb. "Brandon is only invited because he comes attached to you. You're the main attraction."

"But wh-why?"

He smiled. "Because you're beautiful, Lizzy."

She blinked away the moisture in her eyes. She was not beautiful. She was everyday in looks. Beautiful women were all around him, from Susan Vanderbilt to Brooke, his agent who Elizabeth had noticed accompanying him to his original surgery.

Elizabeth stared at the pocket on Jon's chest. "You could have any beautiful woman you wanted."

"I don't want another beautiful woman. I want the one who will go with me as Jon Farell, the kid from Massachusetts, and not just a baseball star, even a fallen one."

She let that digest. "I thought you were going with your brothers," she murmured.

"Frank has my credit card number. He can book flights for him and Bobby. It's time they step up and take care of themselves."

She put her hand to her mouth. Oh, God, it really was happening. She and Jon were growing closer. "Does…your dad want me to come?"

"He wants what I want." Jon dropped his hand to her hip. "So how about it?"

She was running out of peripheral excuses. There was something more she wanted Jon to say to her. To express for her. But nobody could force that on another person.

"Lizzy, please go with me," Jon said quietly, drawing her by the waist to him. "Don't make me pull rank, because I will if I have to. We have one more date, and it's my pick." He sighed. "Look, you were right. There's nothing long-term between us. Your sister is coming back, what, the day after the wedding, the Sunday we fly home? Consider it our last hurrah if you want. It won't cost you anything but your weekend. And hey, I'm throwing in Brandon as a bonus. If you decide you don't like hanging out with me in Arizona, then you can go off and tour Sedona with your nephew, or even take him to a minor league baseball game. He'd love that. Consider it an escape plan."

"There's nothing long-term between us?" With that one phrase he had crushed all her hopes.

"Like you said." He looked relieved, misunderstanding her. "And thank you for being there for me last night. I wasn't thrilled about hearing my dad is getting married. I don't know anyone else who would understand. You're really someone special."

He rubbed his knuckle along her lip. "So how about it? We leave on Friday."

"Friday," she repeated. That was the date her mother was arriving in Boston.

"Yeah, we'll be home by Sunday afternoon for the Sunshine Club fund-raiser."

And for Ashley's return from rehab on Sunday night. But it was the Friday date that stuck in her mind.

She just knew it would be a mistake.

CHAPTER SIXTEEN

THAT FRIDAY MORNING, they were up in the air.

Elizabeth had taken a vacation day for herself and then signed out Brandon midmorning. She didn't like removing him from school, even for a "family wedding," but he was still young and in a low grade, and his teacher was accommodating. She gave Elizabeth homework sheets for Brandon to complete, which he could work on during the plane ride.

She also had made sure she got all the relevant permission she needed to take Brandon on a cross-country flight. Though Ashley's counselor wasn't pleased that Elizabeth was unable to attend family counseling with Ashley and their mother, Elizabeth had already completed intensive therapy sessions during medical school. She knew herself, and she knew that limited contact with her mom was all she could handle.

But that wasn't her biggest problem. She put her book away in her travel bag beneath her seat and glanced up in time to see Jon returning, coming down the aisle toward her, an easy smile on his face. This man just had an aura that drew people to him like magnets.

He handed her a full can of sparkling water.

"Nice flight attendants we have on this plane," he remarked.

"That's because they're female, and you're a hot male."

He raised a brow. "You think I'm hot, huh?"

She just smiled. As he opened the overhead bin to grab something from his stowed carry-on bag, she watched the sliver of skin that appeared between his waistband and the bottom of his shirt. Those pheromones hadn't yet gone away for her—their force hadn't even diminished. She was beginning to think they probably never would.

She shifted in her seat, mindful to check on Brandon. Her nephew sat in the window seat beside Jon's brother Bobby, his face glued to the window. It was the first time Brandon had flown in an airplane, and he appeared to be beside himself with joy. Elizabeth was grateful that Jon's brother was such a good sport about it all. He kept Brandon busy by letting him watch television episodes on his iPad, and periodically giving him a running commentary of exactly what part of the country they were flying over, from the hills of New England to the crest of the Rockies, to the plains of the desert.

It was surreal. They were all going away for the weekend together. The troubling part was that she was looking forward to it. Spending time with Jon was becoming more enjoyable than being alone with herself.

IT WAS STRANGE, but arriving at the wedding reception with Elizabeth and Brandon, Jon felt as if he was with his own little family. If anyone had said earlier in the summer that he would be in this position at season's end, he wouldn't have believed them. Everything in his life seemed to be turning upside down.

Maybe his father's marriage had thrown him for a loop. Jon only knew that he hadn't wanted to face it alone. He didn't want to think about what it would mean for his future. And the only person he could imagine accompanying him to get through it without having to interact with anybody too much was Lizzy.

He led her and Brandon through the flowering cactus garden at the stucco village where Jon's dad was marrying Mary Angela Curtin. The dry Arizona desert seemed as far away from New England as two places could be. But he was here, and he was going to try to accept it.

He girded himself to meet his father's new wife. His *stepmother*.

But when his father introduced him to her, Mary Angela Curtin wore a huge, beaming smile. Thankfully she hadn't gone all out with a big white wedding dress and all the bridezilla trappings, but instead had decided on hosting a small gathering with just his dad's family and hers.

Jon felt himself relaxing. He put his hand into Lizzy's. It felt…right that she was with him. Though it was true Brandon was not his kid, it also felt right to have Brandon there with them.

The boy tugged on Jon's belt loop. "Can you show me where the men's room is?"

"Sure, buddy." He turned to Lizzy and said, "Will you be okay while I go take care of Brandon?"

"Yes, I'll be fine," she said. Jon settled Lizzy into a garden chair and excused himself.

Inside the village clubhouse, cool in the air-conditioning, he found the restrooms and waited outside for Brandon, just as his brother Francis arrived.

Cleaned up, Jon's brother was shaved and his hair parted and combed back. Like Jon, he wore tan chinos and a short-sleeved dress shirt. He smelled faintly of aftershave.

But it was the fact that Francis had a woman on his arm—a pretty redhead—that caused Jon's eyes to pop.

He clapped his brother on the shoulder. "Hey, Frank." He smiled at Frank's date, waiting for an introduction.

"This is Emily," Frank said. He had a touch of pride in his voice. But when he saw Jon studying him, he tightened his jaw and looked red faced. "Emily, this is my brother Jon."

"I'm pleased to meet you," Jon said to her.

"Hi, Jon," Emily said. "You don't remember me? My older brother is Donnie Gagne."

"I remember Donnie." He had been Jon's third baseman on their high school varsity baseball team.

It made Jon smile to think of him. "What's he up to these days?"

"Construction work with Frank." Emily glanced shyly at Jon's brother.

Frank flushed red again.

Emily squeezed his hand and looked back at Jon. "Donnie bounces at a bar in Quincy Market on the weekends."

Jon would have to stop by and see his old teammate sometime. When Emily excused herself to say hello to Mary Angela, Jon leaned into Francis's ear. "Are you sure you know what you're doing? Donnie will kick your ass if he finds out you took his sister on a weekend jaunt."

"Actually, I've been sort of dating her for a while," Francis said.

"Sort of? What does that mean?"

"Check out her ring finger when she gets back."

Jon felt flabbergasted. "What—you asked her to *marry* you?"

"Last Friday night."

Jon raked back his hair. His world really was coming undone.

"Hello, Emily." Dad came over and kissed Frank's date on the cheek.

"You knew about this?" Jon asked.

"Of course I knew," Dad said. "Emily is by the house all the time. She's from the neighborhood."

It just went to show how much Jon missed, being out of town on the road all season long.

Jon left them and found Lizzy by the garden. Brandon saw him and ran to his side. The boy's new shoes were huge on his skinny feet, and made him look like a baby Frankenstein.

Jon shared a look with Lizzy and leaned close, lingering to inhale the soft scent of her skin. He placed his hand on Brandon's shoulder.

But his whole family had followed him, and Jon was left with no choice but to introduce them all to her. "Lizzy and Brandon, this is my brother Frank and his fiancée, Emily. You've already met my dad."

They took turns shaking hands and greeting each other. Lizzy was doing well feigning the skills of an extrovert. He knew she felt awkward being here with other people. She was making this effort in order to be with him. Brandon, of course, was his usual, curious self.

Lizzy smiled at him. Jon clasped Lizzy's hand and pulled it against his thigh. Brandon took his other hand. And when the music of the Spanish guitar that played out in the cactus garden summoned them, Jon led his makeshift family to their seats.

He was starting to feel that he could get used to this. And that seemed a dangerous way to feel.

OKAY, ELIZABETH THOUGHT, settling into her chair beside Emily, who had thrust out her hand at her. This was a girl thing, wasn't it, to ooh and aah over engagement rings?

She peered at the ring. She didn't know much about

diamonds. It had been one of those topics that she'd always deliberately steered away from. Her mom had never married, and neither had Ashley, even though Elizabeth knew they had both wanted to. In her family, the topic of engagement rings and weddings felt like…

Like it hurt.

But Emily didn't know that. So Elizabeth smiled gamely at her. She was trying hard to learn how to do this—to meet people with whom she had little in common. For a moment, she wished she was at home, or alone somewhere with Jon and Brandon, but that wasn't going to happen any time too soon.

"Your ring is interesting." Elizabeth tilted her head. When the diamond hit the light, a rainbow of colors burst forth. Scientifically, she wondered at the way the cuts had been arranged to get this desired effect.

"You should have seen Frank when he proposed to me," Emily murmured. The guitarist was still strumming away, in the lull before the ceremony started. It was warm outside, and the woman in the chair in front of Elizabeth was fanning her face.

"We've been together for months," Emily continued, "but still, he caught me off guard. It was sweet."

"How did it happen?" Elizabeth asked.

"He got down on one knee. He said I was his *treasure*. Isn't that romantic?"

His treasure? Elizabeth had given Frank that word, the night at Jon's apartment.

She glanced at Jon. He gave her a sheepish look,

as if to thank her for being a good sport. Elizabeth did like that he hadn't treated her like an alien species. He'd introduced her to his family and taken for granted that she was as normal as he was.

Or maybe he wasn't normal, either. He was staring at Emily, listening to her romantic story as if *Emily* was the alien species.

"Do you want to see my ring, Jon?" Emily thrust it before his nose.

"That's uh…yeah," Jon said.

Elizabeth covered her mouth before her laugh could escape.

Jon glanced at her and smiled.

"You don't recognize it?" Frank asked him, seated on the other side of Emily. "It's Mom's ring, you know."

Jon's smile froze in place.

Uh-oh. Elizabeth felt a burst of indignation on his behalf. How clueless could some people be?

"Could you excuse us for a minute?" Jon said to her and Emily. He rose, hooking Francis by the arm. "I need you to show me the bar. I have a scratchy throat and I want some water."

"But the wedding march will be starting soon," Emily protested.

Jon gave his brother a dark look. "Don't worry. This will only take five minutes."

JON INTENDED TO ask Frank just what the hell he thought he was doing. But they had no sooner left the garden where the wedding ceremony was set to begin, than both Bobby and their father joined Jon and Frank at the now-quiet bar.

It was a trap. A trap to catch Jon.

"You're serious about Elizabeth," his dad said to him. "You've never been serious about anyone before."

"Neither have you," Jon retorted.

"I've been watching you two together," Bobby said, piling onto the ambush. "Elizabeth is good for you. She calms you down."

"That's the last time I pay for your airline ticket." Jon scowled at the three of them. "And weren't all of you telling me not too long ago that you didn't want me having a girlfriend because it would screw up my baseball career? Make up your minds."

The three of them glanced at each other. Dad sighed. "It's nice having Mary Angela around," he said gruffly. "The right woman can make life easier. Mary Angela makes everything worth it, and keeps me from screwing up too badly." He shrugged. "What can I say? I'm going to like being married to her."

"Yeah," Frank said. "Ditto." He put his arm around Jon. "Don't you care about Elizabeth? She's a smart lady. I like her. And you must feel something for her too, or else why would you have flown her and Brandon all the way out here?"

"Admit it, big brother," Bobby said.

Frank nodded.

What was this? An intervention? "Of course I care

about her," Jon said, flustered. Why was it any of their business how he felt about Lizzy? "The easiest part of my day is having her with me. Not dealing with you jokers."

"Jokers, huh?" Bobby said. "I'll remember that the next time you need your computer fixed."

"Okay, enough," Francis told his dad and Bobby. "Go back in there and tell the ladies we'll be right out. I want a minute alone with Jon."

"With *me?*" Jon sputtered. "You're treating *me* like the screwup brother? Francis, I'm gonna kick your—"

"No," Francis said. "You're not. This is *my* turn to help *you*. So let me do it."

"Frank—"

"For old time's sake, Jon. For *Mom's* sake."

Jon closed his mouth. Frank had used the "mom" card. They didn't do that in their family—ever.

Slumping onto a stool, he glanced out the clubhouse window. Observed the sunny Arizona day.

Francis reached over and poured them both water from a pitcher on the waitress stand. "We stuck together all these years. The four of us." Frank put a glass before Jon, the ice cubes rattling. "I was talking with Dad about it the other night. Do you really think Mom would want us to grow old being hermits?" He drank his water, giving Jon a meaningful look over the rim of the glass. "I don't. I think she would be happy for Dad."

"Come on, Frank. Admit it. You were upset when you heard about Dad's wedding."

"Yeah, well, I did some thinking and changed my mind. But we're not talking about Dad now—we're talking about you. Do you love Elizabeth?" Frank asked him.

"That isn't fair."

"Why not? You brought her all the way out here to be with us. To be with you, because you're terrified of this."

"You're crazy."

"You're terrified that she'll leave you, too," Francis insisted.

Jon paused, the glass of water midair, the condensation cool on his hands. "Frank…"

"I get it," Francis said quietly. "In a way, I'm leaving you now. Dad's leaving you. Someday, Bobby's gonna leave you, too."

Jon had to admit, it kicked him in the gut a little bit to think of that. Everything was changing so fast.

"And you know who left you first?" Frank continued. "Mom. She left you. Well, that's what you think. I mean, I sorta did, too, so I know where you're coming from. But I manned up…eventually." His chin lifted. "How about you, Jon?"

He drew his hand through his hair. He could not look at Francis.

"I gave Emily Mom's ring," Francis said quietly, "and I hope that's okay with you. But I loved Mom, too. I remember her, too. And so does Emily. She wants to wear Mom's ring for me, and I think I'm pretty lucky for that." He got up from his stool. "And once you're ready to move on, there are other pieces in Mom's jewelry box, if you want them. If there's ever someone special you'd like to give something of Mom's to."

Jon put his hand over his mouth. He was physically shaking.

"I'm sorry to do this to you, Jon." Frank's hand clasped his shoulder. "But Elizabeth started it all. She told me not to live through you anymore. And I'm not. Actually, come to think of it, I should probably thank her for that sometime."

Before Jon could say a word, his brother walked off.

Jon drank the rest of the water in the glass. He couldn't stop the shaking. But Frank was right about one thing—he needed to man up. He'd promised he would be here for the ceremony, and he intended to keep that promise.

He got back to his chair two minutes after Frank. Just as Jon seated himself next to Lizzy, the guitarist stopped playing. Everyone turned in their seats.

Emily tugged on his pitching arm. "The bride is here! Doesn't Mary Angela look so beautiful?" She sighed happily and pulled out her phone, setting it to videotape the ceremony.

Jon rubbed at his pitching arm, feeling physically ill. He felt like walking out. But Frank was sitting on the other side of Emily, staring at him.

The reverend launched into the wedding ceremony. Listening to the words, Jon felt doubtful at first. He cringed whenever the reverend talked about husband and wife, life and love.

But then the reverend spoke of the power of love and renewal. Of the stages and cycles of life. Of death circling into beginning and rebirth. Like the cycles of springtime to summer on an oak tree, from seedling to stripling to mature oak, there were many facets to a man and a woman's journey.

The remainder of the ceremony was quietly simple but effective. The tension in Jon's shoulders seemed to ease.

By the time Jon's dad kissed the bride, Jon had a slightly different perspective—he felt more relaxed, calm and maybe even optimistic.

Inside, he didn't seem to be fighting so much anymore.

"WHAT DID YOU think of the wedding?" Elizabeth asked Jon later that afternoon.

"You're alone with me in my bedroom," Jon replied. "I'd rather think about you, instead."

It was early evening and they were in Jon's very nice hotel room. She and Brandon were sharing a smaller room with two double beds across the hall. It was the first time she and Jon had been alone together like this in days.

Brandon was down in the main courtyard pool with some kids he'd met at the cake-and-champagne reception—grandchildren of the bride. Their mother had reassured Elizabeth that her nephew would be fine. For a rare two hours, Elizabeth didn't have to mind her nephew.

She lay fully clothed on the bed with Jon. Not saying much of anything, he leisurely stroked her hair and played with her fingers. Elizabeth just could not help it—she loved being wrapped up in Jon's arms while he held her close.

She felt languid and comforted. Watching him at the wedding had given her a better understanding of him. He'd seemed…sullen at first, doubtful. But the reverend's sermon made him sit up straighter. And by the end of the ceremony, Jon's face had fewer lines in it, as if he'd let his cares be lifted and taken away.

Maybe there was hope for him. That made her feel safer. And feeling safer was making her brave.

Turning her head, she contemplated the bottle of champagne beside the bed. A gift from Jon's new mother-in-law, the hotel had brought it up, chilling inside an ice bucket, along with a tray of chocolate-covered strawberries and two empty flutes.

Elizabeth had silently fixated on the bottle when they'd first come into the room, fresh from the wedding. All the adults at the reception had drunk a champagne toast to the new couple: everyone except Elizabeth. It had felt conspicuous to her.

Elizabeth had never dared to have even a sip of wine. Which, if she thought of it as a scientist, did seem silly. It wasn't illegal, immoral, or even proven to be harmful or allergenic to her.

And if this was a day of cycling and rebirth, certainly she could allow herself to taste some expensive fermented grapes—part of their culture, after all—with the one man she felt safe to do so beside.

If there was a problem, he would take care of her. She had no doubt about that. And it didn't frighten her, either.

Elizabeth sat up and hefted the cold bottle, the condensation wet on her hands. She had no idea how to even open the thing. "Could you help me with this?"

Jon rolled over and looked at her for a long moment. "Are you sure?"

"I trust you," she said simply.

He nodded. She was glad he didn't make a big deal of it. He just sat up and took the bottle from her, unwrapped the foil and the wire and twisted the cork in his palm. It made a muted popping noise. He poured about a half inch of the sparkling clear liquid into one of the flutes, then an equal amount in the other.

Solemnly, he passed her a glass.

"Do you know standard resuscitation measures?" she asked.

He smirked. "I'm learning." Then he clinked his glass with hers. "To beginners," he said.

"All right, but you have to promise to stop me if I get out of hand." She took a hesitant sip, then immediately curled up her nose. The champagne tasted so…tart. "This is supposed to be pleasant?"

"It's an acquired taste, Lizzy."

She put down the flute, stretched out on the bed and waited for the reaction to come.

He was trying not to laugh. "You really are so damn lovable."

Lovable. That was very, very close to love. But Jon was already kissing her again, working magic with his mouth. She felt herself falling under his spell. He was irresistible to her.

Her heart was gone; she knew it was much too late to fight it. Could she really be in love with Jon? She had to admit that she felt the same way about him as she did about any subject dear to her heart. Consumed. Greedy. And she would happily think only of him all day long if she could.

She ran her hands beneath his dress shirt, over his smooth back. His body was strong and athletic. And it was sad, but she was beginning to feel proprietary over it. She cupped his buns in her hands, enjoying his beauty.

With a groan, he quickly stripped her of her clothing, and she didn't protest, she was ready for him. He found a condom and entered her in one smooth motion. She felt as if she was in heaven. He had such a soulful way of making love to her. The way he loved to give her pleasure, and to receive it from her, too.

When they were together, time passed much too quickly. "Damn it," Jon said, turning to squint at the clock. His new mother-in-law had asked them to meet her and Jon's father for a two-on-two dinner. Jon was the only brother she didn't know well, she'd said.

"Let's get this dinner thing over with and then come back here," he said. "Maybe we can convince

Brandon to have a sleepover with Bobby, if my brother hasn't managed to attach himself to one of Mary Angela's twins."

Jon was making jokes, but Elizabeth noticed the crease in his brow again.

"Jon, I'm sorry," Elizabeth said, swinging her legs over the edge of the bed. "As much as I'd love to spend the *entire* evening with you, I think it would be better if I stayed with Brandon tonight. Actually, I should probably go find him now."

"You're going to make me go to this dinner alone?"

"It will be good for you." Especially since Elizabeth's future with Jon was so uncertain. Why get anyone's hopes up?

She reached for a white terry-cloth bathrobe the hotel had provided. "Is having a new stepmother difficult for you?" she asked Jon quietly.

"No. Let's take a shower, I have time."

But during the shower he remained silent. How could he be so physically honest, and then be emotionally shut down moments afterward?

She fingered the small gold medallion he always wore, now looped backward and dangling behind his neck. "You never take this off," she remarked.

"They made me take it off for the surgery."

"Where did you get it?"

He shrugged, closing his eyes and sticking his head directly under the spray. "My mom." He moved away and wiped the water from his face. "It was a Christmas present that last Christmas she was alive."

Elizabeth had studied the medallion against his neck many times. There was an angel engraved on one side. "It's for protection," she said, understanding at last.

"I don't show it to people. Even in the locker room, it's usually hidden."

"I'm glad you told me about it. Thank you," Elizabeth said.

Jon nodded, thoughtful, as he turned off the shower. He stepped out and handed her a towel.

"I think…it was good that I came for the wedding," he said in a low voice. "That ceremony didn't bother me like I thought it would. I think…I let something go in there."

"I'm glad," she said.

"Yeah." He shrugged.

She waited for the joke. Waited for the retraction. For him to be solicitous to her, or fuss with something in the suite.

It didn't come. He finished buttoning his shirt. "How about you? Are you glad you took a chance and came to Phoenix with me?"

"I…have a confession to make." She swallowed. This was huge for her. Outside of medical professionals, who were sworn to secrecy, she never divulged her inner world to people. Usually.

But Jon wasn't the usual man. His gaze slid to hers. His hand stilled on his shirt button.

She bit her lip and plowed on, before she lost her nerve. "My sister wanted me to attend a counseling session with her and my mom at the rehab center yesterday. I used this trip as an excuse why I couldn't go, and why I wouldn't be able to pick my mom up at the airport."

For a moment, he blinked. Then he shook his head. "It's okay, Liz," he said quietly. "I didn't expect that you were in love with me, or anything like that."

She stilled. *Love.* That word was so powerful. And his assumption stung, because who was to say she wasn't in love with him? She wasn't sure if she was or not...but that was beside the point. And what about him? Was he in love with her?

She swallowed, willing away the sudden stinging in her eyes. So weak of her. So silly. "Where I was going with this, Jon, was to tell you that I already did a lot of that counseling work, in private, while I was in medical school. There was shame and chaos growing up the way I did, and because of my medical training, I knew it was best for me to deal with it at that time rather than later.

"The point is," she continued, "I feel like that stuff is private. Ashley can deal with it how she needs to, but I don't need to be dragged into her drama."

It was clear. She had her inner world, her island of competence that held her together. And he also had his island of competence, which required him to project that air of Mr. Takes Care of Everybody But Stays Aloof Himself.

"What happened to your parents?" he asked. "You never told me before."

She stared down at her hands. "My father was never married to my mother because he was already married to somebody else. He wouldn't divorce his wife because her family was wealthy. But then, his wife divorced him anyway." Elizabeth looked up at Jon, and he was listening intently, which gave her courage to continue. "Ashley told me he eventually moved across country and married somebody else. She recently tracked him down. He has three kids with this woman. Ashley is corresponding with them and getting to know them."

"And you?"

She looked Jon in the eye. "I don't see the point. But I'll tell you this. None of those kids are doctors. None of them have worked as hard as me, or had the focus that I had. I have *that* over them, Jon."

He pulled her close to him. "Lizzy, you don't have to impress me. I don't lo— I'm not with you because you're a doctor. I'm with you for you."

Had he been about to say *love?* Oh, God, what did she want from him? Could this ever work? His off-season was so short....

"Do you think we can figure this out?" she asked.

He pulled back and looked at her.

"Jon, our two weeks are almost up. I don't think I want to stop seeing you just yet."

He nodded slowly. "It's a long way until spring training. We can keep going as we are for a while."

"Is that when I go back to my life as it was before?"

He didn't answer. They were silent as he finished

dressing for dinner. When he was ready, he kissed her goodbye.

She didn't see him again until early the next morning. He met her and Brandon for breakfast to take the private car to the airport, and then they'd be headed home.

Judging by the stillness from Jon's side of the car—which might as well have been an island now, so large was the gulf between them—she didn't see a way to bridge it.

CHAPTER SEVENTEEN

THEY WERE IN the air again. This time, they flew coach, because first-class seating was filled. Jon slept most of the flight, and Brandon watched a movie on Bobby's iPad while Bobby slept in a window seat somewhere near the front of the plane.

It looked like Elizabeth was going to have more alone time than she could ever desire during the six-hour flight—plenty of time to catch up on her reading. But for once, Elizabeth couldn't concentrate, even on her previously favorite topics. Trying desperately to think this thing with Jon through, her lids at last drifted shut. The next thing she knew, she was jerked awake by the pilot announcing over the PA system that they were about to land and to turn off their electronic devices.

Elizabeth quickly sat up. She had fallen asleep against Jon. For how long, she had no idea. Embarrassed, she glanced at him and caught him smiling at her.

"I'm sorry I was leaning on your pitching arm," she said.

He interlaced her fingers in his and brought her hand to his lap. "If I haven't said it already, thanks for coming with me to my dad's wedding. It helped having an ally."

"An ally?" That's what she was?

But he didn't answer. She glanced at the window seat beside her. "Where's Brandon?"

"He's in the line for the bathroom." Jon motioned with his chin, and Elizabeth saw her nephew happily chattering with a grandmotherly looking flight attendant in the galley area. "I told him it was his last chance before landing. I don't think he really has to go, he's just fascinated by the way everything works."

"I must have been sleeping soundly."

Jon smiled. "He climbed right over you."

She shook her head. It was amazing to her that she was sitting in an airplane seat between two males that she had fallen for, head over heels. She realized that if they didn't return to Boston just yet, she wouldn't mind one bit. "I liked this trip. Seeing you with your family all together in one place like that was interesting."

He looked askance at her. "I missed you at dinner last night." He sounded surprised.

"Really?" she asked.

"It went well, but…it just wasn't the same."

She tightened her hand in his. "Thanks for saying that."

"It's true."

"Was dinner hard for you?" she murmured.

"No." He shook his head. "Mary Angela is…well,

she's bending over backward to fit in with us, how we already are."

Unlike me, Elizabeth thought.

"What about you? Did you mind hanging out with my family?" he asked, peering closely at her. "Do you think you could stand to see them again?"

She nodded earnestly. "I was thinking about Emily. I'll bet she plans a blowout of a wedding."

Jon laughed. "Frank is going to have a fit," he agreed.

"When is their wedding, anyway?"

"I don't know. Spring, probably." He looked at her. "Why? Are you interested in going?"

She chose her words carefully. "Do you think we'll make it through to that?"

"Spring training lasts for six weeks in Florida, Lizzy. Then I'm back home in Boston."

And yet, he hadn't answered her question. She took a breath. "So...are you saying we should give it a try?"

He turned his head on the seat back to gaze into her eyes. "You know I saw something in you that day I first met you," he said in a low voice, his mouth close to her.

She licked her lips, her hand tightening in his. "I felt it, too. I guess I just needed more convincing than you did."

He smiled. "I did a good job with that, didn't I? I got you out and showed you the fun things in life and you...you've kept me focused on what's important."

"What *is* important?"

He leaned forward, and then they were kissing. oft, pillow kisses that touched her heart. She made little moan and reached out to caress his cheek.

"I love you, Jon," she blurted.

He paused. Slowly his lips disengaged with hers, nd he looked into her eyes.

She felt unease in her chest. Had she misread him? he was so terrible at this. But without a doubt, she new what she felt.

Her hand was trembling, so she dropped it to her ap. He picked it up and pressed a kiss to her knuck-es.

"Did I...do wrong?" she whispered.

"No. I just...I was just thinking about some things hat I need to get straightened out this weekend."

"Will you tell me those things?"

He swallowed, gazing down the aisle at Brandon.

"My nephew goes home this evening," she mur-nured. "After we land in Boston."

He nodded. Looking into her eyes, he asked, "Will ou be okay without him?"

"Me? Of course I will, I can't wait to get my life ack."

"What will you do differently when he's gone?"

"Spend more nights with you, I hope."

He seemed to be thinking about that. His lips urned up, smiling. "I think I'm seeing that, too."

"What else are you seeing?"

"That...half a week on the road in the spring and

summer isn't too bad. At least I'm home for the oth
half, right?"

Her heart felt like it was soaring. She couldn't sto
grinning at him, even though part of her told her nc
to get her hopes up, that he was far from soundin
settled.

"Okay." Jon nodded, a decision made. "I'll tell yo
what. When we land, let's call Mrs. Ham and ask
she can watch Brandon while you and I take a wal
somewhere and, ah, figure all this out together."

That sounded good to her.

When Brandon returned from the bathroom, sh
wrapped her arms around Jon and hugged him tigh

AFTER THE PLANE landed, Jon walked down the ta
mac, into a gate at Logan Airport when Brandon suc
denly squealed beside him, "Look! That's me! I'r
on TV, everybody!"

Jon and Lizzy stopped and stared at the overhea
television screen that Brandon was pointing at. Sur
enough, it was Brandon's face, bold and confiden
The sound on the television was turned off, but wha
ever he was saying to the camera, it was heartfelt.

Then the shot flashed to the Captains' Sunshin
Club logo.

"I'll be damned," Jon breathed. It was the com
mercial they'd made. He turned to Brandon. "Con
gratulations, buddy. You did great."

"How come you weren't in it?" Brandon asked.

"I'm sure it's just an oversight," Lizzy said.

Jon thought back. Considered the significance of his absence. *Shit*. This didn't bode well for him.

"Maybe there's another spot with Jon it," Lizzy said anxiously.

He doubted it very much. He saw the answer staring at him, plain as day. "Brandon was genuine about what the Sunshine Club meant to him. I wasn't truthful with Susan."

"She doesn't know you," Lizzy said softly.

Jon shifted his carry-on bag higher on his shoulder. She was being too kind to him. "No, I just couldn't do it."

"Do what?"

She knew that he had trouble opening up. He had just proven that to her, too, on the plane. He didn't like to show his true feelings, not even when what he wanted more than anything hung in the balance. "I couldn't put the truth out on the air."

"Why?" Brandon asked.

Maybe he was just plain old *damn* scared.

Jon sat in one of the flat, vinyl seats in the airport lounge, and raked his hand through his hair. He needed to call Brooke. His not being in the Sunshine Club commercial would have ramifications.

Lizzy sat down beside him. "So what do we do now?"

"It's a waiting game. It always is. The Captains hold the cards."

She looked hurt. Too late, he realized that she was

talking about her and him. Their future. The othe
thing that he was scared to think about.

"I have to go to the bathroom," Brandon said.

"You just went on the plane," Lizzy reminded him

"No," Brandon said, "I played on the plane. I *really*
have to go now."

"Come on, I'll take you," Jon said, standing.

When he got inside the men's restroom with Bran
don, Jon discreetly turned on his phone. At least call
ing Brooke was one thing he could take care of. H
needed to know what, if anything, Vivian had said t
Brooke about the commercial, or rather, about Jon'
absence in it.

But when Jon turned on his phone, he got a shock
His phone was lit up with text messages. He clicke
on Brooke's message first:

CALL ME RIGHT NOW!!!!

Jon glanced around. The restroom was empty ex
cept for him and Brandon. Jon stood behind the kid
blocking him from view of the door, and making
sure that nobody bothered the boy while he stood a
the urinal. Really, this wasn't the place or time to b
returning a lady's telephone call.

Then again, the lady *did* want to be a sports agent
Max would counsel Jon to just place the damn call

Jon touched the button for Brooke's phone num
ber. Brooke picked up on the first ring and let out a
string of expletives at him.

"Whoa!" Jon held the phone at arm's length. "There's a kid nearby."

"Yeah?" Brooke said, "Well, listen to this, Farell. The Captains are announcing a trade deal with you tomorrow afternoon."

A *trade?* He staggered backward a step.

Another guy came into the restroom, wheeling luggage behind him, but Jon couldn't move and the guy just drove around him and set up at a urinal.

Jon covered the phone. "Go," he said to Brandon. "Go back to your aunt and tell her I'll be out in a minute."

Jon went into the big, handicapped stall and shut the door. He planted his feet and tried not to touch anything except for his phone. "What can we do to stop this thing, Brooke?"

"Stop it? You're not listening to me, Jon. You need to be preparing for a press conference, especially in response to the whole drinking-in-the-clubhouse mess. Vivian wants you *gone*."

He let that word sink in, the dread pooling in him, weighting him down. "I can't believe I failed," he murmured.

"Actually, you succeeded. San Francisco likes the video we leaked of your changeup pitch. They believe you're serious, and they feel that you're underrated technically. They also think that Vivian is an idiot who isn't going to be winning championships by letting people like you go.

"My suggestion, Jon, is that you suck it up, take the

deal and make yourself into San Francisco's top ace Then, next season, throw strikes and win ball games like you have a limitless supply of win in you. I want you to personally make sure you kick New England's ass every time you face them in regular season. And that's a direct quote from Max."

"Did you say San Francisco?" Jon asked. That was three thousand miles from Boston. "A six-hour flight."

"No crying in baseball, Jon."

He wasn't crying, he—

The door opened, and Brandon stared up at him. Jon covered the phone. "Hey, buddy, can I get some privacy, please?"

The kid didn't budge.

Jon spoke into the phone. "Is there anything else? Because I'm in an airport bathroom here." Guys were hurrying in by droves—another flight must have de-planed. "Brooke, I've got to sign off."

"Just remember that I got you a heads-up," Brooke said. "Most players in your shoes find out they're traded when they're sitting on their couches with their girlfriends in their underwear, listening to *SportsCenter*."

"Thanks," he said grimly. "How much time do I have?"

"Twenty-four hours until the news goes live. And then it's done. You are out of Boston for good."

WHEN JON CAME out of the bathroom, Elizabeth knew immediately that something was wrong. His face was

ray. His bag was skewed over his shoulder and his
air was messed up, like he'd been raking his hands
hrough it.

"What happened?" she asked.

"Let's get out of here." Jon looked left and right,
nd then clasped her elbow with one hand and Bran-
lon's palm with his other. "I need to talk to you when
ve get home."

"My home or your home?"

"I hadn't thought about that," Jon muttered. "Shit."

"You're welcome to stay at my house." Elizabeth
urried to keep up with him, her suitcase wheels clat-
ering behind her. He was herding them out of the
irport like he was race-walking them.

"Fine," Jon murmured absently. His mind seemed
 million miles away.

Elizabeth didn't push him as he rushed them out
of the airport terminal and into the central parking
garage where he opened his SUV with a beep from
is ignition key. It was cold outside compared to Ar-
zona. She lowered her chin inside the collar of her
neager jacket and shivered.

"Get in," Jon said curtly to Brandon. "Buckle up."

This wasn't like Jon. Now she was in full panic
node.

But whatever had happened, now that they were
nome from his father's wedding, Jon was completely
withdrawing again. She could feel that unmistakable
nessage, and it hurt.

She was silent while he drove them to her house

using the best and worst of his Boston city driving skills. Brandon, looking drowsy, lounged in the back seat. Now was not the time for her to initiate a conversation with Jon.

Fifteen minutes later, he wheeled the SUV into the second of Elizabeth's two condo spaces. He got out, popped the rear hatchback and helped Brandon jump down, too. Jon lifted out her suitcase, and she waited for him to remove his bag, but no, Jon shut the hatchback, leaving his things inside.

Her heart stopped in her throat.

"Brandon," Jon said, "take your aunt's key and go upstairs. She'll meet you in a minute."

"You aren't going to watch me pitch today?" Brandon asked.

"No, buddy, I can't." He knelt to Brandon's level. "Why don't you get ready for your mom's homecoming? When I'm finished down here with your aunt, she'll meet you upstairs. I'm sure she wants to spend the last hours before your mom comes home with just you alone."

Brandon hurled himself into Jon's arms. He squeezed him tightly around the waist. "I love you, Jon. Don't leave yet."

Elizabeth put her hand to her mouth. Tears stung at her eyelids. What was Jon doing?

He set Brandon down and brushed his hair off his face. "I love you, too," Jon murmured to her nephew.

Obviously he was capable of saying the words

I love you, just not to her. Elizabeth pulled her coat tighter around her.

Miserable, she waited. Jon watched silently as Brandon headed for the building. They waited until the door snapped shut behind the boy.

There seemed to be a long, horrible silence. Elizabeth didn't dare to meet Jon's eyes. Whatever he was going to say, she wasn't going to like it.

"Lizzy," Jon said quietly. She pressed her lips together and gazed up at him. He had taken off his sunglasses, and his beautiful blue eyes regarded her, looking haunted.

They were out in the open, a windy, cloudy early-November day. Anybody could see them. Rusty red colors were past peak in the oak leaves, and yellows from the birch leaves littered the ground. A few autumn pumpkins were still scattered about. It was a picture-perfect New England autumn setting. And a picture-perfect hero, with his windblown hair, his preppy New England clothes and his leading-man good looks.

"I've loved you, Lizzy," Jon said quietly.

Why was he saying this in the past tense?

"I've loved you like I've never loved any other woman." He swallowed. "But the truth of the matter is, I never thought you would stay. Maybe I was drawn to you because I thought you ran away from people like me. That you preferred to be alone."

This was how he felt? Yes, he had said that he loved

her. But there were other, messy things. Things she hadn't realized.

"The truth of the matter is," he said, gazing directly at her, "I need to focus on baseball." His Adam's apple moved up and down.

"Are you breaking up with me?" she whispered.

He exhaled sharply, as if it hurt him to do what he was doing to her. And it should hurt him.

"Why?" she asked. "Tell me, I need to know."

His gaze shot to hers. "Because I'm getting traded."

"By the Captains? How can they even do that?"

"They can do whatever they want with me. I'm a commodity," he said bitterly, "and I'm sorry I have to leave you to break the news to Brandon, but I trust you'll know best how to do it. The official announcement is tomorrow afternoon. It'll be all over the media." Jon closed his mouth and looked in the distance again.

"Is this because of the drinking thing?" she asked, her voice sounding small.

His jaw set. "That's ninety percent of it."

"What…what can I do?"

"Nothing." He shook his head. "It's done. I'm lucky I got a day's heads-up so I can make plans."

"Why…can't we make it work, regardless of what the Captains do to you?"

He stared at the ground. "They traded me to California, Lizzy. I'll have to move out there. My spring training is in Arizona. I'll have no break until next October. November if we make the playoffs. That gives me only a few weeks a year that I could give to anyone located here in Boston." He looked at her. "That's not right for you. You'd only end up leaving me."

"How do you know what's right for me?" she demanded. "How do you know I'd leave?"

"Are *you* willing to leave Boston? Your job? Your sister? Brandon? Everything you've built here and worked for your whole life?"

She blinked. The tears were brimming now. In a perfect world, yes, she could leave Boston. But it wasn't a perfect world. She had obligations. She had dreams and desires. Responsibilities.

And fears.

Choking, she flung her arms around Jon's neck. She couldn't stand it, couldn't stand to let him go. She was sobbing now, into his chest. His arms tightened around her. She heard him softly swear, a long string of bitter curse words. His mouth was in her hair and he was kissing her.

"I'm sorry," she cried. "We'll find a way around it."

"I don't expect you to adapt for me," he said fiercely. "I don't want you to. I don't want to see you hurt."

He squeezed her tighter. "Look, it's for the best. Have you ever gone on the internet and seen the gossip sites that track baseball players' girlfriends and wives? It's a harsh reality."

"I don't care!"

Maybe she was imagining it, but his eyes seemed

wet. "I'm telling you the truth. I'm not…bullshitting you, Lizzy."

"The highest compliment."

His hands clenched into fists. "Please don't ask me to give up baseball. It's the only place I know I own."

"Jon—"

"Just don't…ask me that."

What could she say after that? In the end, she peeled her hands off his chest and stood woodenly as he kissed her palms and then walked her to the front door of her condo building.

Only when the elevator door slid shut between them did he leave her.

When she got to her apartment, she looked out the window. Jon was sitting in the driver seat of his SUV. But it wasn't moving. She waited, curtain in her hand. He seemed to be in a state of indecision. She held her breath. Would he change his mind?

Finally, he drove off.

CHAPTER EIGHTEEN

ELIZABETH'S NOSE WAS still red and her eyes damp when she answered the knock on her door to find Ashley standing in her hallway. Before Elizabeth could react, her sister reached out and hugged Elizabeth as hard as she could. "Lisbeth!"

Stunned, Elizabeth hugged her back, feeling the strength in Ashley's arms. Her sister seemed healthier and not as thin as before. Elizabeth pulled back and stared at her, speechless.

"Thank you for watching my boy." Ashley gave her a grateful smile. "Can I take him home now?"

"We...had something planned for you tonight." Fresh tears pooled in Elizabeth's eyes. *Jon had left her.* She blinked quickly, hoping Ashley didn't notice. "We were a-all going to take you to dinner. A p-party. But you're early."

"I'm so glad to be here." Ashley gave her a wide-eyed smile. "As it turned out, Sharma came to the therapy sessions with Mom and me. She was so helpful that my counselor thought she should be my sponsor, so he allowed her to process me out tonight. She's downstairs waiting in the car. I thought I'd surprise you."

"So…that's it? You're here to collect Brandon now?"

Ashley hesitated. "Is he doing okay?"

"He's fine, he's—"

Brandon ran past Elizabeth and leaped into his mom's arms, no hesitation, no regrets. "Mama, Mama, Mama!"

Ashley's eyes watered, too. "Oh, honey, I missed you so much." She ran her hands over her boy, his head, his shoulders, his back. She kissed him over and over, as if she couldn't get enough of him.

"I missed you, too, Mama, I missed you too!"

Elizabeth pressed her worn tissue to her eyes. She went to the front door to close it, to give them privacy. In the hallway she noticed the pumpkin that she and Brandon had carved together. The waterworks started anew.

"Brandon, honey, are you ready to go home?" Ashley asked, her hands bracketed on either side of the boy's face. "I'm sorry that I missed Halloween with you, but I've been thinking ahead to Thanksgiving, and how special we can make the holiday this year."

"Let me get my stuff! I'll be ready in a minute." Brandon raced past Elizabeth at breakneck speed, careering into what Elizabeth had come to think of as Brandon's room.

Numb all over, Elizabeth went to the doorway and watched him pack. It was impossible not to feel tightness in her throat. Into a duffel bag went all of his clothes and schoolbooks. His toothbrush and his bubble-gum toothpaste. The baseballs Jon had given him, and the glove Jon had signed for him, too.

She hadn't even gotten the chance to explain to Brandon about Jon being traded to the West Coast. About Jon not being able to be as big a part of their lives anymore.

"Mom!" Brandon called as he struggled out the door with his overstuffed duffel bag. "Can you help me with my pitch-back net?"

And, oh, Elizabeth almost lost it. Brandon was leaving nothing to remind her of their time together. He raced toward his mom, dragging his luggage down the hallway and into the elevator.

Elizabeth shut the door and turned around in her quiet, empty apartment. It was almost as if Brandon had never lived here. But wasn't this what she had wanted: To be alone again? Free to do whatever she wished? To read what she wanted? To watch the television programs *she* liked?

She had no more kid's agenda to follow. No more gluten-free dinners to prepare. No more family fun days.

No more Jon.

Her breath catching in her throat, she turned and nearly cried aloud when she saw the construction-paper card that Jon had helped Brandon make for Elizabeth during their time in the Sunshine Club program. It was tacked to her refrigerator with a magnet from Brandon's school, listing the administration's office telephone numbers.

Tears ran down Elizabeth's cheeks.

This was not what she'd wanted, or expected, to feel. But both her males had left her, and there was nothing she could do about it, because she didn't belong to either one of them. Not really.

She went into her bedroom and lay facedown on her bed, sobbing her heart out. Even now, her pillows still smelled like Jon.

Twenty minutes later, there was a tentative knock on her bedroom door. Ashley walked in, alone, without Brandon. She held out her arms, and Elizabeth sank into them, crying like she didn't think she had ever cried before.

"Lisbeth, honey. I can never, ever thank you enough for what you've done for us."

"Are you r-really okay?" Elizabeth sniffled. "Are you not going to n-need me anymore?"

"I *am* okay. I'm going to be okay." Ashley stroked Elizabeth's hair and soothed her. "Lisbeth, I feel so much hope for us. The program was wonderful. I had sessions with Mom, and that cleared up a lot of things for me." Ashley pulled back and looked at Elizabeth. "Honey, are *you* okay? What's going on?"

"Please don't be sorry for me." Elizabeth stood back, taking deep breaths and getting hold of herself. "It's all right. It's not your problem. Brandon is your boy, and Jon is baseball's commodity…"

"Is he the baseball pitcher Brandon was telling me about? I don't know Jon, but I do know my son, and Brandon seems to have grown even fonder of you."

She rubbed Elizabeth's shoulder. "We'll come visit you often, you'll see."

Elizabeth hoped so. She would miss her brave, perceptive nephew. Still, she couldn't tell her sister that it wouldn't be the same for her. Because Jon would not be with them.

She glanced at the digital clock on her bedside table. Maybe Jon had gone to the charity bachelor auction. Maybe he was trying to fix things with Vivian.

"Do you have somewhere to go tonight?" Ashley asked.

"I wish," Elizabeth blurted. "I have so much to tell you, Ash. Brandon actually made a commercial with Jon, the baseball player..."

"I know that," Ashley said, smiling.

"And Caitlin is aware of where you've been these past weeks...."

Ashley nodded. "Brandon told me about that, too."

"So you're okay with it?"

"Honey, I learned a lot these past thirty days."

Elizabeth sat on the bed beside her sister and took a breath. "Well, that's good, because I've got a lot of questions that I can't answer right now. Like what happens when you're not ready to let someone go? When they have the wrong impression of you, and you want to fix it?"

"First, I'd say that a good place to start is to ask for some help."

Elizabeth digested that. Did she dare? What if she

went to Jon? Showed him that she *could* go public with him?

"Will *you* help me, Ash? I need to find something to wear to meet with a CEO tonight. And I need to do it quickly."

Ashley laughed and tugged at Elizabeth's hand. And the next thing Elizabeth knew, they were standing in front of her closet, Ashley helping her into a silk cocktail dress that Brandon and Mrs. Ham had nixed on their earlier consultation.

"Perfect," Ashley said, with a smile playing on her lips. "And now, do you have shoes to wear with it?"

"Um, yours?" Elizabeth showed her the low heels she'd borrowed from her sister's closet.

"Those will work." A smile spread over Ashley's face, and she hugged Elizabeth again.

The distinctive squeak of Brandon's sneakers rounding the hardwood floor sounded behind her. "Goodbye, Auntie. Thank you for taking care of me," Brandon said in a small voice.

Elizabeth smiled down at her nephew. She was feeling better now. "You're always welcome to visit me. Or to invite me along on a family fun day."

"Where are you going?" he asked, indicating the dress.

"To do something helpful for Jon."

"I'm glad." Brandon lifted his arms to hug Elizabeth, and when she bent down to meet him, he whispered in her ear, "I think you should marry him."

She squeezed him tight. What could she say to that?

"Take as good care of your mom as you took care of me," Elizabeth whispered to him.

"I will," Brandon said.

"We've got to be going." Ashley herded Brandon out the door and down the stairs.

From the parking lot, Elizabeth watched their car drive away, Brandon's pitch-back net tied to the roof of Sharma's car.

CINDERELLA MADE IT look easy.

Elizabeth ran tripping into the Wellness Hospital auditorium, already late for the fund-raiser dinner. She'd brought her hospital badge with her, and had somehow convinced the women standing at the table out front to let her in, even though her name was not on the list, and even though the charity bachelor auction was long over.

Tables were set up in the large room, and hundreds of men in suits and women in cocktail dresses mingled about, talking and laughing. The podium was empty and the dishes were cleared, evidence that the main action had finished.

Elizabeth hoped she hadn't missed Vivian Sharpe. She only knew what the lady looked like from her photo in the Sunshine Club brochures.

Elizabeth circled the perimeter of the room, searching faces, but she didn't see Vivian. Maybe it was too late. She didn't see Jon, either, which, given that he'd been traded, wasn't such a surprise after all.

Dejected, she headed for the ladies' room. There must be something else she could do. But what?

She reached for a tissue on a shelf by the mirror. She had to maneuver around an elderly lady applying bright red lipstick.

Elizabeth tottered on her heels. That elderly lady was Vivian Sharpe.

"Ms. Sharpe?" Elizabeth asked. "I'm Dr. Elizabeth LaValley. I'm an anesthesiologist at Wellness Hospital." She held out her hand and smiled at the lady.

To her shock, Vivian took her hand. "I'm pleased to meet you, dear."

Elizabeth smiled harder. "My nephew was the boy who made the commercial for the Sunshine Club."

"Oh, wasn't that wonderful! It was played for us tonight on an oversize screen."

"I'm glad you like it. I saw it this afternoon on an airport television."

"Your nephew could have a future in show business," Vivian said.

"Actually, he is smitten with baseball."

"Of course." Vivian placed her lipstick inside her purse. "Is he interested in being a batboy for the team?"

"He would jump at that in a heartbeat." Elizabeth licked her lips. *Breathe.* "But that's not why I introduced myself. I want to talk about Jon Farell."

Vivian's lips pursed. "I'm afraid I don't want to talk about him," she said in a dismissive voice. She turned for the door.

Don't stop. Keep going. Elizabeth dug her nails into her palms and followed Vivian. "I got to know Jon through his work with my nephew. What was written about him in the newspaper doesn't reflect his character. It wasn't the whole truth."

"It never is, dear." Vivian stopped and patted her hand. "I'm afraid there's nothing more for us to say. I never talk about team matters in public. I'm sure you understand."

JON BRACED HIS hands on his balcony railing at the Back Bay Towers, overlooking Boston and all its twinkling lights. Two hours since he'd left Lizzy, and he still felt like hell.

Because he was in love with her. He felt it with an ache that pulled at him.

But it was hopeless. Even if he wanted to, there was nothing left to say between them. He'd put it all out there. Told her things about himself he hadn't even realized until this weekend.

And now?

The call he'd been waiting for finally came in. Jon answered it on the first ring.

"I'm doing this under protest," Brooke said. "But my father agreed to see you."

"Thank you," Jon said quietly. "I won't forget it, Brooke."

Fifteen minutes later, Jon met her outside the lobby coffee shop at Wellness Hospital.

"They moved Max out of intensive care." Brooke

led him down a hospital corridor. "But that doesn't mean I'll let you upset him."

"I won't."

Inside the private patient room, Jon's agent was hooked into tubes and IV lines. Max looked like a shell of his former self. It just showed Jon how fragile life was, how important it was to focus on what really mattered.

Jon took the chair beside the bed. "Hey, Max. It's good to see you."

Max reached out and weakly clasped Jon's hand. "Brooke says you want to find an East Coast team to offer the Captains something better in a trade for you?" His voice was faint, but he sounded alert.

Jon nodded, feeling guilty for asking, but Max could say no if it was physically too much for him. "I'm thinking of Baltimore." A short, seventy-five-minute flight from Boston. "Tell them I'll do whatever it takes to get there."

Max shook his head. "My advice is to save Baltimore for when you're a free agent. For now, you should go where the Captains send you." Max waited, expecting, no doubt, that Jon would do what he recommended because he had been following Max's advice ever since the day the man had brought him the deal to be a Captains pitcher.

Jon had grown up watching the Captains with his dad, and that was their team. Jon loved the Captains. His dad loved the Captains. His brothers loved the

Captains. His grandparents before him had loved the Captains.

But maybe Jon was ready to start over someplace new on his own terms, using all he'd learned during his time with the Captains.

"No, Max," Jon said. "Baltimore is the team I want."

"Why? Baltimore is a smaller-market team."

The past weeks had shown Jon there was an advantage to that. He would have the respect of being a top ace rather than a back-of-the-order guy. A smaller market also had fewer sports-talk shows and sports-writers, and less intense fans. The atmosphere was more relaxed.

Lizzy would have an easier time.

"A smaller-market team has actually become attractive to me recently, but that's not the major factor."

"What is the major factor?" Max asked.

Lizzy. The West Coast was too far away to sustain a new, budding relationship with her. "I want the ability to commute back to Boston more easily."

"Ah." Max made a small smile. "Family ties, I presume?"

"Something like that."

"You're in love with a woman?"

Jon gazed back at Brooke, but she shrugged and stayed out of the conversation.

Jon leaned forward. "Yes," he whispered in Max's

ear. It felt like a confession. But he wanted to protect Elizabeth's privacy the way that she'd requested of him.

"What will you do if San Francisco is your only option?" Max asked.

Jon clasped the arm of his chair and tried not to think about this possibility.

His whole life, what Jon had really wanted—not what his family wanted, but what *Jon* had wanted—was to be a great pitching ace. Hall of Fame worthy. If he was going to knuckle down and be true to his goal, then now was the time. Being a bigger fish in a smaller pond might help him, and he'd come to see the advantage to being traded, the way that would help him. Jon had been painted with the tar brush in the Boston media, and there was no convincing Vivian otherwise.

But if the team he went to was San Francisco, then he could not have Liz.

She was what he wanted, too. In his heart, he knew it. She needed this town, this hospital. If he went to San Francisco, essentially, he was choosing baseball over Liz.

Which, on the surface, made sense. The guys on every team he'd ever played with would be yelling at him right about now.

It wasn't as if he and Lizzy had been close lovers for years. He'd known her just a little over a month. A big part of that month was spent not seeing eye to eye.

But, always, there had been that strong connection

between them. She had encouraged him to be true to himself, rather than doing things to please others. He had brought her out of her shell and shown her more of the world, more of what she could be if she only dared.

What if, in a lifetime, Elizabeth LaValley was the one perfect match to his pair? What if she was his destiny?

He had always imagined himself with a great love. He wanted to feel about someone like...his dad had felt about his mom. For Jon, Lizzy was that woman.

And she loved him, too. That was solid between them. He *knew* it.

In essence, he had two things he wanted. Baseball—his life, his purpose, and his dreams from his earliest age.

And Lizzy—a chance at a true life's partner.

If Jon didn't get an East Coast team, then he couldn't have both.

"Max," Jon said, "you're a legend. You know people in management in every clubhouse in baseball. Do what you can for me with Baltimore."

"Would New York work?" Max asked.

The Captain's archrivals? Jon almost laughed aloud. Frank would have a heart attack. Bobby would never wear his team colors. His father would insist that *his* father was spinning in his grave. Even Brandon would pitch a fit.

But New York was close by, and Jon would still

be playing baseball at the highest levels. "New York works for me. Just not San Francisco."

"I understand," Max said. "Any place but the West Coast."

CHAPTER NINETEEN

ELIZABETH FINISHED HER shift as usual that rainy, cloudy Tuesday, and went about her usual routines feeling anything *but* usual.

As she headed toward the elevator that led to her route home, she realized that her gait was slower than normal. Instead of staring at the white hospital floor as she hastened along, she walked more slowly and looked about her. At the couples and families that entered the hospital for their appointments. At the nurses and doctors and support staff that comprised their bustling, scrubs-wearing community.

And she was headed back to an empty, lonely condo?

The ache in her heart intensified. It had been about forty-eight hours since Jon had found out he was getting traded and leaving Boston, and the pain was only getting worse. She missed him like she missed her books if they were taken away from her. Like she missed her freedom if it was curtailed.

But wasn't freedom more enjoyable and interesting with someone to share it with?

An ally, that's what Jon had called her. She'd been insulted at the time because she'd wanted him to tell her he loved her. And he *had* told her. Now she had an unshakable feeling as certain as New England bedrock, that Jon would always be her ally, if she allowed him to be himself, and found a way to integrate him into her life.

She hadn't realized how slowly she'd been softening this month, getting used to seeing Jon, looking forward to his amusing comments that made her laugh, to the stories of his day, the comfort and love of his embrace.

She and Jon and Brandon had made their own little family together and, without the two of them, Elizabeth's heart was ripped in half. It was true that she couldn't have Brandon back because he belonged with her sister, but she could have Jon. She could, if only she allowed herself to let go and shed the old habits that just didn't work for her anymore.

Elizabeth stopped. To her left was a waiting room; a television might be playing inside. She didn't know, because she typically didn't look—it was not part of her routine. But televisions played press conferences, especially press conferences from local sports teams.

She had woken this morning vowing that she wouldn't watch Jon, that she wouldn't torture herself. But she was overcome by a desire to see him, to learn more about his decision. If she learned more, maybe she could adapt herself to it.

An elderly gentleman, assisted by his wife, stopped Elizabeth in the corridor. They made eye contact with her, and she didn't look away. "Can you tell us where to find Outpatient Check-in?" the wife asked. She showed Elizabeth their appointment slip.

"Certainly. We're close by, let me show you." Elizabeth led them to the huge waiting room on the main floor. Not one but two televisions were both turned to the local cable news station.

A feed was being broadcast from the Captains press offices at Captains Field. The camera was focused on Jon—*her Jon,* her heart said—with his mystical good looks and his quiet, calm eyes.

She stood in front of the television between a burly man standing on crutches and a boy about Brandon's age. "Is there any way to turn on the sound?" Elizabeth asked the man.

He shook his head. "I asked already, and they said no."

Elizabeth concentrated on the television screen. If only she could lip-read. Jon sat at a table with his hands folded in front of him. He was speaking in what looked to be a focused, measured voice into a microphone. To Elizabeth, it felt eerily like he was talking to her alone.

"He's apologizing," the boy about Brandon's age said.

"Do you think so?" Elizabeth asked.

"That's what the news on the radio said. They said he wants to make a statement to his fans."

"The team scapegoated him," the burly man

muttered. "Everybody knows it's bullcrap how Jon got blamed."

"Really?" Elizabeth asked. "Is that what people think?"

"My wife's uncle works with Jon's brother. Believe me, that's the inside scoop. But you'll never hear it in the press."

"Still, it's nice he's apologizing," Elizabeth said.

The man grunted, but the boy smiled up at her. On television, Jon certainly seemed more at peace. The line on his forehead that had gotten starker as the scandal wore on seemed smoother now. His eyes still looked pained, though. It had to hurt him to give up his Captains affiliation. That had been his life and his identity and his dream for so many years.

Farell Traded to San Francisco, flashed the headline on the screen.

Elizabeth sighed. "Did the radio say when he is leaving?" she asked the boy.

"I dunno." The boy shrugged.

"This week," the man answered. "I told you, I know the family."

Elizabeth hid her smile. She knew the family, too.

Quietly, she watched the press conference until Jon's face was no longer on the television screen. Seeing him there focused her intent.

She went back upstairs to her station and dug out her iPad. She turned it on, and connected to the hospital internet. Maybe it was crazy, but she searched on Google for San Francisco. The city had an exten-

ive network of hospitals and medical centers. She
went through a few sites, scanned through the doc-
ors' names.

She paused at one name. She knew this person.
Yes, she had one contact. She scanned more lists,
found more names. Cross-referenced those names
with directories, made some phone calls, and…found
someone who would talk to her.

Three hours later, she called her scheduler. "Please,
I need to take off two days from work. It's…a family emergency."

And it was.

ON WEDNESDAY MORNING, Jon sat in the airline's first-
class lounge at Logan Airport, and answered the in-
coming phone call from Brooke.

"I just got off the phone with San Francisco,"
Brooke said. "They want to lock up a deal with you.
Max is playing hardball—the money should be big.
If we don't get what we want from them, then we'll
go to arbitration. Either way, it can only turn out
well for us."

Jon nodded. Half of him was thoroughly crushed.
"Thanks for the update," he said quietly.

"Hold on, Jon—I have another call." Brooke sighed
happily. "You're on your way to the big time, do you
know that?"

He knew. It gave the other half of him a quiet,
humbling satisfaction.

But to leave Elizabeth—that wasn't what he wanted.

He'd tried to sleep last night, but his thoughts kept re
turning to her. Even now, even when it was certain
that the West Coast was his destiny, at least for the
next few years.

He would probably always think about Lizzy. Al
ways wonder "What if?"

What if he had stayed with her and given her what
she needed?

But if Jon had learned anything these past thirty
days, it was that if he sacrificed too much of him
self, then he would have nothing left to give anybody.
Lizzy had shown him that. She knew what was good
for her and how to take care of herself, and he would
always carry that with him.

He leaned his head back on the airport seat and
let his mind drift. To the days and nights spent with
her and Brandon. To the trip they'd taken to Phoenix.

To that last goodbye.

Brooke called him back. "Sorry about that. It was
Max. I thought it was about your contract, but it
wasn't, he's leaving the hospital today and he needs
me to pick him up."

"Thank Max again, for everything."

"He did tell me something interesting," Brooke
said. "After the press conference, he got a call from
Vivian Sharpe."

"Did he?"

"She was appreciative. She called you a 'humble
young man.'" Brooke sighed. "Whatever, Jon, it was
classy what you did, apologizing like that."

He hoped so. "There are a lot of kids in Boston," he said quietly. "I wanted them to hear it from me."

Jon had already heard from Brandon. BRANDON! would always be keyed into Jon's contact list, though he'd switched the number to the boy's actual home phone number. Jon had asked the kid about his aunt, but Brandon didn't say much, and Jon had inferred that Lizzy was living life alone again. He wondered if she missed the boy as much as he did.

"Vivian also said something else that I thought you might like to hear," Brooke said. "She said that a doctor at the hospital—a pretty, female doctor at the hospital—showed up at the end of the bachelor fund-raising auction and cornered her in the ladies' restroom. The doctor wanted to talk about *you,* Jon. What do you think that was about?"

Jon choked and sat up. "*What* did she say to Vivian about me?"

"I don't know. Vivian just said that she told the doctor she never discusses team business with outside parties. Vivian also said that if the mother of that boy in the Sunshine Club commercial wants him to be a team batboy, to call the front office and give them Vivian's blessing."

Brandon, a Captains batboy? The kid would be through the roof with joy.

"What else did Vivian say?" Jon asked. "Did she mention anything else about Lizzy? How is she doing? How is she holding up without Brandon in the house?"

"Lizzy? Is that the woman you were seeing?"

He'd said too much. "Brooke, I have to go."

"You're getting on that plane, Jon," she warned.

"Of course I am." He disconnected the call. Grabbed his carry-on bag and headed to the main concourse, to stretch his legs and think. As he walked, he phoned Lizzy's number.

She didn't pick up. He stayed on the line, waited until the call went to voice mail. On the recorded greeting he heard her voice, and he lost his heart a little bit more.

He spoke into her voice mail: "Lizzy. I miss you more than you'll ever believe."

He dodged a businessman running past, swinging a thick laptop case. "I want to talk to you so badly," he said into the phone. "Can you call me? I'm heading out to San Francisco to get an apartment nailed down. But I've been thinking…"

He moved out of the way of a motorized cart driving a wheelchair passenger to his gate.

"Honey," Jon continued with the voice mail message, "we did pretty good with that nannycam thing we set up with Brandon, didn't we? Maybe you and I could—"

A woman running across the terminal toward her gate almost mowed Jon down. He stepped onto the moving walkway and stood far to the right so people could pass him.

"Maybe, Lizzy, we could call each other on a video screen at night," he continued, speaking into er voice mail. "It's a technology-based world, right? We should be able to figure something out, because, Lizzy baby, I don't want to lose you. That's what *I* want. That's not what anybody is telling me. That's me, not pleasing anybody but myself—"

"Jon?"

"Lizzy?" he said into the phone. "Are you there?"

"I'm right here, Jon," she said. He felt a tap on his shoulder.

He turned, and she looked…beautiful to him, like she always did, only more so, because she was here in person, in the flesh, and he was getting to see her before he left Boston.

He shut the phone and pulled her to him, breathing in that luscious scent she wore in her hair and kissing her as tenderly as he could.

The moving conveyor belt ended, and Jon was nearly knocked off his feet.

Laughing, they collected themselves and moved to the side of the corridor. Both hands bracketing her face, Jon asked her, "Are you flying somewhere today?"

"Yes. Out to see *you,* Jon."

He felt gobsmacked. "But what about your job? It's a workweek. Why aren't you at the hospital?"

She shook her head, a gleam on her face. "I heard what you said to me on the message you left. Guess what? We might not need to use technology. I've got two informational interviews set up in San Francisco this week."

He stared. Joy—pure, unadulterated wonder—wa
bubbling up in his chest. "*You're* going to move t
California with me?"

"I am!" She grinned at him. "Can you believe it'
I'm really very excited." She reached up and threv
her arms around him, looking at him thoughtfully
"That is, of course, only if you're okay with—"

"I love you," he said.

She gave him a teary, happy smile. "I'm glad t
hear you say that in the present tense. I...was tak
ing a leap of faith, to tell the truth. But after I sav
you in that press conference yesterday, I knew wha
I had to do."

"Come on." He tugged at her hand. "Let's get yo
upgraded to first class. You're sitting next to me."

"Aren't you a little bit afraid?"

"Not at all." He looked at this beautiful womar
he had helped draw out of her shell. The womar
who had helped him find the core and center o
his heart. "We're allies. We'll figure out the nex
moves together."

* * * * *

LARGER-PRINT BOOKS!
GET 2 FREE LARGER-PRINT NOVELS PLUS
2 FREE GIFTS!

HARLEQUIN®

super romance®

More Story...More Romance

YES! Please send me 2 FREE LARGER-PRINT Harlequin® Superromance® novels and my 2 FREE gifts (gifts are worth about $10). After receiving them, if I don't wish to receive any more books, I can return the shipping statement marked "cancel." If I don't cancel, I will receive 6 brand-new novels every month and be billed just $5.69 per book in the U.S. or $6.99 per book in Canada. That's a savings of at least 16% off the cover price! It's quite a bargain! Shipping and handling is just 50¢ per book in the U.S. or 75¢ per book in Canada.* I understand that accepting the 2 free books and gifts places me under no obligation to buy anything. I can always return a shipment and cancel at any time. Even if I never buy another book, the two free books and gifts are mine to keep forever.

139/339 HDN F46Y

Name	(PLEASE PRINT)
Address	Apt. #
City	State/Prov.	Zip/Postal Code

Signature (if under 18, a parent or guardian must sign)

Mail to the Harlequin® Reader Service:
IN U.S.A.: P.O. Box 1867, Buffalo, NY 14240-1867
IN CANADA: P.O. Box 609, Fort Erie, Ontario L2A 5X3

**Are you a current subscriber to Harlequin Superromance books
and want to receive the larger-print edition?
Call 1-800-873-8635 today or visit www.ReaderService.com.**

* Terms and prices subject to change without notice. Prices do not include applicable taxes. Sales tax applicable in N.Y. Canadian residents will be charged applicable taxes. Offer not valid in Quebec. This offer is limited to one order per household. Not valid for current subscribers to Harlequin Superromance Larger-Print books. All orders subject to credit approval. Credit or debit balances in a customer's account(s) may be offset by any other outstanding balance owed by or to the customer. Please allow 4 to 6 weeks for delivery. Offer available while quantities last.

Your Privacy—The Harlequin® Reader Service is committed to protecting your privacy. Our Privacy Policy is available online at www.ReaderService.com or upon request from the Harlequin Reader Service.

We make a portion of our mailing list available to reputable third parties that offer products we believe may interest you. If you prefer that we not exchange your name with third parties, or if you wish to clarify or modify your communication preferences, please visit us at www.ReaderService.com/consumerschoice or write to us at Harlequin Reader Service Preference Service, P.O. Box 9062, Buffalo, NY 14269. Include your complete name and address.

HSRLP13R

ReaderService.com

Manage your account online!

- Review your order history
- Manage your payments
- Update your address

*We've designed
the Harlequin® Reader Service
website just for you.*

Enjoy all the features!

- Reader excerpts from any series
- Respond to mailings and special monthly offers
- Discover new series available to you
- Browse the Bonus Bucks catalog
- Share your feedback

Visit us at:
ReaderService.com

RS13

REQUEST YOUR FREE BOOKS!
2 FREE WHOLESOME ROMANCE NOVELS IN LARGER PRINT
PLUS 2 FREE MYSTERY GIFTS

HEARTWARMING™

Wholesome, tender romances

YES! Please send me 2 FREE Harlequin® Heartwarming Larger-Print novels and my 2 FREE mystery gifts (gifts worth about $10). After receiving them, if I don't wish to receive any more books, I can return the shipping statement marked "cancel." If I don't cancel, I will receive 4 brand-new larger-print novels every month and be billed just $4.99 per book in the U.S. or $5.74 per book in Canada. That's a savings of at least 23% off the cover price. It's quite a bargain! Shipping and handling is just 50¢ per book in the U.S. and 75¢ per book in Canada.* I understand that accepting the 2 free books and gifts places me under no obligation to buy anything. I can always return a shipment and cancel at any time. Even if I never buy another book, the two free books and gifts are mine to keep forever.

161/361 IDN F47N

Name _____ (PLEASE PRINT) _____

Address _____ Apt. # _____

City _____ State/Prov. _____ Zip/Postal Code _____

Signature (if under 18, a parent or guardian must sign) _____

Mail to the Harlequin® Reader Service:
IN U.S.A.: P.O. Box 1867, Buffalo, NY 14240-1867
IN CANADA: P.O. Box 609, Fort Erie, Ontario L2A 5X3

* Terms and prices subject to change without notice. Prices do not include applicable taxes. Sales tax applicable in N.Y. Canadian residents will be charged applicable taxes. Offer not valid in Quebec. This offer is limited to one order per household. Not valid for current subscribers to Harlequin Heartwarming larger-print books. All orders subject to credit approval. Credit or debit balances in a customer's account(s) may be offset by any other outstanding balance owed by or to the customer. Please allow 4 to 6 weeks for delivery. Offer available while quantities last.

Your Privacy—The Harlequin® Reader Service is committed to protecting your privacy. Our Privacy Policy is available online at www.ReaderService.com or upon request from the Harlequin Reader Service.

We make a portion of our mailing list available to reputable third parties that offer products we believe may interest you. If you prefer that we not exchange your name with third parties, or if you wish to clarify or modify your communication preferences, please visit us at www.ReaderService.com/consumerschoice or write to us at Harlequin Reader Service Preference Service, P.O. Box 9062, Buffalo, NY 14269. Include your complete name and address.

HWDIR13R